D1311179

· KASHKA ·

KASHKA

Ellen Kindt McKenzie

HENRY HOLT AND COMPANY | NEW YORK

Published by Henry Holt and Company, Inc.,
521 Fifth Avenue, New York, New York 10175.
Published in Canada by Fitzhenry & Whiteside Limited,
195 Allstate Parkway, Markham, Ontario L3R 4T8.

Library of Congress Cataloging in Publication Data
McKenzie, Ellen Kindt.
Kashka.
Summary: The son of a royal musician tries to
prevent Lady Ysene and her brother from using their
evil powers to gain control of the kingdom of Darai.
[1. Fantasy] I. Title.
PZ7.M478676Kas 1987   [Fic]   87-8559
ISBN: 0-8050-0327-4

First Edition

Designer: Victoria Hartman
Printed in the United States of America
1 3 5 7 9 10 8 6 4 2

ISBN 0-8050-0327-4

To Beverly Baron
for her humor, her warmth,
her compassion and her courage

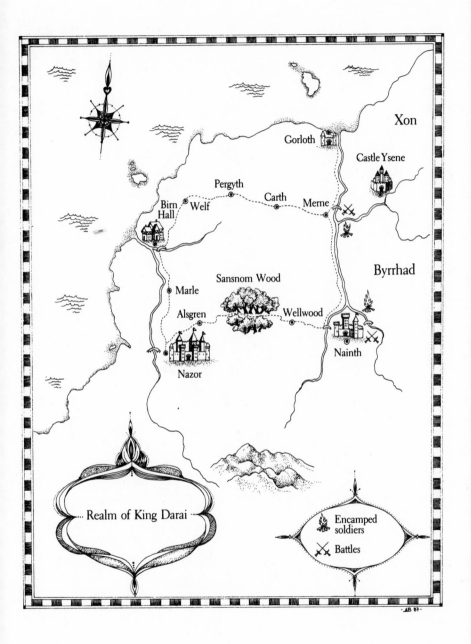

·KASHKA·

· I ·

↘↘↘ For hours the black coach had jounced and rattled over the ruts in the road. Now hooves drummed and wheels clattered over a wooden bridge. After some moments the soft throdup, throdup of horses galloping on hard-packed dirt returned. The road here had neither ruts nor holes. The coach rolled smoothly.

The three passengers, a man, a woman, and a child, rode in silence. The man, long-faced and thin-lipped, rode backward. His hard eyes were fixed upon the child. The woman's eyes, cold as an adder's, stared beyond his right shoulder. Clearly her thoughts were not upon the back of the seat where her look rested. The child, a little girl of nine years, sat rigid, her black-gloved hands folded in her lap. A long strand of pale gold hair escaped from beneath her black bonnet and curled against the shoulder of her black traveling coat. There was an intolerable itch where the wool of the coat chafed her wrist. She moved her fingers slightly toward it.

"Don't fidget!"

"No, my Lord of Xon," the child whispered, her lips scarcely moving.

"Speak so that I can hear you!"

"Yes, my Lord of Xon."

"Look into my face when you speak to me!"

The child lifted her eyes and opened her lips once more, but no words came from them.

1

"You defy me!"

He lifted his hand swiftly. Even more swiftly the woman leaned forward, caught his wrist, and held it.

"She'll not have a bruised face!"

For a moment their eyes locked. Then the Lord of Xon jerked away. He straightened his sleeve and turned his face to stare at the curtained window.

The little girl had managed to scratch her wrist during the exchange, and now sat as still as before, her hands folded in her lap. She scarcely dared breathe. After a while her eyelids drooped. Her head nodded and fell sideways against the woman's arm. The woman pushed her away. The child slept on, her head against the hard corner of the seat.

"I thought you were going to leave her at the last court." The Lord of Xon addressed the woman.

"It was not the place for her."

"We have seen enough. We will leave her here."

"Brother, we shall see them *all* before I decide which is suitable." She moved the curtain with a finger to look at the passing country. A narrow strip of sunlight fell across her throat and glinted on a link of heavy gold chain otherwise hidden by her dress. The Lord of Xon winced, then spoke bitterly.

"Isn't it like you, Ysene! To put me in an unbearable position, promising it will only be a day or two, and then prolonging it for months! To me, the last court looked suitable! They would have taught her!"

"It would have served us no purpose. She meant nothing to them. There would have been nothing for bargaining or—whatever. I hope you came away with a thorough knowledge of the strength of their arms," she added.

"I always do what I set out to do. I know their strength. It is less than mine . . . ours. Of all we have seen, Mogrud alone is stronger. He has plans for his army. We shall be dealing with his overblown ambition."

As he spoke the child's head fell back, her lips parted.

2

The Lord of Xon gestured impatiently. "I cannot tolerate this child any longer! Make an end of your folly. Give her to me. I'll see to her . . . *education* . . . better than you ever will."

"Watch your tongue, brother, concerning who does better! The child is mine to do as I will!" The woman's voice rose. Her eyes narrowed, her lips hardening to an even thinner line than his.

The Lord of Xon recognized the first sign of his sister's rising temper. Peeved, he fell silent. Her unmanageable fury was always directed against him!

It was long before either of them spoke. At last the lady again moved the edge of the curtain.

"I like what I see here," she murmured.

I've seen enough of it, thought the Lord of Xon. Dull, common. Nonetheless, he drew a breath of relief. Her temper had passed. The coach rolled on.

"Welcome, Lady Ysene. My Lord of Xon! King Darai is in council or he'd have met you himself. . . . And this is . . ."

"The Princess Ekama."

"Princess! Welcome to Nazor!" The man bowed low and handed her from the coach with a flourish. A look of pleased surprise crossed the little girl's face.

The palace before her filled her with wonder. It was of a warm yellow-brown stone with countless white towers and turrets. Bright flags curled against the blue sky.

"I'll show you to your chambers," the man went on talking to Zena and my Lord of Xon. "You'll have time to rest. . . ."

A commotion caught the Princess's eye. Two boys at a run ducked beneath the horses' heads, then stopped to stare at her. They were dusty and barefoot. Bits of grass and leaves were tangled in their curly hair as if they had been rolling on the ground. They were exactly alike. Suddenly one winked his right eye at her, the other his left. Both grinned, their mouths curling a little higher on one side.

The Princess's mouth dropped open, and her eyes widened almost as much. If Zena should see—or my Lord of Xon! Would he whip her for looking at them? Would Zena stop him as she had in the coach? She turned her head straight, clamped her mouth shut, and held her breath, her cheeks puffing out. But her eyes stayed as round as before.

She scarcely heard the man call, "Tettie! Come show the Princess to her room! You take care of her now. Step lively! Gailen, see to the trunks!"

My Lord of Xon and Zena walked ahead of her. Princess Ekama peeked sideways, but the boys had disappeared.

Inside, the palace was even more wonderful. The great entrance hall was high and light. The Princess could not tell where the brightness came from, there was such a confusion of people walking about, talking and laughing. She followed Zena and my Lord of Xon up a broad staircase that led to a balcony. She would have followed them down a long hallway, but the girl beside her said, "This way, Princess," and touched her shoulder as she pointed to the right. When the Princess looked back, Zena and my Lord of Xon had vanished. She could only continue to follow the girl, Tettie, who led her through a maze of wide corridors.

Tettie had bright pink cheeks and hair that stood out from her head in such tight curls she looked like a thistle gone to seed. "Here, Princess. Do you like it?" she asked as she pushed open a door.

It was a large room, cheerful, with tapestried walls. A finely carved wardrobe stood on one side. There were handsome chairs and a writing table. The Princess's trunk was already in the room.

The next moment Tettie was into the baggage, taking out Ekama's dresses. "There's nothing but brown and black!" she exclaimed. "We'll have to see to that! There's to be a ball in three days more. You'll need something pretty!"

4

Ekama stared at her without answering. Tettie seemed not to notice. She hung the dresses in the wardrobe and turned to the tall french doors.

"You'll want some air, Princess." She threw open the doors. "Palace rooms do get stuffy. Look—your balcony is over the court. The ballroom is just across—"

"Oh, no no! Please!" Ekama cried and ran to the doors, pushed them shut, and turned with her back against them.

"It *was* aired this morning." Tettie's eyebrows lifted into the frizz of hair covering her forehead.

But Princess Ekama did not hear her. Her eyes were fixed on the high bed across the room. Only the filmiest of curtains hung from the canopy—no more than gauze! Panic-stricken, she looked from one corner of the room to another. If there were no heavy drapes, where could she hide? When night came how would she be able to keep *them* from finding her?

·2·

➹➹➹ "You will come with me." The Lady Ysene, her narrow face expressionless, watched as Tettie helped the Princess finish dressing.

Weavers, spinners, woodworkers, metalworkers in silver and gold—blacksmith, of course. Swords. A horse being shod. They went on.

Here was something the child knew nothing of. She stared at the hollow silver rod.

"It's called a flute," Master Wondry told her. "You blow to make music with it." He peered at her, nodding and smiling. His shaggy eyebrows lifted as if asking, don't you agree that this is the most wonderful thing in the world?

"Here you, what's-your-name. . . ." He turned and gestured. The same two boys she had seen three days ago were here. How did they know which one he wanted? the Princess wondered. They looked so alike, perhaps it didn't matter. "Play for the Princess."

The little girl listened in astonishment when the Lady Ysene snatched up the stick Master Wondry had used to tap with, and brought it down with a crack over the hand of the young flute player.

"*That* is for the wrong note!" she said.

The blow knocked the flute from the boy's hands, but he was quick and caught it before it struck the floor.

"And *that* is for dropping the instrument!" A second stinging

6

blow landed across his shoulders even as he bent down.

"Music is annoying enough. I have never cared for it," she said, handing the broken end of the stick to Master Wondry. "But a student who is unprepared and must be interrupted and corrected has to be properly dealt with. I—"

Her sentence was interrupted by a crash. The tower of books and music, the mugs, inkwell, quill pens, plate of half-eaten cheese, chicken bones, and apple cores, the candlesticks, knife— everything spewed across the floor as the table fell. In the midst of the debris the two boys rolled and kicked.

"I will. . . . I will!" panted one.

"You . . . ouch . . . won't!" gasped the other.

"Boys!" cried the distraught master, his hands thrust into his thinning hair.

The flute player and the boy who had been waiting quietly on the bench beside the door continued to struggle, one trying to pull away, the other tripping him, holding him. The lady drew back her skirts, a look of disgust on her face.

"What are they, twins?" she asked, for no matter how they turned, there seemed to be only one face. She looked hard at Master Wondry. "Your lack of discipline is unforgivable. If this were Castle Ysene, you would be flogged and dismissed. I want those boys flogged. Such behavior in front of the Princess is reprehensible. My brother will see that it's done. Come, Ekama." She turned to the little Princess who stood frozen, her eyes wide, her hand over her mouth. The woman seized her wrist and pulled her toward the door.

"Why did you hit him, Zena?" The child began to wail. "Why did you hit him? The music was nice. I liked it!"

"Be quiet! Don't ever say such a thing again! You are a princess! You have nothing to do with rabble." The lady stopped, shook the child until she was silent, and then pushed her ahead through the door.

Master Wondry took up one of his crutches and tried to poke the boys from where he sat on the wooden stool, but he could not reach them. He groaned, put his hands on his knees,

7

and waited for the pair to stop their snorting and tussling.

At last they were still. One of them pushed himself to his knees, then to his feet.

"I will," he muttered, pressing a knuckle against his bleeding nose.

The other boy sat on the floor. "You wond," he said, "even if you wand do. You wond becauth she'th gone." The bitten tongue blurred his speech.

"You will what, Kashka?" asked the master wearily as he handed the boy a rag to hold against his nose.

The boy shook his head. There were tears in his eyes, not, Master Wondry knew, of pain but of rage.

"He 'wond' what, Piff?" he asked the other boy. "What did he 'wand' to do?"

"I don know. He wand to kill her, I thin."

"Agh!"

"He wand do!"

"Why . . . ?" Master Wondry began, and then with an exclamation, "Let me see that hand!"

Kashka held out his arm. Master Wondry took the hand gently in his own. "Can you move your fingers?"

The boy curled his fingers to his palm, straightened them, spread them wide.

"Well! No damage done at all! Not even swollen! I thought she'd broken every bone!" Master Wondry stared in amazement.

"She hit hith other han," Piff said flatly.

A look of exasperation crossed the master's face. "Kashka! You . . . ! Show me that other hand! Ah. Now, can you move those fingers? No! No! Don't move them that way! Don't touch them! If they're broken. . . But I can't tell. Your hand is so swollen. What a welt! Get water from the well. It's colder than this. Soak your hand—and your nose. Then come back. Maybe I can tell. You—Piff, help pick up this mess." Master Wondry bent to pick up a book at his feet when a shadow fell across the floor. He looked up.

8

A man stood in the doorway.

"My sister told me there were two boys here in need of a flogging. These are the boys?" he asked, pointing a heavy riding whip first at Kashka and then at Piff.

"No, no." Master Wondry straightened his back. "They have been punished. We don't need any more."

"These are the boys." The man's voice was final. "Out— and put your hands against that wall. *At once.*

"Stand there. You will learn not to insult the Lady Ysene or the Princess Ekama!" His arm rose and the whip came down across Piff's shoulders. The blow knocked the breath from him. At the third blow, Piff closed his eyes and slipped to the ground.

"A weakling!" said the man. "Let's see what kind of man *you* are!" He turned to Kashka, raised his arm.

Master Wondry dragged himself across the floor to where the stranger had kicked his crutches. Painfully he pulled himself up on them and swung himself to the door at last.

"Stop!" he cried. "Stop! They are my best!"

But the arm was raised again. And again.

"My Lord of Xon!" A clear young voice cut the air. The man whirled, his arm still raised. "My lord, the King awaits you." The youth's eyes were calm and steady, his face composed. He did not glance from the man's face to the boys behind him. For a moment Master Wondry wondered if the man would strike him too, but he lowered his arm slowly.

"Is the Crown Prince a messenger in this court?" he asked coldly.

"My Lord of Xon," said the youth, "I do you a favor. I know that the King has been waiting for you for five minutes at least. I could have gone on, said nothing, and let you finish your task. However, with respect for the crown, I repeat, the King awaits you. He does not like to be kept waiting."

"Your Highness!" The Lord of Xon bowed his head shortly and stalked away.

The Prince watched until he was out of sight, then turned quickly to the boys and the anguished master.

9

Kashka, on hands and knees, leaned over Piff. He tried to speak but could not.

Piff opened one eye. "Hath he gone?" he asked and sat up.

Kashka, swaying slightly, sat back on his heels, and stared at Piff.

"You're all right?" the Prince asked.

Piff pushed the curling hair back from his forehead. "No. I've had three too many. Why should I make him feel good by ledding him whip me?"

"I . . . thought . . . he'd . . . killed . . . you," Kashka whispered, glaring at him.

"He would have killed *you!*" Piff countered. "He would have beaten you thilly. One more and I would have had to take your plathe."

"Stop it, you two," Master Wondry muttered, rubbing his thumb and forefinger over his eyes.

The Prince helped Piff to his feet, then leaned down to take Kashka's hands. But the boy pulled away with a groan.

"She hit hith han with the thtick," Piff said.

As the Prince helped the crippled master to his chair, Kashka crept to the doorsill and sat there, his head on his knees.

"I didn't play a wrong note." His voice was faint. "I know I didn't. Did I?"

"No. You didn't. I stopped you to question the phrasing there. It was different from the way I do it. I wanted to hear it again." Master Wondry sighed. "Now I don't remember where it was in the music."

"She didn know one node from another," Piff muttered. He sat down next to the huddled Kashka, stretched out a hand, drew it back again. "She wouldn know a wrong node if you threw it at her."

"Sheeza witch," Kashka mumbled into the knees of his breeches.

"Keep your mouth shut, Kashka. It gets you into trouble every time you open it," the Prince said bluntly. "For

10

witches . . . you'd better go to Bargah. It'll take some witching to peel your shirts from your backs. Wait! I'll get someone to help you. You'll never . . . You can stand up? Are you sure? Go on, then!"

The Prince set the table back on its legs, picked up a book, and looked with dismay at the mixture of spilled ink and blood on the strewn papers. He sighed. "I'll find someone to clean up for you, Master Wondry. Why did he come here?"

Master Wondry shook his head. "*She*—his sister—she sent him to whip them."

"What was *she* doing here?"

"I don't know. Yesterday she was poking her nose in other places. Four good pots were broken before she left Podra's workshop."

"I brought my flute." The Prince held up a soft leather case. "I thought we might play—the three of us. I argued all morning to get out of that council meeting—for this. . . ." He waved his hand.

"If you'd argued a minute longer there would have been but two of you ever to play again."

The Prince nodded. "I'd better see that they come to Bargah's. Kashka wasn't very steady. I didn't think he'd be able to get to his feet. He made himself stand. You could see it in his face."

Master Wondry rubbed the back of his neck. "It's being so slight. He has to prove he's ten times the man anyone else is. It doesn't seem to bother Piff. Go on, Your Highness. He'll never come to Bargah's, whatever he's trying to prove."

The master watched the Prince hurry after his two pupils. Prince Aciam will rule well some day, he thought. He sees, he cares, but he knows how to keep his head. What a difference in boys! Who would believe the Prince is only a year older than those two? He carries himself like a man. Kashka—how that boy can play! If only he doesn't get himself hanged before he's thirteen! Piff's a scamp too, but not impossible. Lucky he doesn't play the flute. He'd not blow a note for weeks with that lip! And I didn't hear a note from his lute today. . . .

Curse that woman! If she broke Kashka's hand. . . . Devil on her, she and that brother! Hell hag and ghoul, the pair of them! I can't understand why that little princess . . . Such a sweet child to be in their hands! A pretty little girl too. What a shame! What a shame!

The master was right. When the Prince rounded the corner of the smithy, he saw Kashka flat on the ground. Piff was already bringing the smith to help.

"Kashka is it now?" said the broad-shouldered man as he squatted down to pick up the boy. "I'm not surprised. Though this is more than he deserves—I think." He frowned. "Great fires of the mountains! Who did such a thing? Is he still alive?"

"I . . . I think so."

"Where shall I take him? To his father?"

"N-no. To . . . to Bargah." Tears were running down Piff's face.

When the smith stood up, the boy in his arms, he saw Prince Aciam.

"Take him to Bargah." The Prince nodded. "Quickly!"

His face grim, the smith spoke. "By the look of it, I'd say he had a meeting with the Lord of Xon. I've seen the man cut up a horse in just the same way. For Kashka's sake—if he lives—I hope they never meet again."

·3·

There was warmth, brightness, music! Lords and ladies circled the ballroom floor. Lips apart, eyes full of wonder,
Ekama's gaze went from the dancers to the musicians to the
glowing lamps.

". . . Princess?"

"What? Oh!"

Prince Aciam stood before her, waiting for her answer.

"I . . . I beg your pardon?"

"Would you like to dance?"

She felt her cheeks grow hot. Tears rose to sting her eyes.
She looked down quickly. "I'm sorry. I don't know how."

"I'll teach you."

There was no sharp disapproval in his voice, no biting tone
that belittled her for not knowing.

She looked up. There was no frown, no anger. He was
smiling but not laughing at her. His look seemed to tell her
that he knew just how she felt. He held out his hand.

"Dance with the Prince, Ekama." Zena's voice was smoother
than she had ever heard it. She stood up quickly so Zena
would not touch her arm where my Lord of Xon had held it
so tightly. His finger marks were still there, dark on her skin.
She was glad the sleeve of her new dress covered them.

"Put your hand on top of mine," the Prince told her.
"Do you see Lord and Lady Tarel? How her hand rests on his?

Now, step and step—no, the other foot. We'll start again."

Ekama caught her lower lip between her teeth and drew her brows together. It didn't help her feet at all.

"Wait a bit, Princess. You aren't listening to the music."

"Should I?" She was surprised. "How can I when I'm thinking of my feet?"

"Stand still. You'll hear." He held the tips of her fingers in his hands. "Do you hear the pulse? So?" He pressed her fingers lightly in a way that fit perfectly with the music.

"Yes! It does that, doesn't it!" She looked into his face, delighted with the discovery. Then she saw that everyone was stepping to the music. "Now I understand!"

They tried again and it went so much better that the Prince smiled at her. Her feet tangled up at once.

"Keep listening!" he told her.

"Then I shall have to not look at you."

The Prince laughed at that, but again, he wasn't laughing at her, he was laughing with her. He put his hand at her waist and turned her rather quickly, and then the music stopped.

Prince Aciam bowed. "Thank you, Princess Ekama."

"What for? Where is the music?"

"That's the end of the dance. I'm thanking you for dancing with me."

"Oh. Thank you, Prince Aciam!" she cried, and curtsied as deeply as Zena had told her she must do before the King.

There was laughter around them. The Princess was delighted that everyone liked to dance as much as she did.

"We don't have any music in my country," she confided to Prince Aciam as they walked toward Zena.

"None at all?"

"I've never heard any. Perhaps it's too cold." She thought how hard it was to move her fingers in the dark chill of Zena's castle.

The Prince bowed to Zena and then excused himself. Ekama explained how one must step with the music.

"Of course," Zena said shortly, then added, "The Prince must dance with so many people, I hope you understand how difficult it must have been for him to dance with you."

Princess Ekama wilted. If only she had known how! She watched the Prince whenever she could see him in the crowded ballroom. He would never ask her again. She lifted her hand to her mouth.

Then, suddenly, there he was before her.

"Will you dance again, Princess?"

"Princess Ekama is tired. She must go to bed." Zena answered so quickly, Ekama had scarcely time to open her mouth.

"I'm sorry," said the Prince. "Perhaps tomorrow evening?"

"Oh, yes!" Princess Ekama exclaimed.

"Princess!" Zena squeezed her arm.

"Oh yes, *Your Highness*!" she cried, hoping that was what she was supposed to say.

But before they could leave, the King stopped beside the Prince. He said some words to Zena and smiled at Ekama. Then he turned to Prince Aciam.

"Where are my two scapegraces, do you know?"

"There was an accident," the Prince replied. They both bowed, excused themselves, and began to walk away together.

"An accident?" the Princess heard the King ask. "Both of them?"

"I'll tell you about it, or better, after . . ."

That was all she heard because the music started again.

"Come away, Princess."

For once, Ekama did not notice Zena's tight grasp on her arm. She could think only of Prince Aciam's look, his smile. He had asked her to dance again!

Once in her bed, she lay listening to the music and voices that wafted across the courtyard. Light coming through her windows dappled the ceiling. She could see towers and a small piece of the sky outside. She was beginning to like having something to look at before she fell asleep.

The music stopped. There was applause. If only she had been able to stay longer at the dance!

The next moment she was out of bed and pulling at the tall doors. She could hear better with them open. She could also see into the ballroom. In her nightgown the Princess sat cross-legged on the balcony, her face pressed against the iron grille.

Shapes moved past the bright windows. Now and then couples came through the wide doors to walk about in the warm summer night. One couple came through the door and kissed. The music started and they kissed again, laughed, and began dancing there beneath her.

Why was it so different here from Castle Ysene? Why was everyone here so happy? When the people of Nazor laughed, their eyes crinkled. It was not the way my Lord of Xon laughed. My Lord of Xon made a strange hard sound and scarcely moved his lips. Zena never laughed. She smiled, but her smile made the Princess wish there were someplace she could go where no one could find her.

At the thought of Zena's smile, a chill went down her back. With a frightened gasp, Ekama leaped to her feet, catching her toes in the hem of her nightgown, tripping so that she almost fell. She ran to her bed, jumped into it, and pulled the quilt over her head.

What had she done? How could she have forgotten! Gone out onto the balcony in the night where *they* could find her—*the cold ones*! At Castle Ysene when she lay in the suffocating darkness of her bed, she did not even dare blink her eyes! If she did, *they* might hear. If they heard, they would come.

She clenched her fists tightly, digging her nails into her palms, held her breath. The chill had been the first sign of them. Now would come the strange whispers, the moaning, the crying. . . .

She must pretend to be asleep. They only came to her when

16

she was awake. She must not hold her breath. People who were asleep breathed!

Close to crying from fear, she now held herself rigid and struggled to make her breath come evenly. All the while she listened for the first terrifying whisper, waited to feel the coldness touch her face, her neck, her arms. Then would come the fear, the horror of a half-knowledge of unnamed things.

But there was no whisper, no moaning, no coldness. Had the chill come from something else? Little by little she relaxed.

Weren't they here in Nazor? Perhaps they came only to Castle Ysene where it was cold and dark and frightening things happened! Here, it was warm and bright and lovely things happened.

Just two days ago the Queen had bent over her, kissed her, and said, "I wish you were *my* princess!"

The next moment Ekama found she had put her arms around the Queen's neck and could not let go. The Queen had said, "There, there!" and unfastened her arms so gently! Then she took Ekama's hand and they walked together through the garden among the flowers. She hadn't even asked Zena's permission! But of course, she was the Queen.

The Princess held to the memory, repeating it over and over for the warm feeling it gave her. If only . . .

No, she must not dream. She had given up dreaming long ago for it made the rest of the time so difficult to bear, especially when the cold ones came in the middle of a dream. It was terrible then, for they caught her when she wasn't expecting them.

Tonight, however, she could not stop herself from dreaming. If she could stay here she would spend all her time laughing and looking at flowers and . . . and . . . She would dance with Prince Aciam! There was the warmth of his hand and his smile. . . . Did it start in his eyes or with his mouth? She frowned. She couldn't remember. But all the air was bright when he smiled—as if the sun were shining. Perhaps that was

17

because his eyes were as blue as the clear sky of Nazor. She sighed and thought of how his mouth turned up at the corners. She tried to remember the sound of his voice.

It had sounded different when he spoke to the King. *An accident*. . . . Princess Ekama knew about accidents. They happened often at Castle Ysene. When someone had an accident he was never seen again.

She wondered . . . what a scapegrace . . . was. . . .

The Princess woke. It was so still! There were no more voices. There was no more music. The square of light had vanished from her ceiling. There was light in her room—different, however, from any she had ever seen. It came through the windows, pale, white, steady. Though she could see the objects in her room quite clearly, there was no color in any of them. Only light and dark shapes and shadows. There was no lamp, no candle.

Her curiosity grew until she would risk even *them* to see what this strange light was.

Taking a deep breath and collecting all her courage with it, she slipped from the high bed and a cautious step at a time, silent as a little ghost, tiptoed across the room to the window.

Half a silver globe hung high above the palace roof and shone down over everything, edging towers and turrets with its light. It spread its whiteness across walls on this side and cast those on the other side into deep shadow.

It was so beautiful, so quiet, so peaceful, that the Princess stood for a long time looking, wondering, trying to think how the King could have such a light for his palace, when something below took her attention. A door opened. Yellow light spread out into the silver and then vanished as quickly as it had appeared. Two figures walked into the whiteness. She recognized them at once. It was the King and Prince Aciam. They walked quietly without speaking or looking at one another, but the King's arm lay across the Prince's shoulder.

They crossed the court and went out through the gate at the far end.

She watched them disappear. An ache grew and pressed within her. It had to do with something she had put away with her dreams so long ago. When she was no longer able to help herself, she flew to her bed, buried her head under pillows and quilts, and cried herself to sleep.

·4·

⤙⤙⤙ Beyond the carriage gate, King and Prince turned into the narrow street below the wall.

"There's a candle in Bargah's window. She's still awake," Prince Aciam murmured.

The King tapped lightly at the door. When it opened, neither King nor Prince was surprised to see Mareth, the court harpist, before them. Or was it Piff's father, Camin? For there, rising to his feet, was . . . The King looked from one to the other. So much alike! It was Camin, the poet, who had opened the door. Wrong the first time, as usual, thought King Darai.

"Piff is here too?" he asked, surprised.

"Piff is at home asleep. Cara is with him. He's doing well enough. Kashka gave him almost as much in the mouth and the shins as the Lord of Xon did to his back." Camin shook his head.

"And Kashka?" The King looked at Mareth.

"Bargah has done all she can. The court physician was here too. Between them . . . Now we're waiting." Kashka's father turned his face aside. "Of all the scrapes that boy has been in, all the pranks, all the mischief—he's deserved a whipping a dozen times over. Heaven knows, there's probably not a man in the court or the town who wouldn't have liked to get his hands on him at some time or other. I've had at him myself! But this was brutal. This . . . he didn't deserve this. The boy has never been malicious. I don't—"

20

"What happened? Aciam had only a brief word."

"No one knows exactly, Sire, not even Master Wondry. They were having a lesson and . . ." Piff's father related what he knew. He spread his hands to the side and shrugged his shoulders. "Of course Wondry would never do what the lady asked—or order it done. It's not his way to beat music or anything else into people. Besides, their scuffling had already done enough damage to them. Then Xon arrived. As usual, Piff had enough sense to know he couldn't take such a flogging. . . ."

"As usual, Kashka didn't."

The curtain across the door at the back of the room was pushed aside. An old woman stood there, tiny, wrinkled, her shoulders slightly rounded.

"I thought I heard your voice, Your Majesty. Kashka is awake. A word from you may do more for him than anything I can give him."

The Queen sat up in bed. Dawn paled the eastern sky.

"Where are you going?" she asked the King. "You've scarcely slept!"

The King sat down on the edge of the bed and pulled at his boot.

"I've just come in. I haven't had any sleep at all."

"Where have you been? I've been sleeping so soundly I didn't know! What is the matter? You look so distressed! Has something happened?"

"Yes," the King said sadly, "something has happened." He sat on the bed holding his boot in his hand.

"You should have called Winnow to pull off your boots," the Queen said gently. She waited for him to speak.

"I've been thinking," he said at last. "Do you suppose we can find a way to keep the Princess Ekama with us?"

"I've been thinking the same thing myself!" she exclaimed. "Yes, I think we can! Just yesterday Lady Ysene said that the child was tired of traveling. She wondered if it was wise of them to take her on so long a journey. They've still weeks ahead of them. It's the first time I've heard her say anything human."

"Does the idea please you?"

"Indeed it does! The child is a love! But has something happened to her? Is that why you were out?"

"No, no. As far as I know she is all right. I was out because of Mareth's son. You know, the one who tumbles and plays the flute? He was badly hurt."

"Everyone knows Kashka!" the Queen exclaimed. "Though I'm never sure if it's Kashka or Piff unless I see his eyes. Yes, Kashka's are blue and Piff's are brown. How was he hurt? Did he leap from the roof to see if he could fly? How badly hurt is he? Where is he? Did you have him brought to the court physician?"

"It was through no prank of his. No, he learned he couldn't fly a long time ago. Aciam told me of it. If he and Piff hadn't insisted Kashka leap into a haystack, he would have broken his neck." The King shook his head. "He's with old Bargah. The physician has seen him. He has had all the help anyone can give him."

He paused, then in a sudden burst of anger said, "If only I didn't have to face that assassin, Xon, in the council meeting today! I don't know if I will be able to control myself!" His voice trembled. He threw his boot across the room, jerked at the other, and threw it after the first.

Startled, the Queen again waited for him to speak.

"But I must," he murmured after a time. "And I must be civil to him. Mogrud to the east with twice—three times— our strength. And who knows what game Xon is playing—if he will stand by our side or be against us?" He shook his head, his shoulders slumped. "To think . . . how Mareth played this evening. I have never heard him play more beautifully. And for all he knew, his son was dying."

"Dying! But how . . . ?"

The King shook his head. "Later, my dear. I'm tired. I only hope the boy has too much spirit to die."

"I'm so sorry. . . ." Tears came to the Queen's eyes. "I don't know what to say. He's such a piece of mischief, but at the same time he's so full of charm and brings such laughter. Oh, and I had such good news for you!" she sighed. "Now I think perhaps it should wait. It *can* wait."

"Good news? If there is anything I need . . . ! Tell me now!"

"I would have told you last night, but I fell asleep. I need all the sleep I can get, we're going to have so many cares— Prince Aciam and Princess Ekama. . . . And this—the child we shall have sometime early in the new year."

Delight in her news crowded all worry from the King's mind. He held the Queen in his arms. Then a thought came to him.

"Let's not make the news public just yet," he murmured, "at least not until the Lord of Xon and his sister have left."

·5·

↘↘↘ Bargah was old—so old she understood the beginnings and endings of things; so old she understood the time allotted them between their beginnings and endings. She was not so old, however, that an end-come-too-soon for young living things did not disturb her. She watched beside Kashka as he lay on the cot, his face bright with pain and fever. She waited until his eyes turned vacant, dark with the drug that eased the pain. When they closed to give him rest, she rose from the chair beside him to take her anger to the other room. She thought of the Lord of Xon and his sister and tasted the bitterness of that anger on her tongue. That there were those who could be so cruel as to destroy—no, worse—to take such pleasure in their cruelty in destroying that which was so alive, so bright, so eager. . . .

To see him now . . .

Bargah was old. She was wise enough to know not to bring anger into a room where the thread of life was stretched so thin. She stood in that other room with her hands tightly clasped, her mouth set, her thoughts fighting themselves until she could leave her anger at the door.

Otherwise she was with him all of the next day, gently sponging his back with water strained of the herbs that had steeped in it, changing the poultice on his hand, keeping a cloth cool on his forehead.

"If we can keep him through this night . . ."

Late in the evening, his time at court finished, Mareth came. He brewed a cup of tea for her.

"Rest, Bargah," he told her. "I'll watch. I can't sleep."

She sat in the chair before the fireplace and sipped her tea. Her head was nodding when Mareth called her.

"Bargah, for the love of all the earth, help him!"

She was beside the cot in a minute and wondered on seeing the pallor of the boy's face and the stillness of him if she weren't already too late. At the same time she saw the grief in Mareth's face. His wife was dead; Kashka was his only child. Piff, his brother's son, was dear to him, but Piff was not Kashka. No one was Kashka.

A sudden terrible anger, like white fire, went through her. She had never felt such an instant of rage. Her very skin seemed to burn, every muscle, every bone, every nerve with it.

Then she saw the faintest rise and fall of his chest.

"Get out!" she said, her voice hard. "Leave me with him." She pushed Mareth through the door and drew the curtain shut.

Bargah was a healer. She knew every herb in garden, meadow, forest, and swamp. She knew the herb for headache or heartache, for a quinsy throat or the gout. For fever, for wound, for the dreaded cough, rash, pox, or fit. For a young woman's faintness for love, for an old man's whim for youth. She knew which cured and which killed.

She was much sought after for her knowledge of herbs.

Bargah was much more than one who healed with herbs. Remedy dwelt in her hands. The touch of her fingers at the temple or the side of the throat, and pain was gone. Her palm held over a burn, and there was healing.

For this too, she was sought.

Bargah was more than a user of herbs or a healing touch. But this more—this *other*—was different. For this *other*, no one ever sought her, for no one knew of it. It was a thing she seldom used, or if she did, she hesitated, mulled over it.

Tonight, however, she set about it at once.

The old woman unlocked the door of a small cabinet and took from it a box of black glass, the lid inlaid with curiously shaped figures of gold. From it she took a small key. The key fit into the center of a certain flower in the ornate frame of a mirror hanging on the wall.

The mirror swung aside at her touch to reveal three shelves backed by another mirror. She lifted down a tray of the same gold-inlaid black glass, a silver cup set with sapphires, and two packets of a fine translucent paper tied with silk thread. Finally she lifted down a crystal flask, the contents of which curled and folded upon itself, now dark, now light in color.

When the flask was taken from the shelf a curious thing happened. All reflections were lost from the mirror behind the shelves and in the same instant, the glass itself vanished. A window was left open in the wall, but it opened upon no town of Nazor. Nor was the sky seen through that window, for no clouds or stars were there. Endless space stretched beyond it, empty, silent.

Now the old woman moved with great deliberation. And while she went about what she did, the room became more and more quiet. The stillness grew and thickened and wrapped the movement of her hands into something that was without time or place. Bit by bit the room faded. Furnishings melted away. Walls thinned, turned translucent, disappeared.

Fire remained. The boy remained. Bargah remained. The contents of the black tray remained. All else vanished.

Bargah's hands moved. Her lips moved. The only other movement was the restless fire and the occasional faint rise and fall of the boy's chest.

After a time of no time, of endless time, Bargah raised her head.

"Mareth!" she called. "Come here."

Mareth turned from the fire in the sitting room and went

quickly to the door. He drew back the curtain, sucked in his breath, froze.

There was neither floor nor wall nor ceiling. Only space with no end.

"Don't be afraid." Bargah's voice came to him. "I need your help. Step forward. You will see us."

Not certain if he were awake or dreaming, Mareth stepped from the floor of the sitting room into what had been the small bedroom. He felt nothing beneath his foot, yet he did not fall. Another pace forward and he saw them. Bargah and his son. She stood beside the boy, holding a goblet of blue fire in her hands.

"You must lift him so that he can drink this," she told him.

Now Mareth felt the cessation of time. Again he stepped forward. There was no feeling of motion. He tried again.

It might have been but an instant, it might have been a thousand years until he was standing beside Bargah. She spoke to him. He raised the boy, held him against himself, drew his head back upon his shoulder.

Drop by drop, Bargah poured the liquid from the cup into the slack mouth.

"Two . . . three . . . four. . . ." Her voice pierced him through. His eyes were fixed upon her hands. The blue flame shone through the flesh to reveal the bones.

Mareth felt the boy shudder. The cold emptiness of death touched him, and in an agony of despair he thought, *He'll have no more pain. . . .*

But Bargah was speaking to him. "Draw your breath, Mareth. He will breathe with you."

Mareth was powerless to do other than her bidding. He felt the boy's chest rise and fall against his own, heard the sigh of a breath that came and went with his own.

"Hold him close, Mareth. Your hearts are one."

The father became aware of his own pulse at his wrist, the

base of his throat, beneath his ear as he had never been aware
before. How long . . . ?

"Enough," Bargah said to him. "Put him down. Carefully,
gently."

Now he could see the pulse at the boy's temple.

"Yes, how else would a father treat his son? Now you may
go. There, that way." She turned him, gave him a slight push,
and Mareth found himself stumbling over the rug in the sitting
room. He sank into a chair and began to tremble. He shook
so his hands could not grasp the arms of the chair to steady
them. Then he was overcome by a great weariness. His eyelids
drooped, his head fell forward, and he slept.

·6·

⟍⟍⟍ Most in the palace slept soundly through that night. A few woke suddenly.

King Darai opened his eyes to the deep silence. He sat up, bent over his sleeping queen, touched her cheek with the back of his fingers, caressed her shoulder. She breathed quietly. All was well. Even so, he lay awake and alert, listening, waiting. Then, just as suddenly, a great drowsiness came over him and he slept.

Prince Aciam leaped from his bed. He had been in a deep sleep and was somewhat confused. "I need my boots!" he cried. "Where is my . . ." and then he stubbed his toe on the curved leg of a chair. Gritting his teeth, hopping on one foot and holding the toes of his other with his hand, he returned to his bed and sat down on the edge of it.

"What's the matter with me?" he muttered. "I must have been dreaming!" But he could recall no dream. He only knew he had awakened to a command so compelling to . . . to do what? He sat there for some time, wondering at the weight of the silence and darkness that pressed upon him. When he lay down at last, sleep came quickly.

Lady Ysene too awakened, at once alert, every inch of her body aware.

"What power is this?" she whispered. "It's very near. It's very strong." Her hand went to her throat, her fingers slipping

29

along the golden chain that she wore even at night. They curled around the circular pendant, a golden band. "Is it this?" She lay motionless.

"No," she continued to whisper after a time, "but this answers to it! It burns my fingers! Still . . . An unlike power! Where is its center? What does it seek?" The lady probed the night with all her senses, but try as she would, she could only press so far and then her power was blocked. She found no answer. Suddenly the force lessened. In another moment it was gone. She remained wakeful. "I don't understand. I have never heard of anyone in Nazor who might have such . . ."

The lady did not sleep again that night.

The coach left early the next morning and traveled far. At times the Lord of Xon studied the pale, unlined face of his sister, but the sun was low in the west before he addressed her.

"Are you sure you are doing the right thing? What made you change your mind about the child?"

"If you are not free to change your mind, you miss opportunities. You didn't question me this morning," she replied.

"Why should I argue? I hate children. It's a relief to be rid of her. But will you be able to keep your *very special* control of her?"

"I do not have control of her in the manner you speak of. I could have, of course, but I decided against it."

"Why? It's dangerous to leave her free. We may lose her."

"*We?* No, brother, *we* will not lose her. Her fear is too great. *That* is the way I hold her. By fear. From time to time I shall renew it. Later—when the time is right—if the other is necessary . . . But at the present, *that* way is too dangerous."

"You will lose her." How was it she held her possessions? Why must he always guess at her methods? He chewed his lip.

"No matter." The Lady Ysene was silent. It was not until they had had their evening meal that she spoke again.

"The child is a tool. We will take this country in the same way we took her own."

"Bah! That insignificant buttonhole in the mountains! It wasn't worth the bother!"

"I liked that country. I wanted the palace. I've never seen one that seemed to float in the air among the mountain peaks as that one did."

"It's crumbling now. And you went to such lengths! Getting rid of the King—that child's father—an accident, as usual. And the Queen. You cannot tell me it took no effort to induce her to marry our father, insane old man that he was!"

"She had no choice. He fancied her."

"A short enough time he had her."

"Long enough! Though not by blood, we are now the child's closest kin."

"A burden! Why didn't you do away with her too?"

"Your stupidity is appalling! The child is true royalty. She is the key to *this* country. Through her the crown of Darai will come to us. Marriage and death and we, the closest kin. . . . This was the best place we have seen to leave her. I cannot imagine one better. The court is soft. The whole country is soft. It would be easy enough in any way we tried. But we have other countries to see to that may take more doing. If no suspicion falls on us here we shall be that much stronger. With little effort we shall come to this one in a way no one will question. By then we should be strong enough to face even Mogrud."

"Yes," he agreed, "the country is soft. There is little respect for royalty. The Crown Prince runs around as if he were a commoner. The King is no better. He speaks with anyone, everyone! Consults a council! It is no way to rule. No strength. A country should know that it is ruled. A people should fear its ruler! I should rule it with a fist of mail."

"You would rule with a bloodied mace, brother. But this country is mine!"

The Lord of Xon again fell silent.

When they were about to retire, Lady Ysene asked her brother, "Did you sense a change in them these last two days?"

"No. What kind of change?"

"What should I call it—reserve, perhaps."

"No. They were as stupidly hospitable as ever."

"Something changed. I felt it."

"Do you think they regretted keeping the child?"

"Not at all. They were pleased to keep her. Sweet, they called her. Sweet! Bah! I loathe that word. Sticky sentiment oozing like honey through stale bread. It was something else. I cannot imagine what. But I felt it in all of them—the King, the Queen, the Prince—even the servants."

"You imagine it. There was no reason. We did nothing that was not completely proper."

"That's true. Well, perhaps I did imagine it."

There *was* something different, she told herself after closing her door. I may lie to my brother, but never to myself. Something changed.

And that force! It was so close—almost in the palace itself. Yet . . . once it was gone, there was no trace of it. Perhaps someone passing in the night. . . . But I must be careful. I was right to leave the child free of the power of my bond— of the power of my *band!* If she weren't, such a force might learn of it. I must be very careful. I will have this my way! This country will be mine!

Xon does not understand. He would cut his way through with an ax as he does through everything. There would be nothing left. But *my* way. . . . Agh! He has so little sense of my power!

She slipped her hand beneath the collar of her dress, fingered the golden chain.

"All for my collection," she murmured. "I shall lose none of this kingdom, least of all the Princess Ekama!"

·7·

For the Princess Ekama the next weeks were filled with delight. She was allowed to play, though she knew little enough of how to do so. She walked among the flower beds, smelling the fragrance and looking at the bright colors. Sometimes she carried the doll the Queen had given her, but she had no idea what to do with it. Often she sat on the wall behind the palace and watched the river far below.

"Where does it come from?" she asked Prince Aciam.

"I've never thought to find out," he told her. "They say it starts somewhere in the southern mountains. Someday we shall follow it to its beginning."

The Prince explained the moon to her, how it waxed and waned. One night she stayed up late to see stars appear one after the other. A new world was opening to her.

Tettie of the pink cheeks and dandelion-seed hair helped her with buttons and laces. Every morning, giggling and throwing her hands in the air and rolling her eyes, she brought Ekama the latest gossip of town and palace. The Princess came to know some folk by sight and many by hearsay. Another world opened to her.

One day the Queen called her. "I have a book for you," she said, and turned the pages to show her the beautiful illustrations.

"If only I could read!" Ekama cried, and from then on there was a governess for her.

In the evening, of course, there was music and dancing.

But the nights, after she went to bed, were not a part of her pleasure.

Fearful, she would wait for the cold ones.

One night while she waited, she suddenly murmured aloud, "They've never come here and they never will."

With that, she put them out of her mind in the same way she had put so many things out of her mind. From then on her nights were as peaceful as her days were filled with pleasure.

For Kashka the next weeks were filled with pain. Day and night were alike to him. He would come from somewhere, he did not know where, to a sense of pain—his back, his hand, his arm, the back of his neck—sometimes, it seemed, his entire body. With each breath he drew there would be a sharp agony in his chest and then the air would leave his lips with a cry. He could not help himself.

Bargah would come then. He knew it was Bargah. He knew the touch of her hand on his brow. She would rub his lower lip with her finger and his mouth would be filled with a terrible bitterness. Then she would slip a spoon between his lips. He would swallow the liquid, gagging on it, a feeling of nausea passing through him. After that the pain would fade. All sense would fade until he came back again to the pain and to Bargah's presence.

Sometimes, his sense of himself returning, Kashka would think someone other than Bargah was there beside him. He imagined a voice—his father's or Piff's, Piff's mother's voice, so like his own mother's yet not hers. Once he thought Prince Aciam was there saying to him, "You must get well soon. Piff and I want you to play the flute with us for the Princess."

Once he thought the King was there and it came to him that he was supposed to be playing his flute and tumbling for all the court. There was a great celebration and he was late for it. He hurried, running and running. When he finally arrived he was too late. The company was gone, the torches and lamps were out, the great ballroom was dark. He stood in the middle of the empty hall, alone, a terrible feeling of failure spreading through him. He had disappointed the King! He had failed his father! He had failed Master Wondry! He lifted his flute to his lips, but his mouth was so dry he could not blow into it. His lips felt swollen, his fingers would not move. They were stiff and hard and knew nothing of what they were supposed to do. The music he was to play would not come to his mind. He began to cry. He had even failed the music.

"I can't play," he sobbed. "I'll never play again."

"Oh yes you will!" His father's voice came to him. "Your hand is healing well. Your fingers are as straight as ever. You'll need to practice, of course. It will take a while. But I promise you this. When you are well again and ready to play, your first performance for the King will be with me."

How could he ever play well enough to accompany his father? It must have been a dream, but it comforted him. Now, sometimes, he was able to sleep without the bitter herb Bargah gave him. When he woke, it did not seem that he had come from such a distance.

One day he woke to see Piff sitting next to him and reading a book.

"What are you reading?" he asked.

Mouth open, Piff stared at him.

"Well?" Kashka asked impatiently.

"A . . . a . . . book," Piff stammered.

"Imagine that!" he said. "A book! I never would have guessed. Does it have words in it?"

"A few." Piff began to smile. His eyes sparkled.

"What do they say?" Kashka lay on his stomach, his cheek to the pillow, his hand beside his face. He watched Piff lazily.

Piff leaned over the bed and took Kashka's thumb. "It says, 'This fat piggy had a palace. This fat piggy had a sty. This fat piggy ate—' "

"Oh, keep still!" Kashka's mouth pulled up in half a grin.

35

He wanted to throw the pillow at Piff but it would take too great an effort. Besides, the pillow felt good beneath his face. He yawned. It hurt to yawn, but it was a good hurt and when the yawn had finished, the pain left. He closed his eyes, drifted, woke again to find Bargah and Piff both standing beside him.

"So you're feeling better! Do you want anything?" Bargah was smiling down at him, her amber eyes almost lost in the wrinkles.

"This fat piggy wants roast hen," he murmured. He could see his hand lying in front of his nose. With an effort he wiggled his middle finger. Then with an even greater effort he lifted his hand and pointed at Piff. "But that fat piggy can cry! I'm hungry. I get it all."

But when Bargah returned with a cup of warm broth, he was asleep.

The old woman took a honey cake from the shelf for Piff and then sent him to tell Mareth about Kashka. She brewed a cup of tea for herself.

Bargah had set her anger aside, but her thoughts often turned to the Lady Ysene. That woman—I have heard she has power. I don't know how much. She must have felt mine. I shall have to be careful. And the Princess . . . Why did she leave the child? Innocent as she seems, we shall have to watch her.

·8·

↘↘↘ "Wake up, Princess! Wake up! What do you think? I know it's the middle of the night but you told me to wake you. The Queen has had her baby! It's another prince! There are the trumpets again! Do you hear them? You told me to wake you, Princess, so I'm waking you!" Tettie gave Ekama's arm another shake.

Princess Ekama sat up in bed and rubbed her eyes. She shivered and drew the feather quilt up to her neck.

"There was such a noise in the quarters behind the kitchen! You never heard the like! Everyone shouting! At least Master Dury and Master Gann were shouting. They've been toasting each other with wine all night while they waited, and now they're noisy. The baby . . . They say he's beautiful with eyes like stars and hair like . . .

"But I'll tell you, Princess Ekama, babies are all pretty much alike. My sister has three and I've seen them all new. I love them—so tiny and soft you can't believe it. But they've scarcely any hair at all, usually, though one of them—it was Bru, I think—had a head of black hair like a curly puppy. For eyes like stars, I wouldn't believe that at all, Princess. They scarcely open them at first and their faces are so red. . . . It's all right, though, Princess, because they're so small and warm and comfortable to hold and . . . and . . . they smell like babies!"

"Oh, Tettie! It's a prince, then!" exclaimed the Princess

when Tettie finally stopped for a breath. "I'm so glad! I wanted them to have another prince and they have!"

"I should have thought you might like them to have a princess so there would be two princesses instead of two princes. Boys are such trouble! They pull your hair and pinch you and put frogs in your bed and think it's funny." Shivering in her nightgown, Tettie hugged her arms close to her body and crossed the toes of one bare foot over the other. Her hair was more thistly than ever.

"You're cold!" Ekama was wide awake now. "Get up on the bed and under the quilt and tell me all about the new prince. I want to know more. Do you think he will really pull your hair and put frogs in your bed? I don't believe Prince Aciam does such things!"

"Maybe princes don't, but other boys do. Sometimes snakes or toads. You just don't know boys, Princess. I know lots of them." She climbed up on the bed while she was talking and slipped under the warm quilt.

"I know Prince Aciam and Piff and Kashka," said the Princess. "They never would—"

"Oh, Piff and Kashka are the very worst of all!" Tettie cried. She felt more luxurious than she had ever felt in her life in the warmth and softness of the big bed. "And they haven't stopped one bit, even after Kashka almost got himself killed for it last summer, he was flogged that bad! Why—"

"Flogged!" exclaimed the Princess.

"Flogged, yes," Tettie said, remembering suddenly that she wasn't to tell the Princess about that. She glanced at Ekama; her voice had sounded so strange. "But let's not talk about *them*," the young servant girl went on hastily. "Let's talk about the Prince—about the ceremony tomorrow when they give him the amulet—the stone like the one the King and Prince Aciam have. Let's talk about what they're going to name him. What name would *you* choose, Princess? What name do you like?"

"I like Prince Aciam."

"You can't name them both the same."

"I know. Who flogged him, Tettie? Why? What did he do?"

"I . . . I don't know," the girl said. She was sorry now it had slipped out. She hadn't meant to. But *everyone* knew about Kashka!

"The King wouldn't order it, would he?" There was a thing the Princess Ekama had put away from her mind, the way she put so many things away that she might not have to think about them. Now it came to her of its own accord, and though she struggled to keep it on a dark and hidden shelf, it would not stay. It was a long time ago that it had happened, but the smell of the cold damp stone courtyard of Castle Ysene filled her nostrils as if she stood there now. There was the gray sky above and the dark recesses of the arches . . . and the Lord of Xon lifting his arm over and over again. . . . And the man. . . . It was all there just as it had been. Though she had tried, she hadn't been able to run away from seeing it when it happened, and though she had tried, she hadn't put it away at all.

"Princess! Princess! Why are you crying? Of course the King didn't order it! And Prince Aciam stopped it. It will never happen again. The King won't permit it. Kashka is all right now. Maybe it will keep him from hanging Master Pindy's underthings on the flagpole again." Tettie tried to choke back a giggle. "Maybe it will even keep him from putting frogs in the King's bed! You *never* know what he might think of!"

"Frogs in the King's bed?" The Princess sniffed, wiped her eyes with the sleeve of her nightgown. "Would he really dare?" Her mouth wasn't sure if it wanted to turn up or down.

"I wouldn't be surprised! Now, let's talk about the Prince and what they'll name him and what he will be when he grows up." They talked of the Prince until Tettie fell asleep.

Ekama lay awake, eyes open but not seeing the darkness of night. She saw instead the darkness of Castle Ysene reaching out to touch Nazor. She tried to turn her thoughts again to the baby prince, but the shadow reached out to touch him as well.

The Princess put her finger between her teeth and bit down on it so that it hurt. How cold her hand was against her lip! As cold as the silver of Kashka's flute. She pressed against her lower lip and blew across her finger as Kashka had showed her how to blow across the flute. She imagined the sound that came from it when Kashka blew into it.

How was it Piff had put her fingers on the strings of the lute?

"Rest it in your lap, Princess. It's heavy for you. This hand lies here. This one . . ." He had gone behind her, put his arm around her, his fingers over her hand, curling it around the strings. "You press the string with your finger to change the note. There. . . . Pluck it there with *this* hand and . . . That's it!"

Then he had made up a song for her. It was long and she only remembered the end of it:

> *Oh it takes so many fingers*
> *What I really truly need*
> *Is to be a kind of music-playing*
> *Royal centipede!*

Kashka blew a hundred notes up and down, the sun glinting on the flute. The snow was bright on the windowsill. There was no darkness; there were no shadows with Piff and Kashka.

It was summer again. The doors of the Queen's sitting room were opened to the balcony to let in the warmth. The governess stood before the Queen.

"I don't know what to do, Your Majesty. The Princess is very well behaved and as diligent a pupil as I have ever had."

"Then, what is worrying you?"

"It's . . . well, Your Majesty, it's the company she keeps."

"I wasn't aware that there was inappropriate company in the palace!"

"She should keep company with her own kind."

The Queen smiled. "There is no other princess here and

Prince Aciam is busy learning the problems of the throne. He can scarcely keep her company."

"There are the daughters of lords and ladies for her, Your Majesty."

"And doesn't she keep company with them?"

"No, Your Majesty."

"Then, I should have asked at once. With whom does she keep company?"

The governess bent her knee in a curtsy and said unhappily, "If you'll pardon my saying so, Your Majesty, she keeps company with Piff and Kashka."

The Queen coughed suddenly, turned her face aside, and covered her mouth with her handkerchief.

"Are you all right, Your Majesty? It . . . it just doesn't seem proper. I've mentioned it to her, but all she will say is that Prince Aciam performed the introductions and she is sure he would not have done so if it weren't the right thing. Still, I cannot help but worry. I . . . I fear her manners will suffer. Certainly her clothes do."

"Her *clothes* suffer? In what way, for goodness' sake?"

"She sits in the grass and stains the skirts. She goes through the meadows and comes in with burrs in the hems and her stockings torn. And just this morning she came late to her lessons with mud up to . . . to . . . *here*. When I asked, she said she had been to a pond in a . . . a . . . *cow pasture* c-c-catching frogs!"

"Oh my!" Queen Meta looked startled.

"That's exactly what I thought, Your Majesty," said the governess.

"What did she want the frogs for?" asked the Queen.

"I . . . I didn't think to ask!"

"Perhaps I had better speak to her," Queen Meta said. "And I think I had better speak to Piff and Kashka as well. I'll send Doro to hunt for them at once. If you will send the Princess to me. . . . And I'll talk with Tettie too, later."

The governess curtsied once again and left quickly.

41

Within a few minutes Princess Ekama arrived at the Queen's door. The Queen talked with her of this and that, of lessons and music and the palace garden and the weather. Ekama was allowed to peek at the sleeping prince, holding her breath all the while that she might not wake him. The Queen ordered fresh bread and jam and tea sent up. Then, at last, there was a tap at the door.

"Come in," said the Queen.

Doro herded two startled boys into the sitting room.

While they enjoyed the bread and jam and tea, the Queen still talked of this and that. Of Master Wondry and tumbling and juggling and practicing.

Piff and Kashka sat on the edges of their chairs and did the best they could. All the while they were careful not to look at one another. Nor did their eyes meet those of Princess Ekama, who sat as straight on the edge of *her* chair.

When all the tea and jam and bread were gone, the Queen wiped her mouth carefully with a napkin, straightened her back, folded her hands in her lap, and said sternly, "Now then, I shall not ask you for whose beds those frogs were meant. I hope neither the King's nor mine nor Prince Aciam's. From this moment on, in fact, they are meant for no bed at all unless it is the riverbed. You will march straight back to the pond, or to the river, with your crock of frogs and let every last one go. Yes, *every one*. There will be none for Doro, or the cook, or Tettie, or Mistress Palet. And the next time such an idea comes into your heads, consider it from the frogs' point of view. How very stuffy for them!"

Only two minutes later the King had reason to stop by the Queen's sitting room. He found her seated in a chair, her head bowed into a handkerchief pressed to her face with both hands, her shoulders shaking. Alarmed, he hurried to her.

"My dear, what is it?"

She looked up, her eyes streaming with tears.

"Oh my dear!" she cried, her voice ten notes higher than

it ordinarily was. "You should have seen their faces! All three of them—a map of guilt! I have never seen anything so . . . so . . . f-f-funny in my life! I do believe they meant one of those frogs for you! I can't prove it, of course, b-but you should have *seen* them!" She threw her arms around his neck, laughing so hard that she wept anew.

It took the King several moments to have the story from the Queen, laughing as she was. Then he said, "Lucky for them that they didn't! I would have had their skins!"

He went to the balcony, drawing the Queen beside him. The town lay below, the river and meadows stretching beyond.

Suddenly the Queen pointed. "Look! There they go across the meadow! And . . . and I do believe they *each* have a crock! They must have a frog for every bed in the palace! I wonder. . . . Perhaps we should not let her be so free."

King Darai rubbed his cheek over the top of Queen Meta's head, feeling the softness of her hair against it. For a moment he looked out over the land, here bright under the sun, there shadowed by the white puffs of clouds that drifted across the blue sky. He sighed.

"No, let her run. There is little enough time left her, poor child."

They watched as the three small figures moved into a shadow on the meadow. The Queen shivered suddenly. The King's arms tightened around her.

"Is there no way we can keep her?" she asked.

"No way we can insist upon it."

↘↘↘ "This is the highest place in the world, unless you go to the mountains," Piff told the Princess Ekama. "It's higher even than the highest tower in the palace. You can see farther from here than anyplace."

"But you can't see the beginning of the river." Ekama was disappointed. They had come so far, crossed the bridge over the river, scrambled through so much brush, clambered over such rocks, climbed so steep a path! She had torn her dress and scuffed her shoes terribly. She had even scraped the skin from the heel of her hand. It stung, but she didn't say anything about that. And now there was no beginning of the river.

"That's hundreds and hundreds of days away," Kashka told her. "You can never find that."

"Not that far," Piff disagreed. "You'd find it after a few months."

They sat on the high bluff. Beyond the river the harvested fields lay brown under the late summer sun. The Princess joined in throwing stones downward toward the river. "Swing your arm this way," Piff told her. "The stone will go farther." Then he pointed to the north where the forested hills were softened by a blue haze. "Prince Aciam says the river goes into the ocean near Birn Hall. That's that way."

"That's where it goes, not where it comes from," Kashka

argued. He was standing on his head so close to the edge of the bluff that it made Ekama's hands feel queer.

"It comes from that way." Piff turned and pointed south. "It comes from past Gynnis because boats come from Gynnis on the river."

"It doesn't start at Gynnis," Kashka said.

"I didn't say it did." Piff stood up. "Shall I push him over, Princess?"

"Oh no!" she gasped and went on hastily. "What road is that?" Eastward a road wound through the rolling countryside.

"That goes to Nainth," Piff told her. He began tossing stones into the air and catching them.

"We've never been to Nainth, but the Duke of Nainth has been to Nazor. I like him," Kashka said. "I'm glad they named the Prince for him." He sprang to his feet, did a somersault and a handspring. Ekama bit her lip. She was sure he would turn over the edge, but he didn't.

"Prince Aciam?" she asked.

"No, the baby prince. Prince Mittai. Look, there's a coach coming." He pointed to the north.

"It's no hay wagon," Piff said after watching a moment. "Those horses are going fast."

"I didn't say it was a hay wagon. I said it was a coach."

"I'll know whose it is before you do," Piff said.

"No you won't." Kashka squinted his eyes.

They both watched the coach come nearer and nearer down the road on the far side of the river.

"I don't know," Piff admitted at last. "I can't tell. Can you?"

"Give me a little more time." Kashka strained to see.

The Princess Ekama sat very still, her hands clenched in her lap. She had recognized the black coach at once and her heart beat quickly. It came nearer the town, entered the gate.

"I don't know either," Kashka grumbled at last. He turned. "But . . . what's the matter, Princess?" he asked, alarmed.

"Are you afraid up here? Are you going to be sick? You should have told us!"

At his words, Piff too turned, his eyes widening with concern.

The Princess shook her head. "No." Her voice was small, lost. "It's—the coach. They've come for me."

"Who?" both boys asked, though they knew before she answered.

"Lady Ysene and the Lord of Xon."

Kashka was speechless.

Piff found his tongue. "You can't go with them!"

"I'll have to."

"We'll hide you!"

She looked from one to the other. Both boys had paled. Slowly she shook her head. "They would find me. And . . . and they would . . ." The dark cupboards of her memory threatened to reopen. She stood up quickly. "I . . . I have to go back now. They will be asking for me. I'm sorry we couldn't see the beginning of the river. Thank you for bringing me."

Tettie hurried the Princess into the bath.

"Just look at you!" she cried. "You've torn your dress and you're all scratches! Last time you were covered with mud. Why do you do it? Where have you been this time? It's so late!"

Tettie could do nothing but scold. She wasn't angry with the Princess; she was frightened. The news of the arrival of the Lord of Xon and the Lady Ysene had spread through the palace as quickly as flame through gauze. It could mean only one thing. They had come to take the Princess away.

"She's ours! She's been here over a year! I won't let them take her!" Tettie had cried.

"What do *you* have to say about it?" the servants in the kitchen had asked.

"Then I'll go with her!"

But at that, she began to hear stories about Castle Ysene—how bleak and cold the place was. Worse, how miserable everyone was who lived anywhere near Lady Ysene and her brother, the Lord of Xon.

She scrubbed and rubbed the Princess. She pulled her hair while brushing the twigs and leaves from it. The dress went on backward and the Princess's chin was scratched by the silver buttons as they twisted and turned the frock around her neck.

Through it all the Princess said little, answering only one question. She had been out with Piff and Kashka. Tettie almost cried.

"Again? Why do you go off with them that way? Why did the Prince ever let you meet them! Someday they will get you into terrible trouble and then what will we do? Look at the scratches on your arms! You must say you were out riding and fell in a rosebush. No. We'll have to change your dress—put on one with long sleeves."

And she scratched the Princess's nose in pulling off the dress with the silver buttons.

The Princess remained silent. She thought of the times she had sat in the grass with Piff and Kashka, and Piff had played his lute and Kashka his flute. Each time they had showed her how to play a little more. She thought of the time Kashka had stood on his head and his shirt had slipped down—or was it up?—and she had seen the crisscross of scars on his back. She knew with no more doubt at all who had flogged him. She had wanted to run away and never see either of them again. She found Piff watching her and, when Kashka had gone off to chase something, he had said to her, "It wasn't your fault, Princess Ekama. He was going to throw the inkwell at her and I had to stop him. If I hadn't, it would have caused Master Wondry all sorts of trouble."

She had nodded. "I know. I saw him pick it up. I saw you jump."

How easy it was to talk to Piff! She could talk with him

about great wide thoughts. It was easier even than talking with Tettie. He never laughed at her.

When Tettie had finished with her, Princess Ekama said, "You're my friend, Tettie. They're my friends."

Then she turned away to go to the stiff and formal hall where visitors met with the King and no one ever said what he really thought.

Tettie knelt down to pick up the torn dress and then buried her face in her hands and wept.

·10·

➘➘➘ "You will stay here in this room. You will not go out until they have left, and half the day after that!"

Kashka had never heard his father speak so sternly. He fingered his flute, slumped back in his chair. "I'm supposed to play—Piff and I together tonight."

"I don't care. I'll tell the King you are ill. He will have to do without you. Piff can play well enough by himself, but it may be that Piff will be ill too."

Kashka shrugged, sighed.

"You can practice your flute. It's not perfect, you know."

Kashka scowled.

"I'm not doing this to punish you." His father's voice softened.

"I know."

"I don't want them ever to lay eyes on you again."

"What if they stay here—on and on?"

"Then we shall go to some other court. You and I. We play well together. We would find a place."

Kashka was shocked. He looked into his father's eyes and saw that he meant his words.

"But . . . but . . . *this* is your place. *Our* place. You can't leave King Darai! And what about Uncle Camin and Piff?" To be without them would be to lose half of his life!

"They will have to decide for themselves. I've made up my

49

mind. If they stay here you will have to find someone other than Piff to fight with."

"We don't fight! We've never fought in all our lives!"

"Oh, haven't you!" Mareth threw back his head in exasperation.

"We agree on absolutely everything!" Kashka insisted.

"All right. All right. Camin and I agreed in the same way when we were your age. I don't know how many bloody noses came out of our agreements! All I ask is that you stay in this room. Is that so much that you would risk leaving Nazor forever by disobeying?"

"No. I'll stay." But he squirmed in his chair.

"You don't have to sit on the chair all day," his father said as he opened the door to leave. "I've not glued you to it. You can move around the room. You are permitted to eat. . . ." He waved his hand toward the bread and grapes on the table. Kashka saw a gleam of humor in his father's eyes, but it vanished at once. "Don't go to the kitchen. I'll bring your supper. They're expecting me now. I'm late already. I want to find you here this afternoon."

Kashka nodded his head.

He practiced his flute until he was tired and began making mistakes. He threw himself on the cot and stretched out for a few minutes. If he were Piff he would read or study his numbers, but he could never be still long enough to read and study. If he were Piff he would write a poem. But words did not come as easily to him as music did, so it took more thinking, and he was tired of thinking.

He bounced to his feet, pushed the two chairs against the wall, shoved the table into a corner, and then began the exercises to limber his back and legs.

Half an hour of that and he was ready for something more. There was room to stand on his head, his hands, to balance—so—to walk on his hands, just a little way. But what about a handspring? A somersault? A run and leap and turn and flip . . . ?

There was a crash. Kashka looked with dismay at the broken plates and mug. Why had he left them so close to the edge of the table? He bent to pick up the larger pieces, then, with his foot, scraped and kicked the smaller fragments under the table.

He went to the window and stared through it. It was scarcely noon, the sun not quite overhead. The afternoon stretched a monotonous eternity before him.

What was Piff doing? Why hadn't he come?

Piff was probably spending the day with Prince Aciam or the Princess Ekama. He was out there running free, doing whatever he pleased. He could at least have stopped at the door and said hello. Perhaps he was playing the lute for the King. He wouldn't be singing for a while, though. His voice was between times, sometimes high, sometimes low. There would be no singing for him all year. But he could play. He could juggle. He wasn't a prisoner as Kashka was. No ceiling pressed down upon him. No walls shut him in. Kashka ground his teeth and glared into the yard.

It was a small courtyard he looked into, cobbled on this side, a short strip of grass on the far side. The more he looked at it, the more he longed to do his tumbling on that bit of grass. It was green. It was soft. No tables or chairs cluttered the space. No shards of pottery accused him from the corner. There were walls all around, a gate at the end. But the sky opened forever above. He padded around the room, scowling at his prison walls, and returned to the window.

If only . . . He would know if anyone were to come to the gate. In two steps he could be back through the door. Three steps down the short hallway and he would be in the room.

Who would see him?

In all this time no one had even passed through the yard, and he had been standing here forever! He glanced again at the sun. It had not moved in the sky. Was it bewitched? His eyes came back to the green, the enticing grass. Why, it was

51

so close to the door and window it was almost part of the room! The yard was *almost* the room itself!

The next minute he was out on the grass. The air was fresh and cool with a taste of autumn in it. For two hours and more he practiced. At last, worn out, he went back to the room and slept. When his father came in the late afternoon with a bowl of stew from the kitchen, Kashka was again playing the flute.

They ate with spoons from the bowl.

"Piff has had to stay in too," his father told him. "I was sure Camin would decide as I did. The King didn't ask for either of you. But you will have to stay in again tomorrow. They will be leaving the day after that, and then you will be free."

Kashka nodded. "What about the Princess?" he asked, not quite able to meet his father's gaze. "They aren't going to let them take her, are they?"

"I don't know. It hasn't been decided. There's one hope. It seems the Lord of Xon has married the sister of Jevis of Toth. Jevis has since died, so Xon has proclaimed himself Duke of Toth as well as of his own country. The hope for the Princess is that the new lady would rather not have the Princess underfoot."

"Wouldn't she stay at Castle Ysene? She did before."

"I don't know. Lady Ysene seems to think she will be safer with her brother and his wife."

"Why?"

"Mogrud threatens, and Castle Ysene lies close to his border. Mogrud! He wants gold, not the mold of Castle Ysene. I would fear more for the Princess's life with the Duke of Xon."

"What does the King say?"

"Of course the King and Queen want to keep her here. But they are being careful not to press it. Lady Ysene—who knows what she wants—or why?"

"And Princess Ekama? Doesn't anyone ask her what *she* wants?"

"The Princess? Poor child! She sat there through the evening, pale, not a word out of her. You wouldn't know her for the same child who runs through the palace or bounces the baby prince on her knees, both of them laughing, making faces at each other. She had to sit there listening to all that jousting with words—others jousting with her life." Mareth snorted. "You're lucky you deal with music. The more deeply you seek out its meaning, the more truth, the more of what is eternal you find. There is no deceit. You search a lifetime through what is great and the revelations are only greater.

"But what truth do you find in the sudden death of Jevis after his sister's marriage? Or Mogrud's passion for gold that leads him to destroy? Or the Lady Ysene and her brother with their—whatever it is that gives you a crawling sense at the back of your neck of something wrong, something slimy. For the love of all the earth, why did the Lady of Toth marry that . . . horror of brutality?"

Kashka wiped the bowl with a piece of bread, soaking up the last of the gravy. "Poor woman," he said, his mouth half full, "married to the Lord of Xon! I don't think I want to know anything about it." He licked his fingers.

"The whole thing is as sticky as your fingers." His father paused, then remarked, "Practicing has given you an appetite."

"Practicing always makes me hungry."

Mareth left with another warning to Kashka. The boy stayed in the whole evening. Piff, after all, was also a prisoner.

"Why did you go out?" The lamp was shining in Kashka's face. His father stood over him and was shaking him. "*Why did you go out?*"

Kashka blinked, struggled his way out of a deep sleep. He had never seen his father so angry.

"*Why?*"

The boy sat up.

"It was . . . it was only in the small yard. No farther. I *had* to. I couldn't move. . . . I broke the plates. . . ." For the first time in his life he feared his father, the look on his face. "No one came. No one! I came right back in. I didn't go out again."

"She saw you! The Lady Ysene's windows overlook the courtyard. She saw you practicing and she asked the King for you."

Kashka could not speak. His blood seemed to dry and shrivel in his veins.

"She said, 'Who is the boy who does the tumbling in the little yard in the corner? I thought to see him here tonight.' "

Kashka could only stare at his father.

" 'I watched him this afternoon for some time,' she said. 'He is very quick, very agile, very graceful. I should like to have him. We need someone to amuse us at Castle Ysene. I shall pay you well for him.' "

"*Pay* for me? *Buy* me?" Kashka whispered, horrified that she might purchase him like a clay pot. "What did the King say?"

"At first he didn't know what to say. I have never seen the King so startled. Then he lied. He said he didn't know who she meant! The whole court knew who she meant! Your king lied before the entire court for you!

" 'You don't know? Then you have treasures here that are kept well hidden!' " Mareth imitated the voice of Lady Ysene. " 'For myself, I know exactly what treasures I have gathered for amusement. I call it my—*collection*.' "

Kashka shivered.

"That woman has the eyes of a snake!" Mareth went on. "When she looks at you, you feel as if she is wondering whether you are worth her swallowing you whole!

"Do you know who saved you *and* the King? Prince Aciam! 'You must have seen that boy who was with the mountebank Suvio and his troupe. He was excellent.' 'Oh, of course,' the King said. 'It must have been he. But I thought they had left. Are they still here?' 'No,' Prince Aciam said as cool as you can believe. 'They left this afternoon rather late. They had

meant to leave this morning but were delayed by some misfortune—a broken wheel on their wagon, I believe. The smith
repaired it for them. They could have stayed and performed
again tonight but they were in a hurry to get on. They had
promised the Duke of Nainth a certain day. They'll travel half
the night to make up the time now.' 'Ah,' the King said. 'So
that is who it was.' And they talked of other things. So the
Prince too lied for you."

Kashka swallowed. "She didn't know who I was . . . from
before?"

"No. It had nothing to do with what happened before. But
she saw you. She wanted you—for what I don't know. Her
collection? What kind of collection does she have to amuse
her? No kind of amusement at Castle Ysene I can think of
but turns me cold as death's tomb. It's as if a demon were in
it, plotting with her to be at you one way or another! *You will
stay in tomorrow if I have to tie you!*" He shook Kashka again.

When Mareth finally loosened his grasp, Kashka lay back
on the cot. His father set a small pan of water over the lamp
to heat. He paced the room twice around, turned back, sat on
his cot, got to his feet, took off his shirt. He put a mixture of
things into the remaining mug and, when the water was hot,
added it to the rest and stirred it. He sat down again and sipped
at the steaming drink.

Kashka stared at the ceiling the entire time. Now he spoke.
"I should go away. All I do is make trouble. If she wants me,
maybe I should go to Castle Ysene. If they take the Princess,
maybe I can help make it not so bad for her."

His father sat with his hands around the mug as if trying to
warm himself from it. Then he set the cup on the table and
leaned forward.

"Listen, Kashka. There is much to be loved in this world.
Much to be cherished. I cannot count the number of things
I love." He paused, took up the mug, put it down again, and
pushed it away. He spoke again, quietly.

"Before your mother died there were six things I loved be-

55

yond all others. Now there are five." He held up his hand and bent one finger after the other to his words. "You, my brother Camin, his family, the King, and music. You are first.

"Now, I don't know how many things the Lady Ysene and her brother hate in this world. I am sure the number is endless. But if you were to go to Castle Ysene, I am just as sure you would soon be first on their list as well. If you lived one day in that dank, ill-omened, funereal crypt they call Castle Ysene, you would be fortunate. If they killed you at once, you would be even more fortunate."

Kashka ran the tip of his tongue over his lip. His mouth was dry. "And the Princess Ekama? How can she go there to live?"

"The Princess? I am not sure, but from the sound of their words I think they mean to leave her here, for whatever their reasons. It is clear that the lady at Toth does not want her and the Lady Ysene will not have her. Lucky for her!"

Suddenly Mareth struck the table with the palm of his hand and cried, "For the love of all the earth, your father included, stay in tomorrow! That's all I ask! *One day!*"

Kashka sighed. "If you lock the door and take the key—and—and put up the bar across the window on the outside. . . ."

"And tie you?"

"And tie me."

"And a gag so you can't cry for help?"

"And a gag."

"A guard at the door?"

"Two!"

"The King's best!"

"The Margrave of Tat and Sir Andros!" Kashka's mouth pulled up on one side.

"Done! And two more at the window. Doro and the smith."

"That should take care of it." Kashka nodded as his father blew out the lamp.

"No." His father's voice came through the darkness. "You must *want* to stay *in!*"

He did want to stay in. But what if he had to escape to rescue the Princess from the Duke of Xon?

Kashka fell asleep wondering how he might free himself of gag and bonds, how he might get through the locked door and barred window, how he might elude four guards as formidable as those mentioned. It would take some doing, he told himself. But there might be a way if . . . Of course! Piff! Together they could. Piff would . . . But first Piff must escape. . . . then. . . . Then it was not Piff before him. He was face-to-face with Lady Ysene.

"There you are at last," she said. "My brother is waiting for you. We were so pleased the King was willing to trade you and Piff and your father for the Princess."

My father! Piff! He turned cold. Why?

She seemed to read his mind. "Because you put frogs in his bed. Here is my brother now."

The Lord of Xon walked into the room, cutting the air with his whip. At the sound Kashka woke with a start. His back was tingling and he was cold and sweating and trembling all at once.

·11·

꙰꙰꙰ Through the morning the nightmare clung to him like a wet shroud. Nothing he did could take his attention completely. Shock, fear, and despair hung upon him so that the usually cheerful notes from his flute only surrounded him with gloom. He had no desire to go out, though as the morning passed he became more and more restless.

His father's words kept returning to him. Was he really something that might be bought or sold? He loved the King—when he thought about it—and respected him. As for belonging to him, he had never felt anything but duty and allegiance, and that of his own free choice. *Could* the King sell him? *Would* he? But the King had lied for him! Who was he that the King should lie for him? A boy who caused no one anything but trouble! Only last week. . . . And then, just three days ago. . . . He groaned. There was an iron chain inside of him that twisted and turned and knotted. He had never been so miserable in his life.

"Kashka, are you there?" The whispered words came through the keyhole. "It's me, Piff. Are you there?"

Kashka was kneeling at the door at once, eye to the keyhole. "Of course I'm here! Where else would I be?"

"I don't know. Let me in."

"I can't. My father locked the door and took the key."

"No, he didn't take it. He hung it here on the wall. Wait! I'll be back!"

Though he listened, Kashka heard no sound of Piff's leaving. He waited, first eye, then ear to the keyhole. What was Piff doing here? He wasn't supposed to be out any more than Kashka. Where did he go? What was he going to do?

Then there was a sound, breathless whispers, a giggle, a "shhh!" The key was turned, and in the next instant Piff was dragging a bulging sack into the room. The door closed behind him, the key turned in the lock.

"Finished!" A whisper came from the hallway.

Piff bent to the keyhole and asked, "Did you hang the key back on the wall?"

"Yes. Remember what you promised."

"I promise again. Thank you! Don't tell *anyone!*"

"I won't!"

Kashka listened but no more whispers came from the other side of the door. "Who was that?" he asked, whispering himself. "What is that stuff you're wearing? Why did you put it on?"

"Tettie. Because I didn't want them to know me in case they were looking. They're always looking where they aren't supposed to. That's why we have to hang something across the window. What is there?"

"Blankets," Kashka said, joining Piff's spirit of urgency at once.

They found a pair of tall stilts and jammed them into the upper corners of the window, the blanket caught between stilts and frame. It made a fine curtain.

"Now we have to disguise ourselves." Piff untied the knot in the top of the sack and began pulling things from it.

"You're already disguised! Where did you *find* those clothes?"

"They're just rags that were lying around. You should have seen me limp all the way here with the sack on my back. You would have thought I was born that way. Step and drag a leg, all uneven and hunched over. It gave me a pain. . . ." He rubbed his thigh. "But now we're going to be something else, so if they saw me the first time they won't think I'm the same one."

Kashka's eyes sparkled when the contents of the sack were spread out at last on cots and table and floor. They set to work at once with all the care that the best actor would take in preparing himself for the stage.

"A little more wax there. Another line here." Stopping now and then to sit back and examine their work, to hold a mirror up. A nod or a frown.

"How did you talk Gamel out of this?" Kashka asked, holding up a piece of limp pinkish-yellow cloth stuck with furry pieces.

"I didn't exactly talk him out of it," Piff told him. "He wasn't exactly there when I stopped in to ask for a few things."

"Uh!"

"I only *borrowed* them. We'll take everything back as soon as we've finished with it. After all, we've worked enough with him. Helped him out. He wouldn't want us floating dead in the river and all his fault for not lending us a little paint!"

Piff's reasoning was as logical as his own, and Kashka now felt only a twinge of his earlier fear at the mention of lying dead in the river. Had Uncle Camin spoken as harshly to Piff as his father had to him?

"I thought you were supposed to stay in today too," he said.

"Nobody really said so. They were too busy talking about you to worry about me. So after my mother left this noon I thought . . . well, it's boring to sit in a room all day and all night forever. Can you look stupid? Like this?"

"This way?"

"Yes."

Kashka nodded. "What will they do when they find you're gone?"

"What did your father do?"

"He . . . he shook me until I thought my head would fall off."

"Uncle Mareth? He did that?" Piff was silent a moment. "Ooof, he must have been angry!"

"He was." Kashka nodded, some of his discomfort returning. But with Piff there nothing seemed as dangerous, as frightening, as terrible as it had been when he was alone.

They began picking up and putting away all that was left unused when they heard a door close and footsteps in the hallway.

"Is Uncle Mareth home already?" Piff looked up. "What time is it? Tettie should have come to warn us."

"I don't know. I can't see the sun." Kashka glanced at the covered window. All they had done had been by candlelight. Had they been at it all afternoon? "It must be late, but that's not my father's step."

"They've stopped at the door." Piff's voice too dropped to a whisper.

"Maybe it's your mother. She'd look for you here."

Piff shook his head. "I don't think so. I mean it doesn't sound like . . ." They looked at each other.

The latch rattled, then stopped. They held their breaths in the silence. Then the key scraped in the lock and turned.

"Rub your eyes," Piff whispered.

The door swung open and they froze to their chairs. The Lady Ysene stood before them, her eyes sweeping the room in half a second, then fixing themselves first on one face, then the other of the two terror-stricken boys.

"I never would have locked him in, but he insisted," Mareth told his brother as they walked together with Cara through the wide palace courtyard. He shaded his eyes against the late afternoon sun. "I hated to leave him there alone. I've never seen him more dejected and I'm sorry to have been so harsh with him. Yet, somehow, the boy *must* be made to understand.

61

You would think after the beating, the pain he suffered, that he would remember and be careful."

"You would think so," Camin agreed. "But he was unaware most of the time. It was you who sat by his side and suffered for him minute by minute. You had nothing to give you sleep or rest or healing. You hate and fear them more than he does."

"And you?" Mareth turned to his brother.

"I hate and fear them as I do nothing else on this earth. But I have my Cara, and Piff is not quite the worry that Kashka is. It's not that I don't love Kashka as if he were my own—as you love Piff. It's just that minim of difference"—he held up finger and thumb a hair's breadth apart—"that drives you mad and leaves me sane.

"I trusted Piff to stay home today even with Cara gone. It's no matter of good behavior or sharpness of mind. It's a matter of . . . of reflection on what the outcome will be. Kashka never stops to think of that. Piff does. Just now we wish Kashka would show some of Piff's caution. There may be a time when Kashka's way would serve Piff. He might stop to think just at the moment he should jump."

Mareth sighed. It eased his mind to talk with his brother. "To think how much they look alike, almost as much as we do, and yet they are so different."

"Not that much different," Camin disagreed. "Have we ever known which to blame for the deviltry they get into? And they are both always in it up to their eyes. Does one play music better than the other? Simply different instruments. You know how they argue that one! Tumbling—juggling—they try for every perfection, young as they are. It's not the few differences that's so surprising. It's how much alike they are!"

"And they need each other. Camin, if this matter with the Lady Ysene and the Duke of Xon . . . If I felt I must take Kashka and go some other place with him, would you stay here or go with us?"

"I knew you'd come to that! Last night I thought it over.

Where would you go? To Nainth? Birn Hall? Gorloth? Do you think you might escape them there?" He shook his head. "You would have to go much farther. You would have to cross the sea to escape them, and who knows what lies across the sea? No, Mareth, what lord or duke or *king* of some foreign court would lie in the teeth of that pair to protect the life of a young scalawag? Don't let your fear carry you beyond reason! King Darai is one king of a thousand kings. Stay with him."

They had arrived at Camin's door. Cara opened it and called, "Piff!"

There was no answer.

"He must be asleep," she said to Camin and Mareth, who stood outside for a few words more. She tiptoed across the room and looked into the alcove. There was no one there. She opened the door to the bedroom.

"Piff!" Her voice rose.

Camin and Mareth turned from their good-byes.

"He's not here."

Three pairs of eyes swept the courtyard. Then someone came running across to them. It was Tettie. She was pale, out of breath.

"Hurry! Oh, hurry, Mareth! She . . . she's at your door. That terrible lady. The key is right there. She can go in. They're there! Piff—Kashka, both of them. Locked in! They . . ."

"Hecate's tomb!"

The Lady Ysene stood in the doorway, eyes piercing every corner of the ill-lighted room.

Seated at the table, a deck of cards and several children's toys lying on it, were two wizened old men. One, hunchbacked, fingers curled clawlike, twisted awkwardly to stare at her. The other, bald, red-eyed, slack of mouth, drooled and turned a lump of yarn around and around in his hands, some-

63

times pressing it gently between his palms. "Soft, soft, soft," he murmured to himself in a hoarse and crackling voice.

Suddenly the hunchback's lips twisted in a distorted smile showing a mouth almost devoid of teeth.

The lady stepped back quickly, a look of fury replacing that of surprise. She slammed the door and whirled around to stalk through the hallway and yard. At the gate she almost collided with three persons who were hurrying as quickly toward it as she was hurrying out of it. Too angry to notice who they were, she muttered a curse and hastened on her way.

Tettie had said something more but none of them heard her. Mareth, Camin, and Cara flew to the other side of the courtyard and to the gate opening into the small yard. They drew back as the Lady Ysene strode past them, her face livid. Then three steps across the little yard, two down the hallway, and Mareth flung open the unlocked door.

Cara covered her mouth to muffle her scream. Mareth and Camin gasped.

"Don't cry, Mother!" Piff's voice came from the strangely distorted mouth. Two bodies straightened. Four hands were raised. Two pink scalps, one bald with gray tufts at the ears, one with sparse and stringy hair—both with grizzled eyebrows—were lifted. A tumble of fair curling hair fell over wrinkled brows. A hump slipped down from between a pair of shoulders to catch in a bizarre lump at the belt of the ragged tunic. One hand wiped across its face sideways, streaking it with grays and blues and yellows. The appearance of wrinkles and stubble vanished in a smear of color. Another hand picked and peeled a coating of wax from its face to let lips and eyes grow straight and young.

Mareth, legs weak, stumbled into the room and sat on a cot. Camin and Cara were as glad to sink down beside him.

"I thought, what if she comes after all—to see for herself?" Piff's voice came from behind the still waxed cheeks. He continued to pick at his face with trembling hands. "He'd be trapped even if he hid under the bed or in the wardrobe."

"We never thought she really would come." Kashka's voice shook.

"Wait," Mareth said holding his head in his hands. "One at a time—slowly!"

"She came right to the door. Right here and unlocked it." Even more breathless than before, Tettie came through the doorway. "I'd just come down the stair. I was going to tell Piff it was time to go, that you would all be back in a few minutes, and I saw her. She came in from the yard and went right to your door, Mareth, and started to unlock it. I had to go around the other way to find you."

Mareth raised his head to meet Camin's look.

"Someone told her!"

By the time she reached her room, her rage was at its peak.

"I know they were lying! Why they should, I don't know. What is a boy that they should want to keep him for themselves?

"But *he* . . . He made a fool of me! He must have been watching to see if I went to that place. The servants' quarters! Me! Old men! Senile! Imbecile! They keep them here! Give them games to play! Disgusting!

"Well," she went on, muttering to herself, "we shall see. I'll find . . . Yes, if it's games they want, let them play this one."

She threw herself into a chair, grasped the arms with her hands, and stared hard at a place where the two walls met.

Bargah was kneading a loaf and had just added another handful of flour when she paused, lifted her head, and grew very still. What is this? She stood motionless for several seconds. Then, leaving the dough in the middle of the board, she rinsed her hands hastily in a basin of water and, drying them on her apron even as she hurried out of her cottage, made her way as fast as she could to Mareth's.

·12·

↘↘↘ Bargah lived in a small cottage just outside the garden wall at the back of the palace. When there was reason for her to visit the palace and there was neither hurry nor worry for her being there, she would take the road that skirted the wall all the way around to the wide front gate and the great central courtyard. Though the walk was long, she found it pleasant to look out over the roofs of Nazor as they stepped down the hill to the river with its bridge and high bluffs beyond. She might pause to smile down at a lone buttercup growing between the cobblestones or pinch a bit of rosemary between thumb and forefinger to smell the fragrance. Folk would stop to pass a moment with her, asking what to do about a grandfather's rheumatism or a baby's colic.

If she was in a bit more of a hurry, she would go through the side gate next to the stables and carriage sheds, where the smithy stood and the craftspeople lived and had their work-places. Here she would nod to Janis the silversmith or Podra the potter, mention to the weaver a swatch of cloth she had ordered, or ask the tailor if his stiff neck was any better. At the far end of the row against the inside of the wall, she would cock an ear for the sound of music coming from Master Wondry's workshop.

But today Bargah was in a great hurry. There was no time to enjoy a walk nor did she want eyes to see her or tongues of gossip to clack over her going. She went through her own garden to the gate at the back of it.

Hers was the last cottage on the narrow cobbled street. Beyond it a cliff of granite dropped to the street below. There was room at the top only for a narrow path, along which she now hurried to the corner of the wall. There, hidden from view, she pushed aside a tangle of ivy. With a key of her own she unlocked a small door that everyone but herself had forgotten.

With growing dread, she hastened down the narrow space between a row of thick cypress and the windowless back of the craft shops. The path turned into the same courtyard of shops as the carriage entrance, but she took only half a dozen steps beneath a thick-leafed oak before entering a passageway.

There was no concealing herself now. She passed through both second and first kitchens. But at this time of the afternoon everyone was too busy to ask why she was there. Having spoken to no one, she came to the steps and, finally, the hallway off which Mareth's room lay.

Bargah tapped at the door. It opened a crack and then swung wide for her to enter. She looked quickly around, her anxiety changing at once to relief mixed with astonishment.

"What is this?" she asked. "A council of war? Or some kind of ancient rite called washing?"

The room was crowded. Camin rose at once and moved the chair for her to sit down. Then he turned again to scrubbing the back of Piff's neck. There were still streaks of color on his jaw and around his ears. Cara rubbed grease from a jar on Kashka's face, handed him a rag to mop at it while she rubbed more on his throat. Mareth stood with a towel in his hand and so bemused a look on his face that Bargah decided to wait before asking any more questions.

It was Tettie, as she rinsed out cloths and poured fresh water into the basin, who told Bargah all about it.

Camin gave up on Piff's neck and turned to Bargah while

he dried his hands. "She came here for him. There's no other way to explain it. She knew exactly where to come and that means someone told her where to find him. We would like to know who it was."

All eyes turned on Kashka as he pulled on a clean shirt. Head through the neck and sleeves hanging armless from his shoulders, Kashka paused, looked from face to face of his questioners. With an expression of "why-are-you-looking-at-me?" innocence, he shrugged his shoulders, shook his head, and spread his hands to the sides from beneath the shirt.

All eyes turned on Piff. Piff looked at Kashka and then back to the others. With an identical look on his face he too shook his head, lifted his shoulders, and spread out his hands, palms up. Then his eyes met his father's and Piff looked down with a sigh. It could have been anyone within a day's walk of the palace.

Mareth's face was grim. "It's a small man who would take such revenge on a boy."

"Perhaps not revenge," Bargah said thoughtfully. "And I think we shall learn soon enough who it was."

"Why do you think so? Who do you think it was? How do you know? Why did you come? Did someone tell you she was here? Who else knows of it?"

Bargah held up her hand. "Never mind how I knew! In fact, I *didn't* know. I thought . . . Well, I thought something might have happened—and it did. But it was not what I feared. I don't know who might have told her, but I think we shall find out. And I think the reason may not have been revenge, but greed."

"Greed?"

"She offered the King money for Kashka. Another might sell more willingly than the King."

They were all silent.

"How do you think we'll find out who it is?" Cara asked.

"I think the lady was angry that she didn't find Kashka,"

Bargah said. "I think someone will meet with some kind of accident. Something not ordinary. You'll hear about it, at least by tomorrow. And tomorrow she will be gone. I can't say that I'll be sorry. I'm going home now. I left my bread without covering it and it's drying out. I'll have to knead it all over. I hope it rises again."

Tettie left the room with Bargah. The old woman put her arm around the girl's shoulder. "It would be best to say nothing about any of this, don't you think?"

Tettie nodded. "I saw her face when she crossed the court-yard. It would have been awful for Kashka. I wonder how the Princess lived with her so long without . . . without something terrible happening to her."

Bargah held Tettie's hand and patted it. "That's so. I wonder too."

"She wanted the boy," Grabe muttered. "If she'd pay the King for him, she'd pay another. So why shouldn't *I* have it? The money is all the same to *her*!"

He had gone to her. Now he would have the money and she would have the boy. Not a pleasant lady, though. Grabe licked his lips and stopped counting his gold pieces to rub his hands together. She'd have the boy by now. She'd pay him soon. Then he, Grabe, would have more. He looked lovingly at the heap of coins on the table. It would grow today. There was yet another debt due.

Grabe drew a piece of parchment from a drawer and glanced over it with a smile. There was the amount. To be paid in gold! Today was an excellent day.

He looked through the window. There he came now, his debtor—the potter's ne'er-do-well cousin—with his hands in his pockets. A worried look! With good reason! He was holding the last money he would have for a long time. Everything he earned from now on would come to Grabe. His children? Grabe shrugged. You can't feel sorry for a donkey who gambles. A gambler must be able to lose. A wife who was ill? They all had excuses! He thought he'd win! The man was a fool!

But he'd be at the door in half a minute. Grabe scooped the coins into a leather pouch. He would make him wait, give him an instant of hope. . . . Ahieee!

A sudden pain shot through Grabe's ear and down the edge of his jaw, the side of his throat, shoulder, armpit—all the way to his wrist. The pain grew more intense. Grabe fell to the floor, writhing.

There was a knock at the door. He could not answer it, only choke with the pain that now filled his throat, his chest.

"Hello! Hello! Are you in there? What's going on?"

"The ph-physician!" Grabe managed to gasp. "Bring him!"

The latch on the door rattled, but the door was locked.

"The key!" Grabe cried hoarsely. "Under the loose brick. . . ."

After a moment the door opened. There he was, money in his hand. Gold pieces to pay.

"The physician!" Now the pain went down his back and into his leg. He groaned. From head to foot, where it was the worst he could not tell.

The visitor stared. "What is it? What should I tell him?"

"How do I know? I'm dying!"

"Then you won't need this." He held out his hand.

"No, no! Keep it! Take the parchment—there on the table. Take it! Tear it up! Go. Fetch the ph—"

The visitor nodded, picked up the parchment, tore it into two pieces, four, several more, and put all the little pieces into his pocket. He saw the leather pouch and picked it up, his eyes widening. Then he nodded his head. "I'll go for the physician. Looks like you need him." He slipped the pouch into his pocket and pulled the door shut behind him.

Tettie was behind in her work. She hurried twice as fast to fix a tray for the Princess, who did not feel well and was staying in her room. As she carried the supper up the stairs she thought, it's because she's so . . . so . . . She is just a dear sweet thing! That's why! All the wickedness in the world can't hurt her!

Then, because Tettie was not sure that being a dear sweet thing would protect even the Princess from one with such a look as she had seen on Lady Ysene's face, she cried a little. When she came to Princess Ekama's door, she had to set the tray down and wipe the tears from the silver dish cover with her sleeve.

"What do you think brought Bargah here?" Cara asked. "When she first came in she looked as if she expected to find us all dead on the floor. I never saw anyone look so relieved in so short a minute!"

"I don't know. She was out of breath, as if she had been running. Yet she didn't know that Lady Ysene had been here." Camin wiped an overlooked bit of paint from behind Piff's ear.

Mareth rubbed his brow, said nothing.

"You know something, don't you?" Camin spoke suddenly to his brother, then added quickly, "I'm sorry. I don't mean to pry. It just came to me all at once. We've always known . . . There's that between us. . . ."

"Yes," Mareth said quietly. "It's that way with Bargah too. She senses things."

"We all know that," Cara put in.

Mareth looked thoughtful. Camin knew there was more than that to Mareth's knowledge but he did not press him.

Bargah kneaded her bread again. There have been rumors of Lady Ysene, she thought. Today I learned why. I'm glad she has never seen me. I shall have to be careful to keep out of her way when she comes again. She would know me as I know her.

She shaped the bread into two loaves and put them in pans to rise.

Tettie is right. The Princess is free of any taint of her step-sister's powers. I'm certain of that. Still, there's something brewing with the child or she wouldn't have been so eager to leave her here. The old woman frowned as she washed her hands. And if she wants her here, there is something brewing with the rest of us. That woman does nothing without a reason, and her reasons have no good intent.

She wants Kashka. Why? I don't know. I cannot imagine! Mareth senses it in his bones. He must also know that he cannot protect the boy by himself.

Mareth woke early the next morning. It was still dark but there were the sounds of voices and horses and the clanking of harnesses from the stables. He rose quickly, lighted a candle, and dressed. After pulling on a jacket he paused to bend over his sleeping son.

How could a boy with so much mischief in his mind during the day sleep so soundly at night? You would think he would have to lie awake the whole time, hatching schemes, concocting ideas for the next day's pranks. No, that wasn't Kashka's way. It all came to him in a minute, was executed the next minute, and regretted—perhaps—the following one! What would become of him? If only I can keep him alive until he's a man! Mareth straightened his back.

He pinched out the candle and moved quietly to the door. Practice, that's what would become of him! The boy had more than his share of gifts. He must not waste them. Practice on the flute and at the tumbling. More performing for the King. Anything to keep him busy and out of trouble!

Mareth locked the door behind him and pocketed the key. He walked quietly down the hallway and out into the side yard, then through the gate to slip into the shadow of a doorway.

As yet there was no hint of the dawn to come. Wisps of fog

from the river drifted across the stones of the courtyard. Mareth waited.

The coach drawn by two black horses came through the courtyard and stopped near the wide palace doors. Servants with torches lighted the way for a man and a woman and helped them enter the coach. The iron gates swung open. At a flick of the reins, the horses started forward.

Mareth watched until the gates closed. He waited until he could no longer hear the sound of hooves and wheels. He waited even until the sound died from his imagination. Then, with a sigh, he stepped from the doorway.

Someone touched his arm. He turned, startled.

"Were you holding your breath the whole time?" It was his brother. "I came to see too, to be sure they were on their way." He pointed toward the garden. "If we watch from the wall we can see them even farther on their way. It should be light by the time they come to the river road."

Mareth nodded and together they went to the back of the garden. There they sat on the wall, the earliest gray of the dawn beginning to show in the sky behind them. And there Mareth at last told his brother of the night Bargah had called to him.

"I still wonder if I dreamt it, but I don't think so."

"Did she . . . did she bring him back from death itself?" Camin's voice was hushed.

"I . . . don't know. So close to it. . . . I try . . . not to think of that night. I still shake."

"No wonder, no wonder!" Shaken himself, Camin embraced his brother. "I knew something had happened," he murmured. "I didn't imagine anything like . . . that."

For a moment they held to each other. Then, "Look! There at the bend where the road comes out of the fog!" Camin pointed. "The coach . . . gone!"

"I hope I never see them again." Even as he spoke, a knot of fear tightened in Mareth's chest.

·13·

↘↘↘ It was a time for growing, not as things grow in the spring, bursting forth green upon green, shooting out, all busy with blossoming and song. It was a time for winter growing, for things wrapped in woolens, simmered in covered kettles, brewed in crocks, ripened in barrels, aged in cupboards to grow unnoticed. It was a time to absorb, to grow inwardly, the mixing and melding of flavors, minds, feelings. It was a time to gather around the fire of a hearth, to share hopes and fears, to give comfort and counsel, to grow closer to others.

Storms came head to heel, snow falling so thick that those peering from the windows on one side of the courtyard could not see the palace towers on the other. The gray days of the storms passed and the snow lay deep and glittering, covering the earth with a quilt that shut out the bitterness of the air. Those peering over the countryside from the palace windows would look at the smooth white covering, at the ice-blue sky rimmed with a pale orange light, at the bare trees fingering the cold air. They would shiver and turn back to the warmth of the fire.

Mareth drove Kashka. To the boy it seemed his father was never satisfied. A note was too long or too short, too high or too low, the line not clear, the sense muddled. When Mareth fell ill he spent even more time, was more insistent. He would prop himself on pillows on his cot to listen, to shake his head no, or to clap his hands to an even more subtle rhythm. Unable to speak for coughing, he would draw his harp to his side to play the passage for Kashka. The boy, wrapped in blankets, his heels hooked over the rung of the stool, would play it over. Then, once more, he would repeat it. And repeat it, setting it in his mind and fingers, setting it even more deeply in that place of understanding that recognizes the shape of what has meaning, what is beautiful. *That* was what told his breath, his lips, his fingers what to do in the fumbling reach for perfection.

When Mareth nodded and murmured, "Good!" their eyes would meet and Kashka knew that he had not only pleased his father but had also touched the essence of the music.

The boy spent other hours practicing his tumbling in the dark hallway. In the evenings there were performances for the court. He joined Piff and Camin, and if his father felt well enough, Kashka carried his harp up the stairs and through the passageways to the dining hall where there was warmth and laughter and music and dancing. Let the winter wind blow!

March came, and the winter did not let go. Sleet driven sideways by fierce gales hissed and rattled shutters, coated trees and ground with ice.

Camin opened the door, stuck his head into the room.

"You're wanted for supper. Cara has enough for ten! Your favorite, Mareth."

Kashka put down his flute, helped his father with his coat, and held the door for him.

"Go ahead," Camin told Mareth, and then to Kashka, "You carry this." In an instant he bundled the quilts from Mareth's bed into a roll and thrust them into the boy's arms. Then he hurried to catch up with Mareth and walk beside him.

"We've been talking, Cara and I," he began when the wind struck them as they stepped into the wide court. Camin put his arm around his brother's shoulders. Heads down, they crossed to the other side.

"Ahh-hooo! That's a cold wind and almost spring! Here!"

Camin flung open the door and hurried Mareth into the warmth. Kashka followed, his arms full. Piff took the bundle from him and vanished with it into the second room. Kashka trailed behind.

"You're staying with us—both of you." Their eyes met. "Uncle Mareth's been ill too long. It's cold in your place. Just until he's better—until it's warmer. It's only across the courtyard. . . ."

"*I* didn't say no." Kashka hunched his shoulders and blew on his fingers.

"*He* will. Help us argue with him if he does."

Mareth shook his head. "It's too much work for you, Cara. You have enough." But he argued little more. "There are too many of you," he said, giving up on being told that he had no blankets for his bed.

Less than a week had passed when Camin asked his brother, "Have you been doing this all winter? You're driving the boy too hard." He frowned. "He's as thin as you, and almost as pale. The only thing he doesn't have is that miserable cough. Have you seen Bargah?"

"What am I supposed to answer first? No, I haven't seen Bargah. How could I—or she—in the weather we've had? The physician bled me twice. I felt worse both times. No more of that for me! As for Kashka. . . ." Mareth paused. "You don't throw away the gift."

"You don't throw away the boy!"

Mareth smiled. "That's not what I heard you say to Piff yesterday."

"Piff would lie on his back until the end of the world came, making up verses in his head and never bothering to write them down for the pen being on the other side of the room. He needs prodding now and then."

"I've heard him play. I've seen him juggle. You don't lie on your back and gain his skill."

"I just said he needed prodding. I don't exhaust him."

76

Mareth lay back against the pillows and stared at the ceiling. "Do you remember when Kati was alive—how we'd laugh?" he asked at last. "She and Cara—they would start something and we'd all be off. We'd end up rolling on the floor, crying with laughing so hard."

"I remember!" Camin smiled. "I'll never forget the dance at Gandy's. The riot."

"Kati and Cara started it."

"We helped it along."

"When Gandy went begging for the guards from the palace and the King sent them down . . . Do you remember how we had to boost Kati and Cara through the back window to get away? So we wouldn't spend the next two weeks locked up?"

Laughing, Camin threw back his head. "Cara gave me a black eye for the boost I gave her!"

"So that's where it came from! We were married the next day, you with a black eye! The next summer Piff and Kashka were born only a day apart.

"Did you listen to those two last night? Did you *hear* them? Did you hear us laughing? They were too young when Kati died to remember how it was between her and Cara. It's just in them. Born in them. Minds like quicksilver for the fun of it. And the way they move—the agility. You always dance with Cara. Have you watched her dance? Do you notice? Kati moved the same way. Sisters—twins—as like each other as we are! I see it in Piff and Kashka, the way they hold their heads to one side when they're thinking up some bit of deviltry. I shudder when I see them do it—both at the same time. Heads on one side, a look of in-the-cradle innocence, and you know something's coming. You pray it won't be a disaster!"

"I know. I know. I've seen it! But what has this to do with working Kashka to the marrow of his bones?"

"It has this to do with it," Mareth said slowly. "There are Kati and Cara in Kashka and Piff. And there are you and myself in them. And there's what they are themselves, the

77

combination and whatever else. What they have from their mothers, they have. What they have of themselves, they will deal with. What Kashka has of me, I will add to. What else have I to leave him? No wealth, no kingdom—only my harp, and he chose to play the flute.

"But the music—he has the gift for it. His sense of it astounds me, excites me. He understands everything I say, almost at once. And so I will give him everything I know, everything I have, as much as he can soak into his bones in the time I have to give it. What he does with it—that is up to him." He paused. "I hope he will give it to others. That's as it should be."

"You're telling me more in what you don't say about yourself than in what you say about Kashka." Camin turned his face away. "You *must* see Bargah!"

Mareth shook his head. "I am only saying that I must give him all I can as quickly as possible. The time is so short. There is no use going to Bargah."

For Kashka it was a dark emptiness, his father's place never to be filled. He would waken expecting to hear his father's voice. And the minutes would go by. He would lift his flute to his lips, waiting for the sound of his father's harp. And then, in the hollow silence, put down the instrument without blowing into it. Weeks went by with no sound from it.

It was Camin who spoke to him one day.

"I grieve too, Kashka. He was half of me—my brother, my twin. The loss is infinite. But so was his gift. Think what a man does who leaves his son only gold! It can be squandered in a year, a month, or even a week! A king can be turned beggar overnight! But Mareth has given you that which will make you richer than any mine of gold or jewels, stronger than any place of power—whatever rags you may wear upon your back. He has given you himself, his own gifts, talents, and his love. Those will never be lost to you, will never die, will always be within you."

Summer passed and fall came. A new rhythm of life replaced the old. Some of the newness was clear and bitter and lonely, some almost unnoticed.

There was word that Mogrud and the countries of Byrrhad and Xon were even more restless. The borders were filled with dark rumors of war. King Darai and Prince Aciam journeyed that fall to the east and north. When they returned, there were new lines in the King's face. His country was small, vulnerable.

Piff and Kashka were asked to stay near for the fun, the laughter, the quick words as well as the miming, the music, the unexpected leap or twirl. Even the King held his breath during the stumble, almost spill, almost break in the precarious balance of crystal glass and wine bottle to be served him. The chase would go on to the final serving with never a drop spilled, no single chip from the glass. Of course there was no word of the hundreds of puddles wiped from Cara's floor, or the tin practice cup with an uncountable number of dents in sides and edges.

There was less mischief, perhaps because there was less time for it. But if there was less mischief, that is not to say there was no mischief.

One afternoon Kashka and Piff met the Princess Ekama crossing the courtyard. She came close and whispered, "I heard there was a dance in the town tonight and I should so much like to go and pretend I'm not a princess! I'm so tired of being a princess and I do love to dance."

Blue eyes met brown eyes. What harm was there in it? If no one knew. . . ? Heads on one side, they looked at her critically.

"A cousin from Nainth?"

"Our mothers' cousin."

"A wig?"

79

"Better black dye."

"A dress borrowed from . . . Who is the same size, Princess?"

Piff counted on his fingers. "Tettie is too tall, Ana is too fat, Nathilla is a lord's daughter and her dresses are too fine. . . ."

Brown eyes met blue. "Darcie!" in the same breath. "Darcie, the baker's daughter!"

"Leave it to us, Princess Ekama." Kashka put his finger to his lips.

Piff's eyes stayed on Ekama's face.

"Do you mean it?" she asked. "I didn't really think . . ."

"Of course we mean it, if you really want to go. Don't we?"

"Of course," Piff echoed, shaking his head as if to clear it of a buzzing. "We'll have to give Darcie something, do something for her."

"We'll dance with her! She's sure to be there."

"Who'll dance with the Princess?" Piff asked.

"Why, we will, of course! We can't let her dance with just anyone! Don't look so worried. We'll go for only a little while. Then we'll bring her back. It's a different kind of dancing, though. We'll have to teach her."

The Princess's smile was wide. Her eyes sparkled. She caught her underlip between her teeth and hunched her shoulders.

Kashka leaned on his elbows on the long board in the baker's shop. Darcie leaned on her elbows on the other side of the board. Their eyes were level, faces close, voices low.

"I've come to ask you a favor, Darcie."

"I can't give you any more honey rolls. My father will whip me."

"I've not come for honey rolls, Darcie. I've come to borrow a dress from you."

"A dress! What do you want a dress for? You can't fit into one of my dresses!"

"It's not for me to wear!" Kashka straightened up suddenly. "That would be a sight!" He grinned and leaned down again, his face a little closer to Darcie's. "It's for a cousin. She's come from Nainth with not a thing to wear."

"Not a thing! I'm surprised she got this far!"

"That's not what I meant, Darcie."

"That's what you said, Kashka."

"Not a thing to wear *to a dance*, Darcie. She has but one dress—well, two for a change when she washes the other. *You* have pretty dresses. I've always noticed. Pretty girls always have pretty dresses. Yours are the prettiest in Nazor. That's why I came to you."

"I know exactly what you're doing, Kashka! You're saying all that to get the dress!" But Darcie was beginning to melt. She wished he would smile again. He did. A little more on one side than the other.

"That may be, but there's no harm in saying the truth, is there?" He wrinkled his nose, leaned a quarter of an inch closer. "I'll dance with you, Darcie." His voice was soft. "Three times at least. I'll have to dance with my cousin, and they may ask me to play the flute. But all I don't dance with her, I'll dance with you."

"You will?" Her voice too began to melt.

"And Piff will dance with you too. Three times at least."

"He will?" Almost a sigh.

"He'll have to dance with our cousin too. And they may ask him to play his lute." His voice was even softer. "But the rest he'll dance with you, Darcie." He leaned closer yet.

"Ohhh," Darcie sighed and then murmured, "When do you want the dress?"

"Now?" he whispered and touched the tip of his nose to hers.

"I can't now. I have to tend the shop." She was whispering too, though there was no one there to hear them.

"When will you be off?"

"At noon."

"I'll come back at noon." Still whispering. "You *are* pretty,

81

Darcie." He tilted his head the slightest bit. Was he going to kiss her?

A door slammed at the back of the shop, Kashka straightened quickly, blew Darcie a kiss, and was out of the shop all in an instant.

Darcie's father came in from the back room.

"What was *he* doing here? You didn't give him a honey roll again, did you?"

"No." More a sigh than a no. He *might* have kissed her!

"You're sure? I'll lose my shop with the honey rolls you give him! Which one was it?"

"Kashka."

"Aaagh! I was hoping it was the other. What did he want?"

"He's going to the dance tonight. He wants to dance with me."

"Oh, he does!" The baker looked closely at his daughter.

"And so does Piff."

"Both of them! You'll come home right after the dance! Your brother is going too. He'll bring you right home! No dillydallying on the way! You hear me? Home at once!"

"Yes, Papa. Oh, Papa, can you imagine what it must be like, dancing with Kashka?"

"No. But I can imagine everything you can think of with Kashka and all worse than dancing. Home at once! Go on, now. Your mother wants you in the back."

When she was gone he pulled at the tufts of hair above his ears and groaned. "First my honey rolls and now my daughter! I can't watch everything at once! Why doesn't he stay in the palace where he belongs?"

·14·

↘↘↘ The dinner was finished, the music for dancing not yet begun. There were a few moments for a diversion.

"Charming," remarked the Count of Belnez. "Those two work well together. They have doubtless done this often for you, Your Majesty, yet it seems so fresh."

"No," said the King. "This is the first time we've seen it. They may have practiced it—it went so smoothly. Though often Piff has not yet written down the words and Kashka is improvising. Their minds seem linked."

"Did you like it, Princess?" Prince Aciam leaned forward to catch Ekama's attention. She sat with her lips parted, her eyes fixed on Piff.

She turned to look at the Prince. "Oh, yes, Your Highness. I liked it very much!" And then fearful that something in her expression might have given all away, the message was so clear—the baker's daughter, the dress, the disguise, the dance . . . oh, the dance! . . . and remembering it afterward! She smiled her widest smile, frantically searching her mind for something to say.

"The dancing is starting. I shall have to leave soon. Will you dance with me? The first one?"

"Oh yes, Prince Aciam. I should love to."

The Prince led her to the line of dancers. King Darai and Queen Meta watched them.

"They're fond of each other," said the King.

"No doubt of that. But she's still only a child. A few more years . . ."

"The way she was watching Piff—I almost thought I heard a touch of jealousy in Aciam's voice. He has eyes only for her."

The Queen laughed. "They've all been such good friends. It's a little sad, their growing up. They will go such separate ways, though they all stay right here in the palace. They are already going! Aciam and Ekama—give her time! I'm sure they will be king and queen one day. And Piff and Kashka . . ."

"Piff and Kashka will keep the world from madness, my dear. There may not always be kings and queens, but there will always be music and laughter. Now, I too will soon have to go to that council meeting. Shall we dance? They are waiting for a sign from us."

The Queen rose to her feet, placed her fingertips on his raised hand. "It's serious then, in the east?"

"Yes. Mittai of Nainth will add to his strength over the winter and the Baron of Gorloth is looking to any weakness in the walls and arms there. We know the armies of Byrrhad—Mogrud's forces—have returned victorious from the east. The rumors now are that they are moving to the west. That they are gathered in the castles closest to the forests across the river from Nainth. But for five minutes, my love, help me forget those rumors."

Princess Ekama turned sedately under Prince Aciam's hand.

"I've been gone the whole summer, Princess, and have scarcely seen you since I came back—until tonight. What have you been doing?"

"Nothing that I can think of."

"Has it been dull, then?"

"Yes, very. Though Little Prince Mittai says all kinds of things now. I play with him in the garden or in the palace. When it rains we go exploring. Do you know how many rooms there are in the palace? I always lose count. We can never visit them all in one day."

"I used to do that!" Prince Aciam smiled. "And I never found out. Perhaps one of the keepers of the keys knows. I shall ask the next time—"

"No, no," the Princess broke in quickly. "Don't ask him. Then I'd not feel I must go and count them and look into them."

"You're right. It's much better not knowing."

"Are there other things that it's better not knowing?" she asked suddenly, seriously.

Prince Aciam was surprised. "I don't know, Princess. What kinds of things were you thinking of? Some things—unpleasant things—war—but it's better to know about them too. Often you have to know."

She nodded.

"What's the matter? Are you unhappy?"

"Oh no. I'm very happy. I love to dance."

"You looked as if you were about to cry."

"Oh no! How could I?"

"I'm sorry I can't stay. I'd dance with you again."

"I'm sorry too. Tettie is going to a dance this evening."

"Is she! At Gandy's, I'll wager."

"How did you know?"

"All the dances are at Gandy's—the ones outside the palace."

"Tettie says they dance differently there." Ekama bit her lip.

"That's true." Aciam smiled. Then he whispered in her ear, "But you can't expect Lord Benden to kick up his heels the way they do down there!"

The Princess giggled. "That's just what Kashka said!"

The dance was over.

"Thank you, Princess Ekama." Prince Aciam bowed.

She curtsied. "You're welcome, Prince Aciam."

"I must leave now."

"I'm going too."

"Why don't you stay and dance with Lord Gyles' son?"

"I don't like Lord Gyles' son."

"Well then, I shall walk with you up the stairs."

He walked all the way to her door. "I shall see you tomorrow?" He smiled.

"Oh, I hope so!" the Princess exclaimed. She watched him
walk away down the wide hall. If only he had asked her what
she was going to do the rest of the evening! She would have
told him she was going with Tettie and he would have told
her not to go, and she would not go. But he hadn't asked
her. If only they danced here the way she had been dancing
with Piff and Kashka all afternoon in one of those rooms
way off in a corner where no one ever came! But all the
dances here were done only touching fingertips and then,
at the last, a hand at the waist, all of the lords being so
careful not to step on the ladies' wide skirts. But with Piff and
Kashka . . .

"You're not used to dancing this way," Piff had warned her.
"You may not want to. Tell us if you don't, for I don't know
if it's proper for a princess—"

"You know perfectly well it's not proper for a princess,"
Kashka broke in as he put his flute to his lips.

"I'm tired of being a princess," she had insisted. She had
not been a bit frightened then.

"All right. Cross your arms in front of you—so, and I shall
hold your hands this way—so, and now we step to the side
and . . ."

It was quite different dancing with Kashka.

"You know that step well enough, Princess," he said. "Play
faster, Piff, the way you will at the dance!"

He turned her this way and that, hooked her arm in his
elbow, pranced her around, and then turned her again. At
last he whirled her quite off her feet, around and around, so

86

that she had to cling to him when he put her down, she was so dizzy.

Piff was angry. "You're too rough with her!" he said and started after Kashka. But Kashka laughed and turned her around and put her hands on Piff's arms so that she wouldn't fall. Then he went off leaping and twirling and doing hand-springs as she had never seen him do for the court.

"Play, Piff!" Kashka cried, and Piff sat down next to the Princess and began playing as she had never heard him play for the court. His fingers were so quick she could see but a blur. As for Kashka, she was not sure if he was dancing or leaping or tumbling or . . . or flying! But he and the music moved together. Her eyes went from Piff's hands to Kashka, back and forth. Finally Kashka did a whirl around and around in one place, stopped suddenly, dropped to his knee in a low bow, then sat back on the floor, panting and grinning, his shirt wet, his hair matted around his face.

"You gave it to me that time, Cousin Piff," he gasped.

"You asked for it that time, Cousin Kashka," Piff replied with an identical grin.

"We're ready for the dance tonight?"

They both looked at the Princess. Overwhelmed, she nod-ded.

"I think," she whispered, "that it's better to dance than be a king!"

They had to tell Tettie, of course. There was no other way to spirit the Princess from the palace. They had to promise to stay only a short time. If necessary, some of the promised dances with Darcie would have to be paid later.

There was a dampness in the air as the Princess, Piff, and Kashka slipped through the stable yard and out the coach entrance.

"Ring around the moon, rain soon," Piff murmured.

The Princess looked up. She had never seen such a circle

in the sky around the moon, though she had grown used to the moon itself—not so much that she still didn't love to look at it.

The town was so different at night! She walked quietly between Piff and Kashka, even more unsure of what she was doing. Her head felt strange with her hair hanging in the long braid down her back. Though Darcie's dress seemed to fit, it didn't feel the same as the soft cloth of her own dresses. It was stiff and . . . and *itchy*. She moved her shoulders under the cape where the dress was scratching her.

"Are you cold?" Piff asked.

"No."

He took her hand. "Yes you are," he said. He kept hold of her hand. His was warm and it made her feel better. He was looking at her. "Do you want to go back, Princess?" he whispered.

"No," she said, though she was quite sure she did.

"Just two dances, Piff," Kashka said suddenly. "Then you take her back and I'll stay and dance with Darcie. Or you can stay and I'll—"

"I'll take her back," Piff said quickly.

"Or we can both take her back and come down again."

Piff nodded. "Whatever."

Ekama's heart was beating so fast she felt as if she had been running uphill instead of walking so carefully down.

But here they were. This was Gandy's. It was a low, wide building, and when they went in they found a great many people there. Ekama felt better at once. There were so many people surely no one would notice her. They were dancing already. There was music and clapping and the tapping of feet.

When that dance ended and the next started, Piff took her hands in both of his and they took their places while Kashka looked for Darcie. In no time at all they were stepping and turning and whirling about. The Princess forgot at once that she had been frightened. The music was so different from that at the court! Her head was filled with the new sound and her feet were busy with the new steps. There was time for nothing else.

When that dance was finished, Kashka stood ready for the next. "I can't find Darcie," he told Piff. "Look for her." Then they were off skipping and sliding their feet and whirling. The Princess's eyes sparkled and she laughed. She was just a little breathless by the end of the dance. Oh, she could not go back yet! Just one more dance? Please? Piff took her hands again in his. "Did you find Darcie?" she asked.

"No. I don't think she's here."

Princess Ekama could not decide which of them she would rather dance with. Piff was so gentle, so careful, she almost told him that she would not break if he whirled her around. But then, she seemed to float across the floor with him, her feet scarcely feeling the wood beneath them. With Kashka she felt she might be tossed to the ceiling at any minute! And of course she must dance with him again. Two and two.

She begged for the fifth dance. They had taken only two steps, she and Piff, when she heard a voice close to her ear.

"Take her home. At once!"

Piff stopped so suddenly that she stepped on his foot.

"I'm sorry!" she cried and looked around to see where the voice had come from.

Piff's father and mother—they were next to them for a moment. "Kashka's waiting outside. *Now!*" Then they were gone, part of the dancers.

She wanted to watch them. They had moved like no one else here. She wanted to cry, to beg Piff to stay as he pulled her hastily through the crowd of onlookers.

"Camin!" someone cried. "Camin and Cara!"

Piff didn't stop. He found her cape and hurried her through the door. Kashka was there waiting. It had started to rain.

Kashka took one of her hands, Piff the other, and they began walking so fast they were almost running. Indeed, Ekama had to run to keep up with them.

"Stop!" she cried. "I can't . . ."

They went more slowly. The rain came down harder.

And then she felt it.

The cold. The terrible cold.

They were here! The cold ones of Castle Ysene. After all this time they had found her at last. Found her out in the street, in the rain, in the night.

·15·

↘↘↘ Princess Ekama trembled. She wanted to scream. She struggled to free her hands to cover her mouth and stop the sound. But Piff and Kashka held them too tightly.

"Princess, Princess! You can't go back. We've been found out!" said Piff.

"We have to take you to the palace as fast as we can. There's all sorts of trouble waiting for us," added Kashka.

Then they felt it.

She knew they did, for they stood very still and she felt them shudder, both of them.

"What was that?" Piff whispered.

"I don't know!"

"It's *them!*" the Princess cried. "They've found me! They've found me and they've come for me!"

"Who?" asked both boys at once.

"I don't know!" She was crying. "They've never been here. They were at Castle Ysene. At night. They're so cold! They came when they knew I was awake!"

"What would you do?"

A shiver went through them.

"I would hide under the blankets. It's all I knew."

"Did it keep them from you? Would they go away then?"

"I don't know," she sobbed. "There was no other place to hide. I . . . I think it helped. After a while they would go away."

In an instant they drew her into a doorway out of the rain, bundled her cape around her, and made her sit down on the step, her knees drawn up under her chin, her arms wrapped around her shins. They pulled off their jackets and wrapped her in them. Then they crouched beside her, their arms around her, sheltering her, shielding her the best they could.

At first the Princess was too frightened to know how uncomfortable she was. After a time, she had no idea how long—surely forever—she realized that the cold was not reaching her as it had in Castle Ysene. The sounds too were muffled, almost to whispers. If she had not known what they were, she might have thought the wind was blowing through leafless trees.

But the step was hard, the stone cold, and the boys had wrapped her so snugly, even covered her head, that she could scarcely breathe. Beside that, Piff was holding her so tightly she could not move.

"A-are you all right, Princess?" he asked her once, his teeth chattering. She felt him shudder so that she wanted to cry for him.

"Yes." She wondered whether he heard her muffled answer.

After another infinite time she heard Kashka say, "They'll never st-stop. You . . . you must take her, Piff. I can't . . . you must take her to . . . to the palace."

"N-not alone!" Piff answered. "I . . . c-can't without you. I w-won't!"

"I . . . c-can't move," Kashka said, gasping even as he spoke. "I c-can't think. They make such a n-noise!"

"You have to!" Piff argued. "You . . . you have your arms around b-both of us. We can't m-move unless you do. We . . . we'll go to B-Bargah. It's closer. P-Princess, do you think you can r-run a little way?"

"Oh, yes! Yes!" she cried, more terrified now for them than for herself. "But you must run with me!"

"Of course we . . . we wouldn't send you a-alone! I'll count to th-three. We'll all jump up together. One . . . t-t . . ."

"Th-three!" Kashka finished the count.

They struggled to their feet and pulled the Princess up with them. But Ekama's legs trembled so that she fell at once to her knees.

"A ch-chair!" Piff cried. "Hold round our necks, P-Princess!"

They drew her arms around their shoulders and then, clasping hands to wrists, they scooped her up and began carrying her up the hill.

The rain stopped for a moment, but the streets were darker than anything she could imagine. And the cold! Now she felt it. Oh, it came over her the way it had never done before. Wave after wave across her face sent chills through her until she felt she would soon be no more than a shape carved from ice. Beside the moaning and crying there was laughter, not joyful laughter, but a strange distorted cackling that mocked her, took pleasure in her fear.

Kashka stumbled and almost fell.

We can't go fast enough this way, Ekama thought. I *must* run. I will!

"Put me down," she cried. "I can run now!"

They held hands, fought together against the cold that would freeze every step, battled the noise that would drum them to the ground, and pushed against the darkness that would swallow them up.

Where are we? the Princess wondered frantically. It seemed to her they were in some midnight forest of brambles that tore at them, tripped them. The rain began again, an icy deluge.

Kashka stumbled again and fell. Piff and the Princess dragged him to his feet. They tried to run but could only struggle for each step they took against the wall of cold, darkness, and sound.

Just when she thought she could stand it no longer, when she could not take one step more, the sounds began to fade.

The running fingers of coldness touched her less often. The darkness grayed. The rain lessened. All faded, faded—and then were gone.

There was a house before them with light coming from a window. There was a door.

Kashka threw himself at the door, beat upon it with his fist. It opened to them. They hurried into the warmth and brightness of a room. The Princess clung to Piff. The door closed behind them.

"So it was you!"

It was a moment before the Princess could turn from Piff and lift her head.

She was an old woman, scarcely taller than Ekama, stooped, wrinkled, yet with bright eyes. She glanced from face to face, reading the terror in their look. Her eyes came to rest upon the Princess.

Ekama returned her gaze. The longer she looked into the old woman's eyes, the less her fear became. She felt her terror being drawn from her, the coldness with it. She could not take her eyes from the old woman's face. She did not want to.

Bargah reached out and took her arm. "Let go of the Princess, Piff," she said and turned to look at him.

Ekama saw that Bargah gazed as deeply into Piff's eyes as she had gazed into her own. It wasn't until his arms relaxed that the Princess realized how tightly he had been holding her. Bargah took his arm too and turned them both toward the glowing fireplace.

"Warm yourselves," she said and gave them each a little push. Still shivering, Ekama held her hands to the heat.

"Kashka!" Bargah spoke sharply.

Piff and Ekama both turned to look.

Kashka stood just inside the door. He was doubled over, his head bowed, his hands covering his ears. He was shaking as if the cold ones were still running their icy fingers across the back of his neck, around his throat, and down his arms.

94

Bargah took hold of his wrists.

"Kashka! Take your hands from your ears! Listen to me! Hear me!"

It did not seem to Ekama that the old woman struggled to pull his hands away. Rather it seemed that Kashka fought with another to do as she told him, to draw them away. He sank to his knees.

"Kashka!" Piff cried and started toward his cousin.

"Stop, Piff!" Bargah ordered, though she hadn't taken her eyes from Kashka. Piff hesitated. "Stay with the Princess. Stay by the fire. You can't help."

Ekama covered her mouth with both hands. Piff put his arms around her.

"Hear me, Kashka!" The old woman's voice was sharp.

With an effort that seemed to take every muscle in his body, Kashka slowly curled the fingers of his hands into his palms, then drew his fists together before his face.

"That was good, Kashka. Now you must raise your head. Open your eyes. Look at me! Look at me!"

Again he fought to do as she said.

"You can, Kashka. You must!" She still held his wrists.

"I-I'm t-t-trying, B-Bargah! I'm t-trying!" he whispered from between clenched teeth. He turned his head from side to side.

At last he was able to lift his face to her.

"Now! Open your eyes!" She spoke even more sharply than before.

He blinked, then cried, "I can't see! It's . . . so . . . dark!"

"Hear me!" Bargah repeated. "Open your eyes!"

Once again he blinked as if he were coming from a long darkness into sudden bright light.

"There! Good! Try again! Open them, Kashka!"

It seemed to take forever, but finally he was able to look into her face, her eyes. She dropped his wrists and quickly held his face in her hands.

"Now," she said quietly, and for a long time held his eyes with hers.

Little by little Kashka grew quiet. He stopped trembling, sighed, and sat back on his heels.

"Yes," Bargah nodded. "Good!" Still her eyes held his. "There will be none of it left, Kashka. None at all. And now," she went on in a low voice, "you will forget this part of it, Kashka. From the time you stepped through the door to this minute. *You will all forget this part of it.*" Her voice suddenly became the air in the room, the walls of the room, the chairs, the table, the fire. It wrapped itself around Ekama and Piff, though she did not look their way.

"*You will all forget this. This was no more than a dream. If it ever comes back to you, this was a dream.*"

She took Kashka's hands and drew him to his feet.

"Come to the fire and warm yourself."

Princess Ekama rubbed her hand across her forehead. For an instant she was dizzy. It was comforting to have Piff and Kashka standing beside her, shivering with her, rubbing their hands and holding them to the blaze.

"Bargah, we—" Piff began.

"Don't try to tell me yet," the old woman interrupted. "There'll be no sense in it until you've had a chance to collect your wits. You're soaking wet. I'll fetch some towels. What are the black streaks on your face, Princess Ekama? We had better wash them off."

Bargah brought towels and a cloth and a basin, which she filled with water from the kettle that hung over the fire. Piff and Kashka peeled off their shirts and rubbed themselves dry. They were still covered with goose flesh. Ekama put her hands into the basin. Piff squeezed water from the cloth and mopped the streaks from her face, for she would not take her hands from the warm water.

"It's the dye from your hair," he said and managed half a smile. "All down your face and jackets. You look like a funny striped beast. A few whiskers and you would be a . . . a . . . kitten!" He tried to meow but his voice cracked. He took the

96

wet jackets from her shoulders and helped her with the tie of her cape.

"I hope it's not on D-Darcie's dress," Kashka said. "I wo . . . I wonder where she wa-was tonight." He struggled for the words, dropped the towel, picked it up awkwardly.

Bargah watched him. "I think it's time you tell me what happened. Bring a chair closer to the fire for the Princess, Piff, and one for yourself too. Sit down, Kashka." She pointed to an armchair.

"Th-that's your chair, Bargah."

"Sit down before you fall down!" She pushed him gently. "I've things to do."

Ekama was glad to sit down.

"Kashka?" she whispered. He was so white! She didn't know what to say to him.

Bargah heated broth and gave them each a steaming cup.

"Start at the very beginning, of course," she told them.

When they had finished, Piff leaped suddenly to his feet. "We were in that doorway for hours! Father will have the whole palace looking for the Princess!" He looked at the clock, his mouth dropping open. "But . . . but it's only a few minutes—as if we'd come straight from the dance! How could it . . . !"

"Perhaps it wasn't as long as it seemed." Bargah rose to her feet and took up her shawl. How tired she looks, thought the Princess. She had not looked that worn only a few minutes ago when they had come to the door.

"Camin and Cara are doubtless on their way back now. I want you to stay here," she went on. "Don't go out. Lock the door behind me. Don't open it until I return or send Camin for you. You will be safe here. Don't worry."

When the door closed behind her, a look was exchanged. Piff sucked in his breath. What lay in Kashka's eyes? The terror that he himself had felt. . . . It had been worse for Kashka. Much worse.

For a long moment their eyes held. The darkness in Kashka's began to fade. At last their gaze fell to the Princess, who sat between them, her eyes fixed on the fire, her hands wrapped around the warm cup as she sipped from it.

Silent, they too sipped at their broth.

What was it? Why had it come? Piff asked himself.

·16·

➷➷➷ Lady Ysene sat rigid. Her sisters had returned from Nazor with news she did not like. Yes, they had done her bidding this night and frightened the Princess. Their coldness, their cackling—yes. But they had done something more. What was it?

To add to her uneasiness, her brother's words were annoying her almost beyond bearing.

"I repeat, you're wasting time." The Duke of Xon frowned. "These cat-and-mouse games with Darai! We are twice as strong as we were two years ago. Why do you insist we wait? Why do you insist upon *your* way?"

"The kingdom of Darai is to be mine," she snapped. "We agreed upon that. Since the unfortunate accident befell your lady, you have Toth all to yourself. Duke of Xon, Duke of Toth—be content with that for the moment. There are others beyond Nazor for you."

"I did not say I would take it *from* you. I offer to conquer it *for* you!"

"Conquer it! What you want to do is destroy it! You cannot wait, brother, to see the spires of Nainth go up in flames, the gardens trampled to mud by the horses of war. You lick your chops over the blood you would spill at Nazor. Those handsome children of Darai! I know where your pleasure lies!" Her anger grew. "That is not my plan. I want the country as it is—all of it. The only change will be upon the throne. It will be mine to do with as I will. Keep your armies to yourself. You will need every ounce of strength you have to defeat Mogrud!" She snorted. "Mogrud and his lust for gold! Someday *that* will defeat him. Watch yourself, brother, that your lust for blood does not one day defeat you!"

The Duke of Xon struggled to hold his tongue. He longed to throw her words back at her. She too had her desires! Whatever, whoever she coveted, whatever, whoever she took or had brought to Castle Ysene, she destroyed as thoroughly as if she had beaten them to death. He had no understanding of why she collected as she did. But he could see clearly how her plums withered, died at Castle Ysene.

And what a juicy plum the kingdom of Darai was!

If only he did not need her help! If only he did not fear her power! Just two weeks ago . . . Seven of them! Each at one time a favored trinket in her collection. Such an unbelieving horror frozen upon each face! A thousand ants crawled over his skin when he thought of it. He had not really wanted to bury them. It set his teeth on edge. He must not anger her!

"You have your plans set, then? The birth of another prince has not changed them?"

"Of course I have my plans! The infant prince is a part of them." She grew more irate with his stupidity.

"Then what of that—child?" he asked as civilly as he could manage. "Was it not through her you intended to gain your throne? Do you still control her?"

"She is completely terrified, believe me. Having thought herself free of them for so long has made it a thousand times worse for her. I have my uses for her. She will serve me." The lady's eyes flashed.

"Why are you so angry? How am I to know what your plans are? You never tell me of them and I don't have those ways of knowing. . . ."

"I shall tell you of those that concern you. We will stay at

Nazor for more than a single week. We shall spend the winter there."

"Who?" he asked. "You and your weird sisters?"

"You and I!" she snarled.

He looked at her for a moment, then shrugged his shoulders. "It's warmer there than at Castle Ysene."

"I shall see you in the morning, brother." There was a twitching in a muscle of her upper lip. She rose to her feet. She could not tolerate his imbecile words for one moment longer.

She was equally furious with her sisters. What had they done?

The Duke of Xon listened to the lady's deliberate footsteps upon the stair. It was another sign. He would do well to leave the castle at once. He had business elsewhere. Best to tend to it now.

Lady Ysene locked herself in her chambers and dropped the key into a heavy stone vessel with a narrow mouth. Her fingers curled, the nails digging into the palms of her hands.

Her sisters, yes. What had they done? She did not know. They were keeping something from her.

She had felt so safe sending them. Her earlier indiscretion at Nazor, losing her temper with that noxious little man who had promised her the boy for gold—oh, she had made him suffer for his lie, his insult!

There. It made her feel better to think of him. Then her lips grew thin. That had been a mistake. The slight pleasure of it was no balance for the fear she had known afterward. That power she had once felt in Nazor—if it were there! Yet . . . it would have responded to her own lashing out, and there had been nothing. No seeking out to discover her power. No acknowledgment, no whisper of a reply. Its presence that first time must have been someone, or something, passing through. Now that power was gone. What luck she had not lost her temper on that first visit!

101

But her sisters! *What had they done?* She twisted her fingers together. She would call them! She would demand to know!

No! Then they would know that her power was not as great as they believed. She could not question them for this any more than she could for what had happened two weeks ago. Never again must her anger grow as it had then. She still could not remember what she had done because of it. She remembered only her rising fury. The next day she had seen the fruit of it. Seven of them!

It was clearly by her own hand. The terror on their faces! It was not what her brother would have done.

She frowned. Her sisters had been sent out to bring in seven new ones who must be banded and trained to serve. Always an aggravation, that banding and training.

She pursed her lips, narrowed her eyes. *What power had she used?* The question haunted her. Only her own? Her sisters—they were so devious. There was no hint among them that they had helped. . . .

Another wave of anger passed through her.

She must keep control of them. Perhaps they had watched what she had done two weeks ago. Perhaps they feared her for that. Or had she taken . . .

"No!" she whispered. "I could not have used that! I would have known." Fear cut across her anger. She put her hand to the heavy gold at her throat. She was so aware of its presence. "I would have remembered holding it in my hand! I must not wear it so constantly. I must find a place for it." Her eyes went around the chamber and she stirred uneasily. Would she have remembered? If only she understood more of its power! She knew enough now to use it as she planned, but little beyond that. She would have time afterward to search it out carefully step by step. When she knew all of it, she would not need even her sisters!

Her sisters! This wave of fury was greater than the last. Her eye twitched.

"We thought to bring you a gift," they had said after they told her of the Princess's terror. "But we decided against it."

There had been no orders but to frighten the Princess—build her fear to such a peak she would not dare tell anyone of it, even the charming Aciam!

The lady clenched her fists.

When she herself arrived in Nazor she would gain the child's confidence, fill her need. Yes. The child would need her.

Her brother. . . . Her lips quivered.

Suddenly she picked up a vase, smashed it.

What had they done at Nazor?

"She will need me!" she screamed and threw herself at the door to open it. But it was locked and the key was at the bottom of the deep stone vessel . . . her own precaution, though now she cursed herself for it. It would take hours to catch it with a lodestone on a string, manipulate it through the opening.

What had they done at Nazor? If they had let their presence be known . . . If they had betrayed her to that other power!

She grasped the neck of the heavy vessel in her hands, shook it, clawed at it. She would go to Nazor this moment! The Princess would learn who it was protected her from such terror!

·17·

↘↘↘ "Bargah?"

"Yes, Princess. From now on Tettie will sleep in the same room with you and Bargah will have Tettie's room right next to yours. She will be nearby day and night. There will be a guard at your door and one beneath your window. If anything disturbs you, you must call one of them immediately—Tettie, Bargah, a guard—or all of them. Do you understand?"

"Yes, Your Majesty."

"That is the last of what I have to tell you. You may go now."

"Yes, Your Majesty." She curtsied, then asked in a very small voice. "Sire?"

"Yes?"

"It was my fault. I asked them to take me. They asked me ten times if I would rather come back and I said no. I *made* them stay longer because I wanted to dance. They would have brought me home much sooner." She looked into the King's face, hunting for some sign. But he did not smile. His look was grave.

"And . . . and they were very brave. . . ." Her voice faltered.

He nodded ever so slightly. She thought perhaps his face was more sad than grave.

"Thank you, Princess. Now you must rest. Sleep."

She curtsied again. She dared not move her eyes, blink, look to the side. If she did, the tears would come, and she must not cry before the King.

"We cannot always have what we want to have, do what we want to do—princesses or kings," he added as she started to turn away. She looked at him quickly. Yes, he looked very sad.

The guard opened the door and followed her out. They were waiting there, Kashka and Piff and Camin and Cara. Tettie had already been sent back crying. The Princess did not dare look at Piff and Kashka. She would not cry in front of them either. She would not!

"The Princess Ekama tells me that she insisted you take her to the dance."

Piff and Kashka raised their heads.

"She is too young to decide such a thing," Piff said. "We knew that."

"We should have refused." Kashka's eyes went to the King's face. How worried he looked! And he, Kashka, had added to his troubles. Why had he done it? Why? He had not hesitated as Piff had, until it was too late.

"It's my fault most of all, Sire. She . . . It . . ." No! He could not say that!

"She wanted to go so badly. It looked like such a lark!"

Kashka stared at the King. How did he know? "Yes, Sire! And . . . and . . . she is so light on her feet, Sire. Like down floating! To dance with her is . . . If only she weren't a princess, I—" Realizing suddenly what he was saying, he stopped in the middle of his sentence.

Piff broke in. "Oh yes, Sire! If only she weren't! And she so loves to dance! I would die for her, Sire, before I would let any harm come to her!" The words tumbled out.

Cara closed her eyes and leaned against Camin. Why didn't they stop talking? They had already said enough to have them-

selves hanged ten times over! Piff! No wonder he had been
wandering about like a moonstruck owl! She had wondered
who . . . But the Princess! She turned her face into Camin's
shoulder. His arm slipped around her, held her.

It seemed forever before the King spoke.

"I am sending you away. Both of you." How slowly he
spoke. An agony for them between words. He seemed to be
thinking, choosing what he said, deciding what was to become
of them. "Together."

Had he thought of sending them to different places? The
shock went through Kashka from head to toe. He might as
well have them drawn and quartered.

"To Nainth."

Nainth was scarcely a punishment! But, "Forever?" The
whispered word came from Kashka's mouth before he could
stop it.

The King frowned. "Your lack of thought—what you did—
was dangerous for the Princess. I am angry with you for that.
For that you will stay in Nainth until I say you may return."

There was no hesitation now in what he said.

"I only hope that Duke Mittai will not be given reason to
send you elsewhere. If he does, you will never return to the
court at Nazor."

Both boys, already pale, turned whiter yet.

"You will leave for Nainth tomorrow morning with Sir
Andros and Lord Feran. You will make yourselves useful both
on the journey and in the court at Nainth. You will stay the
winter there. When spring comes, I shall consider what to do.
Now you may go.

"Camin—Cara! I would speak further with you."

When Piff and Kashka had left, the King dismissed the
guard. He motioned to Camin and Cara. "Sit down. There.
I am not punishing you."

For a few moments he was silent, head bowed. Then he
raised his eyes.

106

"Before Mareth died I talked with him. His fever was high and I thought his mind was filled with imaginary fears. But I did make him a promise. It was that until Kashka is a man and responsible for his own doings, I would see to it—at least as much as is within my power—that he would never come face-to-face with the Lady Ysene or the Duke of Xon.

"After what Bargah told me this night, I think now that Mareth was not that confused. He had reason for his fear from what had happened. Bargah thinks he had even more reason for it, reason that he did not understand but sensed as surely as he sensed his own approaching death. I believe her.

"For Nainth—I had already decided to send Kashka there to honor my promise to Mareth. Lady Ysene and the Duke of Xon will arrive here within the week. Now I think that it will be just as well for Piff to be absent from Nazor. They both must go for their own sakes.

"I am not pardoning what they did in taking the Princess to the dance. My words to them were harsh that they might understand that. Neither do I have any desire to put a burden upon the Duke of Nainth. However, I want you to know that there is more in sending them to Nainth than the punishment of a youthful prank. Of what has just happened, if they tell you of it, say nothing to anyone."

"You have been more than generous with them, Sire. You always have been. Of course we will say nothing," Camin said.

Cara could only nod.

"The change of masters will be good for them," said King Darai. "One winter is not a lifetime, after all."

When they had left, the King stared at the wall. Bargah's words echoed in his mind.

"*There is a power that threatens the Princess Ekama,*" the old woman had said. "*It may be a power that threatens much more than the child. I know little of it. It is a dark power, unfamiliar to me. It has shown itself twice now in Nazor. The*

107

first time was a year ago. That was the day Grabe went mad. He insisted that he was in terrible pain, yet the physician could find nothing wrong with him. Nor could I. He has since died.

"The second time was this night—not an hour since."

The King turned cold again as he recalled the tale she related.

"They were here the first time it happened, the Lady Ysene and the Duke of Xon," she had gone on. *"They are on their way here again. Her power moves before her like waves in the sea, building before the wind.*

"Both times Kashka and Piff have been involved. Both times Kashka more than Piff. There was, of course, the very first meeting between them, which I do not doubt you remember well enough.

"What does it mean—this connection between them? I am not sure. I must guess, for I cannot see the future. I think there is something in them, Kashka especially, that Lady Ysene senses she must either overpower or destroy. We do not know what that is or why it is, but it is to our advantage to protect it. He is too young to understand anything of it himself. Send him away, Sire. Send them both away. Quickly!

"The Princess Ekama? We will keep her here, of course. We are fortunate that Piff and Kashka took her to that dance.

"Fortunate, you ask? Yes! If she had been alone in her chamber, we would never have learned of this. Terrified by it, she would have hidden it from us. Who knows what poison might have corrupted her because of her fear? In how long a time? Aciam's affection for Ekama and hers for him— Everyone sees it, even you, Sire! Hmm? I should guess it would begin to flower a short time after their marriage.

"We need not fear that now. We know what we must watch for with her. We shall help her face those fears she has hidden away so deeply that she does not recognize them. She will know that she is not alone with them, nor will ever be again.

"Ekama will be safe.

"Others—Piff, Kashka—I do not know. Safe, perhaps, in Nainth."

The king thought a while longer. Then he sighed and muttered, "What an eternal drab winter it will be without them!"

Piff and Kashka said nothing to each other until the door of their own room closed behind them.

"He could have had us hanged," Kashka said then.

Piff threw himself down on his cot, buried his face in his pillow. "He should have!"

·18·

↘↘↘ Princess Ekama lay in her bed. *The cold ones were here in Nazor.* There was no way she could put them away in any place back of her mind and know they would never come again. Would they come to her again tonight? She did not try to keep from blinking her eyes. She did not pretend to be asleep. If they came, they came. Let them freeze her forever. She was already frozen.

Tettie had cried herself to sleep. Ekama did not cry. She had said good-bye to Piff and Kashka. She had said good-bye to Prince Aciam. *I shall see you tomorrow?* No. She would never see him again.

Her face was numb.

What was that? Just a sound. Not the kind of sound *they* made. Perhaps it was the guard below her window.

The drape swung out as if the window behind it had opened. Then it hung straight again. The Princess turned her head. They had never come that way before. She hoped they were here. She hoped they would take her far away so that she would never trouble King Darai and Queen Meta again. She closed her eyes and waited.

"Princess Ekama!" A whisper.

Something—someone was standing in the room! The Princess sat up.

"Piff!"

"Shh! I came to say good-bye. They wouldn't let me see you. They wouldn't let me give you the letter I wrote. They wouldn't even take it to you for me. I wanted to tell you, I'm sorry we got you into such trouble."

"*I* was the one—"

"Shhh! No! Listen! I wanted to tell you. . . . You must tell Prince Aciam all the things you have ever told to me. You must also tell him all the things you have *never* told me. Will you do that?"

"I don't know if I can. If he will want me to. . . ."

"Of course he will! You must!"

"I'll try."

"I wanted to tell you . . . no, never mind. That's all. Good-bye, Princess."

"Piff. . . .Wait! Thank you for . . . Piff?"

But he was gone. The drape had moved again and then hung slack. She listened, holding her breath. But there was no sound at all. Piff was gone.

She lay down and pressed her face into her pillow. The corners of her mouth pulled down.

In the morning the Princess Ekama heard men's voices and the clatter of horses in the courtyard. She went to her window and watched as Sir Andros and a troop of mounted men gathered behind the coach of Lord Feran.

There, behind them all, were Piff and Kashka, booted, spurred—they looked different on the tall horses, as if they had already been gone a long time. The carriage began to move, the horsemen following. When Piff was beneath her window, he looked up. She heard him say, "If I were you, Edry, I would tell the King to have the ivy trimmed from the wall around the Princess's balcony."

"No one will ever get in that way, Piff, without my seeing him."

"I'd tell the King all the same," Piff said.

◆ ◆ ◆

For two days the Princess stayed in her room. The third day she asked Tettie if it might be arranged for her to go out in a carriage. It was arranged and, with Tettie beside her and a guard beside the driver, the carriage wound down through the town of Nazor.

"Would you stop here a minute, please?" she asked the driver.

The carriage halted in front of the bakery. The guard helped the Princess down and Tettie followed. Several people stopped to stare. The Princess entered the bakery and put the small bundle she carried on the long board. Tettie waited inside the door. The guard stood just outside.

"I should like to buy a honey roll," she told the girl on the other side of the board.

"Yes, Your Highness." Darcie bobbed her head, bent her knee, and turned to take a honey roll from the shelf.

When she turned back to the Princess, the roll in her hand, Ekama leaned forward, pushing the packet toward Darcie.

"Piff and Kashka say thank you for the dress," she whispered. "They're sorry they did not dance with you. They promise when they come back—"

"Papa wouldn't let me go," Darcie said, startled.

Their eyes met. Darcie and the Princess were of just the same height, the same size. Suddenly Darcie's eyes widened and Ekama knew that Darcie knew who the cousin from Nainth had been.

"I'm sorry you couldn't go. It was such fun!" Ekama whispered, smiling suddenly. Then she grew serious again, took up the roll, and left the pennies on the board. "Thank you, miss."

"Thank *you*, Your Highness!" Darcie bobbed again and slipped the packet to a shelf under the board.

When Ekama reentered the carriage, the driver asked, "Where would you like to go from here, Princess?"

"Oh, anywhere. To the river and then back." She leaned

112

against the seat, looked at the roll in her hand, and then gave it to Tettie. She wasn't hungry after all.

"Who was that?" the baker asked Darcie as he came in from the back room. He had caught sight of the carriage moving away.

"The Princess Ekama. She bought a honey roll." The pennies still lay upon the board.

"The Princess! You made her pay for it? Why didn't you just give it to her?"

Darcie shook her head. *When they come back!* So they *were* gone! The gossip was true! But why? And where had they gone? When would they come back? She might *never* dance with Kashka. But he hadn't forgotten her. To think . . . the Princess herself had brought the dress! And Piff and Kashka had danced with the Princess! Her head was in such a swirl she did not hear her father's scolding words.

That night at supper Darcie's brother announced, "Kashka and Piff have been sent to Gorloth. They're to be fishermen. They're never coming back here or the King will have them hanged."

"Whatever for?" Darcie's mother asked.

"They say they put glue on Lord Benden's chair so that when he stood up, the chair came with him."

"If it was an armchair, it would have come with Lord Benden and no need for glue. I should think he'd have broken every chair in the palace by now as it is."

Darcie said nothing. She didn't believe her brother's tale. The Princess had said *when they come back.* Had they been sent away because of the Princess? Except for the one smile, she had looked so unhappy! Poor Princess Ekama! She must be almost as sad as Darcie herself!

The next day the Lady Ysene and the Duke of Xon arrived at Nazor. They settled themselves in their own suites of rooms somewhat away from the others in the palace. They would stay until the following spring.

◆ ◆ ◆

Mittai of Nainth groaned and laid aside the third letter as he reached for the fourth.

"Is it as bad as that?" asked the Duchess. "You haven't given me a word of how anyone is in Nazor. The baby prince, your namesake, is he well? He must be walking and talking by now. No mention at all of Aciam?"

"These have nothing but bad news, my dear. Not of Nazor itself, but of other places. I shall be glad to have Sir Andros and his men here for the winter, though nothing will probably happen until the spring or summer, if then. Perhaps we'll have a winter to cool the heels of Mogrud."

"He's threatening us?"

"He's threatening someone! Every man and youth in the country is training to kill."

"Asininity!" The Duchess of Nainth was a woman of strong opinions. "They should have spent the summer raising crops. They wouldn't have to come around stealing and killing for their food. It was a good summer. A good crop. The fishing was especially good in the north. But they spend their time training to kill. Next summer they will spend killing and destroying. We shall have to put our young men to fighting and our crops will be poor. It's too much to expect the women and children to keep the country alive! They need their husbands and fathers with them. Mogrud and his stupid greed for gold! And Xon too—for power! If I had my way with men like that I would . . ."

Suddenly the Duke snorted. He was accustomed to the Duchess's tongue and had opened the fourth letter and begun to read it while she talked.

She stopped in midsentence. "What is it now?"

"Isn't this just like Darai!" exclaimed the Duke. "First warning us to give all our attention to building our strength, looking to fortifications. Beware of spies and plots. Keep an ear open for news of Mogrud and his doings. Keep an eye on Xon. And

114

then . . . and then . . . he says he is sending us a crock full of trouble, a pair as mischievous as a couple of baby goats— into everything. 'Tie down the towers,' he tells me. 'They'll turn them upside down. Watch out for frogs in your beds and above all, lock up your daughters.'

"What did he send Andros and his men for? To be a help to me or to watch these two? By the sound of it, I'll need a whole army just to keep track of them!"

"Who are you talking about?"

"Those two boys who came tagging along with Sir Andros and his men."

"Those twins?"

"They aren't twins. They're the sons of Camin and Mareth. Cousins."

"I was so sorry to hear of Mareth's death." The Duchess shook her head. "He was the finest musician I have ever heard. Doesn't he have anything good to say about these two at all? Why did he send them to you?"

"If I read rightly between what he says and what he doesn't say, he is so fond of them he could not bear to send them to anyone else for fear they would be strangled almost immediately. He is depending upon my good nature to put up with their pranks."

"But . . ."

"Besides which, I gather . . . mmm. . . . They are honest, intensely loyal, bright, quick-witted and—you'll be won over by this, my dear—extremely accomplished musicians for ones so young."

"Why didn't you read that in the first place?"

"Because he doesn't say it in so many words. I am having to pull it out like teeth."

"Well, it sounds as if we'll be kept amused this winter."

"Mmmm." The Duke went to the tall window, opened it, and stared out over the roofs of Nainth. He had more to think about than being amused. Just then the sound of music came up from somewhere beneath him—a flute and the plucking of strings accompanying it. In a moment, he had lost the line of his thought.

"Gracious!" exclaimed the Duchess and came to stand beside him. "No one here plays like that. Who can it be?"

"I suppose," said the Duke, "it is Kashka and Piff."

·19·

⟍⟍⟍ In Nainth they called the winter mild. Yet it was severe enough that few letters had been carried back and forth between Nazor and Nainth. Now the winter was over. The Duke of Nainth, still numb with the shock of the news and with having to announce it, once again took up the private letter to himself from King Darai. He had read it so hastily the first time he could not remember what it said.

My dear Mittai,

By now, of course, you have had the official news of the death of the Queen. I have never known a more unhappy time, not only for myself but for all the people of Nazor. There is no one in the city who has not lost someone to this terrible fever. It has been almost two months since the death of Lord Wegren, the first we knew of. There are still names being added to that list, both daughters of Lord and Lady Rothin being the latest. But now there are fewer and fewer each day, so it would seem the disease has had its time.

I dread the meeting of the council tomorrow. I scarcely know who will be there. Decisions must be made for the welfare of all. Why is it that at the time

117

we feel so empty, so helpless, useless, hollow, we are looked to to give more than ever?

I am more than grateful that I do still have my sons. By some miracle, young Mittai and myself were spared. Aciam was gravely ill for two weeks but has recovered at last. We have announced his and the Princess Ekama's betrothal—I promised this to the Queen before she died—and that too was in the official papers you received, as you know. It will, of course, be at least two years before they marry.

I was glad to have the good news from Nainth a month gone. I pray all things still go as well for you, and above all that this dread malady does not touch you there.

I am in deepest mourning for my Queen.

Darai

He had added, "We have lost the poet Camin too. Break the news gently to his son and nephew. It would be wise if they did not return at once, however much they may wish to. There is still illness."

For a moment the Duke was puzzled. Son and nephew? Then he realized that the King wrote of Piff and Kashka. He put his hand to his forehead. The poet's name had been on the list he had left for Derenth to read to the court. They would have heard. He must send for them, speak to them.

But there was someone at the door. And then there was another and another. It was not until the next morning when Derenth brought him word that Kashka wished to speak to him that he remembered.

One look at the youth's face, and the Duke knew that Piff had gone.

"We talked of it," Kashka admitted, "but I thought he would wait until we asked your permission. He must have left as soon as I was asleep."

"The King advises against it because of the illness that is still in Nazor. However, he does not forbid your returning."

"I have to go, my Lord."

"Yes, I suppose you must. Wait until tomorrow and go with Sir Andros. It's a long journey alone."

Kashka shook his head. "Piff is alone. Now he's only a few hours ahead of me. Tomorrow . . . Let me go."

The Duke studied his face for a moment. "Go, then. You have your horse. Wait a moment! You'll need money. Here. . . ."

Kashka had already made a bundle of his clothes. He had only to sling it over his shoulder along with his flute. He would have liked to bid the Duchess good-bye but he dared not take the time. The Duke would give her his farewell. Piff would ride as fast as he could follow. Only a misfortune might slow his cousin.

It was Kashka, however, who met with misfortune. His horse threw a shoe just before he came to the village of Wellwood. In all, it cost him another hour and a half. He had no word from anyone there that Piff had been seen. A messenger from the Duke of Nainth, in as great a hurry as Kashka, overtook him there, however, and he had company for the long journey through Sansnom Wood. For that he was grateful. He grew even more uneasy for Piff's traveling alone.

When as last they came through the wood and stopped at the inn of young Master Bedlin, he was overjoyed to be taken for his cousin.

"But you were here only yesterday!" the innkeeper exclaimed. "Out of Sansnom Wood and left for Nazor only this morning. I let you out myself at sunup and watched you ride to the west, you were in that much of a hurry! Now here you are, back again out of Sansnom Wood. You give me a chill! Have you lost your lute? I've not found it here."

"No, no. That was my cousin. We're often taken one for the other. He left this morning?"

"At sunup. Six o'clock. Routed me out to unbar the door. I've never seen a youth in such a hurry, and not a penny to his name! But what a song he gave us for his supper and bed! Do you sing too? I would charge you nothing. . . ."

"Yes, but I play the flute better. I'll play. Though I too must be off as early." Twelve hours ahead of me! How did he gain that much? He must rest his horse as often as I. But he's through the worst of it. Sansnom Wood. . . . There was something eerie about Sansnom Wood. All the stories he had heard on his way to Nainth. . . . Perhaps Piff too had remembered them and, being alone, had been in an even greater hurry to get through the wood.

The next morning he was up and away before five, having let himself down from the window that he might not have to waken the innkeeper. Again he traveled alone. But here the way was easier. There were more villages, more farms. Twice he had word of Piff from the astonished folk who rubbed their eyes on seeing him. There was no doubt in his mind now that Piff would arrive safely at Nazor. Kashka had the extra comfort of knowing that the King would not be angry. He wished that Piff knew. The heavy ache of grief for Camin and worry for Cara was more than enough to bear.

It was night as he approached Nazor, as dark a night as he had seen all the way from Nainth. The sky was overcast. There was no light from moon or stars. But Kashka could not bear to stay a whole night in the village of Alsgren only a few hours from Nazor. He rested an hour and then pushed forward, letting the horse take its own pace. He knew the animal was tired.

The horse had a sense of its own, however, and must have had a memory of how close it was to its old stable. It trotted along, ears pricked forward. In two hours they came around a bend in the road at the top of a gentle hill. Against the dark

120

sky rose the darker mass of the hill of Nazor with the palace at the top.

Kashka reined up his horse, a sense of strangeness coming over him. He had been so eager to get here, to find Piff, to see Cara, Aciam, the King—Nazor itself. Now . . . what was it?

As he looked, leaning forward, eyes searching, the feeling of strangeness turned to fear, the fear to dread. What was it? In that instant he knew. There was no flicker of light in that darkness. All of the city, the palace too, was the black of a pit, a hole carved in the lowering clouds that seemed light by contrast.

However hard he looked, he could find no spark.

There *must* be light somewhere, a torch in the street, a candle or oil lamp burning in a window to turn it yellow. He was not too far away for some gleam, some glint to come to him! His horse blew softly, tossed his head. Still Kashka hesitated.

Below the town the river was covered with fog, a white pall that followed the valley as it wound away to the north. On this side of the river the mist reached out, shrouding the low-lying fields. On the other it cut away the base of the high bluffs. They rose black against the clouds, as if separate from the earth.

He could not sit here forever. At a slight touch from his heel, the horse started forward.

Kashka felt that he was moving into the edge of a shadow. The closer he came to the walls of the city, the deeper the shadow grew. The air was oppressive. He could not fill his lungs however deep a breath he took.

Soon he would be at the east gate of the city and there was still no light. Would the gate be locked? Would there be someone to answer his call? He swallowed. His throat was dry.

There was no light in the gatekeeper's window.

Kashka dismounted and went to the gate. He pushed against

it. It was locked. He knew well enough where he might climb over the wall, but he did not wish to leave his horse outside the city. The animal needed rubbing down and a measure of hay. They had come far today.

There was the narrow door at the side of the gate. To his surprise it was open. He led the horse through and closed the door behind him.

"Hello?" he questioned, raising his voice only the slightest. Beside the darkness, a stillness lay upon the city that made even his speaking voice seem loud. He continued to lead the horse, walking through the streets toward the palace. Though he walked softly, his footfalls sounded loud in his ears; the noise of the horse's hooves echoed—enough to call the dead.

Kashka had never known such a stillness in Nazor. House after house he passed with no sign of life in any. Did everyone sleep? Was there no night watch? Or . . . or was the town deserted? Empty? He walked faster, his heart beating more quickly. He was at the palace wall now, almost at the gate. Surely there would be a guard at the palace gate!

The gate was locked.

There was no guard.

He would try the carriage entrance. He skirted the wall. The darkness seemed even more intense here. There was something familiar in it, as if sometime—somewhere—he had known such a darkness. He rubbed the back of his hand across his dry lips.

As he came around the corner of the wall, he thought suddenly of Bargah. A fierce longing to see her welled up in him. He would stop at her cottage first. It was no more than a few steps beyond the carriage gate. Why hadn't he thought of her sooner? She would drive away this darkness as she had when . . . What was he thinking? He rubbed his forehead. He could not remember. No matter. Just recalling her face comforted him and he hurried even more, this time not from fear.

He would have to rouse her, of course. How she would complain at being wakened at such an hour! It was past midnight, he was certain. He could imagine her expression when she saw who it was. Oh, what a hug he would give her!

There, that was the cottage, the last on the narrow street. He paused. Something was amiss. It was hard to tell in the dark what it was. He strained his eyes. The house was there, the shape of it the same, but there was something unkempt about it. Yes, the weeds. . . . He put his hand out to the side. The weeds were tall. There was no garden. He kicked at the clump of high grass at the side of the walk. The ground was hard. Bargah had always kept a garden all around the house.

A few seconds later he found the door boarded shut.

Such a fear went through him he could not think. What had happened to her? For an instant he wanted to run away from this familiar town turned strange. No. He must find Piff.

He turned at once back to the carriage gate and found it open. As at the other gates, there was no one to guard it. By now his heart was pounding against his ribs and his hands had grown cold and wet.

He led the horse to the stable. It was so dark inside he could not see where there might be an empty stall. He felt in his pocket for flint and steel, wondering if he might get enough of a spark to see. He had no luck. At last he rubbed down the horse with a shirt from his pack. While he did so, a horse within the stable whickered and stamped. The sound made Kashka leap aside and then sigh with relief. If the horses were here, *someone* must be here! He led his horse into the stable and, fumbling in the dark, managed to tie the reins to a post. Then he made his way around to Camin's and Cara's door.

He tapped. There was no answer. He pressed the latch, the door swung open, and he stepped into the even greater darkness of the room.

"Piff?" he questioned. "Cara?"

There was no reply. But he could hear someone breathing.

It was the sound of deep sleep. Kashka felt his way across the floor, groping for the table where there would surely be a candle.

Yes! Here it was, and the tinder next to it! He drew the tinder close to him, felt for the candle wick, and again took out flint and steel. Finding the tinder once more, he struck a spark. Again—and again. His hands were trembling. At last the splinter took fire. It flared for an instant, then died. He tried again. Is it wet? he wondered. But it would not light at all if it had been wet. No, it simply would not burn. There! He held it to the candle. The wick flamed and he looked about quickly. Piff! There he was! Asleep at the table across from him, his head on his arms. Then the flame died.

"Piff!" he cried, almost weeping with relief.

Kashka felt his way around the edge of the table until his hand found his cousin's shoulder. "Piff! Wake up!"

Shake him as he would, he could not waken him.

Was he that tired? Perhaps he was. Or perhaps he, Kashka, was asleep and this was all a dream. Ever since he had seen the dark city wrapped in its ominous air of gloom, he had felt as if he were in the midst of a nightmare. Had he fallen asleep?

"I'm dreaming," he said aloud. His voice frightened him. No, I'm not dreaming, he told himself. He stumbled to the door. At least it was lighter outside than in, the air cool, damp. The river fog was creeping up the hill. He could smell it.

What was he to do? He must find someone to talk to! Frantically his eyes swept the dark windows of the palace and were caught at once. There! A light! One of the windows. . . . He started to run toward it, stopped. Wait, he told himself, you can't stand below and shout. Which room was it? He counted the windows. This one belonged to the Princess, the next was. . . .

Mentally he named each room that faced upon the main courtyard. Then that was—the Prince's chamber—the young

124

Prince Mittai. He must have wakened in the night. The nurse was taking care of him. A drink of water, perhaps. The thought was so welcome, so sensible, that he almost laughed. He knew exactly where to go. He would talk to the nurse, ask her . . . anything! She was awake. She had a lamp beside her.

Kashka ran across the familiar courtyard, through the small yard that had so tempted him—a thousand years ago, it seemed— and into the hallway to the first kitchen. Now he must go slowly, feeling his way. Here was the door that opened into the wide passageway. It led to the dining hall on the right, in the other direction to the broad staircase. He turned toward the stairs. How well he knew his way here, yet in such darkness he must run his hand along the wall. His foot touched the stair.

Up he went, and to the right along the high balcony. Again he felt his way until he came to the first passage to the left. Down that, door after door, then to the right again.

This passageway should be carpeted. Yes. Thick and soft beneath his feet. He must be careful here. There were tables and chairs, bric-a-brac along the wall. He went more slowly. He was less sure of himself here. He was certain he was drawing close.

The antechamber to the Prince's room should lie . . . there! There, around the next corner! He could see a glow. . . . He paused. Something odd. Had they painted the walls green? A sickly green—but the light, it pulsed! Was there fire? Fear replacing hope, Kashka hurried noiselessly to the end of the passageway, turned, and then stopped. Everything within him turned cold.

It was a sight that burned itself into his mind so that, though almost instantly he leaped backward to the safety of darkness, it still hung before him like a vision.

The two guards, one on either side of the wide doorway, lay insensible upon the floor—asleep or dead, he did not know which. Beyond, the room was filled with a green light that pulsed like a heartbeat. At one side the nurse slumped in a chair, her head bent down.

All of this rushed upon him, but what sent such a terror through him that his legs melted beneath him was the sight of the Lady Ysene. She stood in the center of the room and bent over the bed of the sleeping prince. Even as Kashka leaped backward, she raised her head.

"He is mine!" she cried. "Mine!"

·20·

Kashka's head whirled. He could not breathe. He could not move. He was not even aware that he had fallen. He was aware of an immense shadow that stretched across the floor and covered the wall of the passageway, the green light dancing around it like flame. And the voice! The wild exultant voice. *He is mine!*

Then came another cry. "Sleep, Nazor! Sleep, palace of Darai! Who is there to hear me?"

A silence followed and then a laugh. She seemed to take delight in shouting her victory to the deafness of sleep.

"It was my sisters put you to sleep, Nazor. I have sent them away, Nazor, but you will not waken until the dawn. They made certain of that. And I . . . Two hours until the cock crows and he is mine forever!

"Two hours!" Again she laughed. "But who is there to come in the night? Who is there to take him? Who is there to wake him? Who is there to break the circle of my power?"

Again a silence. Did she listen for a reply?

The shadow moved.

"Did you hear me?" Was she addressing the sleeping guards? "You sleep too soundly!"

Now the shadow moved out and into the hallway where Kashka lay. The light followed behind, flaring around the lady. Kashka closed his eyes, covered his face with his arm. He felt a sudden great sympathy for a mouse about to be swallowed by a snake.

The light came closer, the undulating green coming through the sleeve of the shirt that covered his face, through his arm, through his eyelids. So did the black of the shadow penetrate his eyelids to fill him with a darkness as it passed over him.

"What is this?" asked Lady Ysene. She touched him with her foot. Cold went through him, spreading from his side through his body to his fingertips, his toes, his lips.

"Shall I make him mine too?" And then, "No, no. I am spent. The child—let the power that encircles him hold him while I sleep. Let that power hold all in Nazor who sleep, keep them blind to what holds him when they waken. Let that power hold him until it is taken from him!

"Now, to bed quickly before I fall asleep as I stand! No one must find me near—they might wonder. There must be no whisper. . . ."

She moved swiftly away from him. Then, where the passage turned into the next, she cried loudly once more. "This I must tell you too, Darai, for the power holds no secrets! If you take him from Nazor, Darai, before the cock crows, you take him from me. Even so, for seven years I may take him back if I find him. And you, Darai, if you take him, I will find him in your mind. I will find him in the mind of any one of your royal family who knows where he is, though he never speak of it! I will find him and make him mine once more! Have my will run in his veins!

"Take him, you who sleep!"

Once more she laughed. More words followed, but they fell upon Kashka's ears in a jumble, meaningless, senseless, so horrified he was at what she had already shouted to the sleeping palace.

Then she was gone.

For a time Kashka lay upon the floor, numbed, unable to move. Then he drew a deep breath, and another and another.

He pushed himself to his hands and knees. He shook so he could not stand. He crawled, crept through the hallway, crept past the guards, crept into the room of the sleeping prince. He had only one thought in his mind. He must take the child from Nazor before the cock crowed.

There was a light burning in the room, an ordinary oil lamp. Kashka pulled himself up at the bed of the Prince, forcing himself to stand. He looked down into the child's face. How beautiful he was, son of King Darai and Queen Meta! That so evil a power should possess him. . . . *He must find the strength to take him.*

Kashka reached out to pick up the child when he thought of what he might need for him. Shirts, a coat, shoes. . . . In great haste, he threw open the doors of the wardrobe, chose the simplest clothing he could find, bundled it up, tied it together, and looped it over his shoulder. Doing this ordinary thing took his mind from the witch, calmed him, let him think, notice what he did. He found he had been sobbing.

Now he wrapped the sleeping prince in a blanket. He lifted him from his bed and, taking up the lamp, went swiftly back the way he had come.

He crossed the courtyard. He must leave Piff a sign that he had been here. When he entered the dark room he was overjoyed to see the flame continue to burn in the lamp. There was paper, a quill, and ink on the table. Piff had been writing a letter when he fell asleep.

Kashka leaned over his cousin's shoulder. His heart leaped. The letter was to Bargah! He scanned it quickly.

Dear Bargah,
    I have just learned that you left only two days ago to go to the village of Pergyth. No one seems to know why. I hoped I would find you here but I didn't have such luck. I had to come. No matter what the King says or does, I am glad that I did. My mother is so

ill I am afraid for her. At least we have been together a few hours. Just now I am waiting for Kashka. He should be here any minute—any second.

I will find someone to carry this to you. You must have . . .

The writing trailed off as Piff had fallen asleep.

Kashka took up the letter, folded it, stuffed it into his pocket. He dipped the quill into the ink and on another piece of paper quickly formed the few notes of music that were a sign between them. Then, taking up the lamp, he hurried to the stable. There he looked for Piff's horse, as much like his own as he and Piff were alike. After leading the animal out, he put his own in the stall. Thinking suddenly of the lamp, he took it to the center of the wide courtyard, blew it out, and left it there. Then, holding the child tightly, he mounted the horse and rode to the east gate. He must be beyond the walls of Nazor as quickly as possible.

Through the door he led the horse with its small burden, remounted, and turned downward toward the river. He would take the river road to the north toward Birn Hall and Welf. Pergyth lay somewhere east of Welf. But before he must go that far, surely he would overtake Bargah.

Once on the road that followed the river, he was away as fast as the wind.

"Prince Mittai. . . . Little Prince Mittai. . . . He's gone! He's not in his bed! He's not in the room. I've looked and looked! The guards have looked! He's . . . just . . . gone!"

The nurse was weeping, frantic.

"He can't be gone. He's in the palace somewhere." The captain of the palace guard gave sharp orders. "Find Prince Mittai! At once!"

The entire guard was soon searching the palace. The King must be informed. Word went through the servants' quarters.

Soon everyone was looking, hunting, calling. Prince Aciam and Princess Ekama, Tettie, the four cooks, the Margrave of Tat. . . .

A young maidservant brought tea and toast to the Lady Ysene. The lady was displeased. She had waited overlong for her breakfast.

The girl curtsied. "I'm sorry, my Lady, but the Prince is missing. We have all been searching the palace."

"The Prince is missing? I should think the Prince is quite old enough to look after himself!"

"Oh, not Prince Aciam, my Lady. Prince Mittai. The little one. We've been searching for an hour at least and he hasn't been found."

"Nonsense! He's there in his bed."

"No, my Lady. He's not. His bed was empty, the blankets on the floor. The wardrobe doors were open and his clothes thrown about. The nurse doesn't know yet if anything is gone, except the Prince."

"Impossible!"

"Will there be anything else, my Lady?"

"Yes. More truth and fewer tales."

The girl curtsied. "I'm sorry to distress you, my Lady. If there is anything else . . . ?"

"Go, go. You are annoying me."

The maid was accustomed to being told that she annoyed Lady Ysene. At first she had cried over it, but all of the other servants told her that the lady was annoyed by every one of them. Some of them would be only too glad to annoy her even more if they hadn't been so afraid of her. The girl felt better on learning that. Now she only wanted to be gone and help again in the search for Prince Mittai. She curtsied once more and left the lady with her tea and toast.

Lady Ysene sipped her tea. What possessed the girl to invent such a tale? Doubtless some stray bit of gossip started by the nurse or one of the guards to cover the fact that they had slept.

131

Such talk passed from mouth to ear by the servants until it reached the kitchen, became a monstrous distortion of wagging tongues. Agh, she was so tired! Should she wake the Prince? It would take such an effort. Let him sleep. . . . She finished her breakfast and called for help with her toilette.

The same tale was repeated. The Prince was missing.

Lady Ysene frowned. Was there something to it after all? She questioned the woman who was arranging her hair.

"Yes, my Lady. The bed was empty. Clothes thrown all about. The nurse is in hysterics. They've had to put her to bed. Everyone in the palace is searching. They still haven't found him—at least they hadn't when I came."

"Dreadful! I had not realized! I shall join in the search. Clumsy oaf! Take care!"

After the woman had left, the lady thought for some time. There is only one answer to this, she told herself. The nurse. She woke muddled and could not waken the Prince. She hid him somewhere. Now she is having her hysterics—false or real—false, of course.

Whatever they were, it had gone on long enough. The Lady Ysene had not planned it this way, but perhaps this was even better. She would join the hunt. How worried she would be! She would find him, of course. This very minute she might— but no. Someone might feel it. They were all awake now. Better to take care. Better to find him. How grateful they would be for it! Perhaps it would do away with that peculiar sense of antagonism they felt here toward herself and her brother. Yes, this would change everything! She left the room.

The palace was in a ferment. Search of the servants' quarters had begun, of the grounds around the palace. The garden, the stables. A cry was heard. The lamp from the Prince's room! It was found in the middle of the courtyard!

Lady Ysene bit her lip. Enough of this! She hurried back to her room, locked the door behind her. It would take little doing. No more than an instant. . . .

Now, my pretty one, she said to herself, closed her eyes, and lifted her head.

Nothing.

She did not believe it.

Again.

Again, nothing.

It was then that Lady Ysene joined the search for the Prince in earnest. No one could say that she was not as concerned as the King himself. She went through every room that had already been searched. She moved through the halls of the palace, swift and cold as the winter wind.

Doro rapped. "Cara! It's Doro. I must come in. We must . . ."

The door opened to him. The boy who stood before him was pale, his eyes red.

"Piff!" the man exclaimed. "What. . . . ?"

"She . . . she has died," the boy said. "In the night. Alone. I was asleep."

"Oh, lad, lad." Doro dropped his jacket on the table and put his arm around the youth's shoulders.

"My father . . . I wasn't here. My mother . . . If I'd only been awake!"

"You had a chance to talk with her before . . . ?"

"Yes. For a while yesterday. . . . I came . . ."

"She must have died in her sleep, Piff. Just gone to sleep not to wake. There was no one awake last night. No one as far as we know except whoever it was made off with Prince Mittai."

Piff looked at Doro as if he were speaking some unknown language.

"Prince Mittai? What is wrong with Prince Mittai?"

"We can't find him. We . . ."

A shadow fell across the floor. The Lady Ysene pushed her way past Doro. "Have you searched here?" she asked, her eyes sweeping the scantily furnished room. A table, some chairs, a harp standing in one corner, two lutes hanging upon the wall. She stepped to the door of the second room, opened it.

Doro held Piff firmly.

Half a minute later the Lady Ysene came from the room. "Not there," she snapped and looked angrily at Piff. Then she was gone.

Doro held Piff a moment longer, then shook him slightly. "I'll send someone to help you, lad. It's a hard time. A hard time for everyone. A terrible time. Did Kashka come with you?"

Piff shook his head. "I thought he would follow. He didn't."

Doro dropped his hands from the boy's shoulders, reached for his jacket.

Suddenly the door flew open. The Lady Ysene returned. "I've never seen you before. When did you come here?"

Piff stared at her.

"When?" she shouted at him.

Doro answered for him. "Yesterday. Come away, Lady. His mother died in the night while he slept."

The lady whirled. Doro took up his jacket, shook it with an angry snap, and went to the door. "I'll send someone," he repeated and closed the door firmly behind him.

Piff stood a moment, trembling. Then he seized the jar of ink from the table and threw it. It broke against the door, the ink running black down the wood and dripping on the floor.

He turned, his eyes blind with tears. Wiping them with the edge of his hand, he sat down at the table and stared at the paper before him. His letter to Bargah . . . he would have to tell her. Now he had no ink to finish. His letter . . . where was it? Had it fallen to the floor? No. Had Doro picked it up with his jacket? No, he had shaken his jacket before he laid it over his arm. Where . . . ?

And then his eye fell upon the other sheet of paper. The blank sheet that was no longer quite blank.

·21·

➘➘➘ Kashka rode as fast and as far as he dared push the horse. Every few hours he stopped to rest, then set out again. No matter how far and how hard he rode, he would not reach Birn Hall until the next day. And then . . . and then . . . He suddenly realized by then word would be out that the Prince was missing. Already they must be searching the palace and the town for him. Surely they would send messengers in all directions as soon as they knew he was not in Nazor.

That means they will be looking for me!

A new mountain of problems now rose before him, so appalling he slowed the horse, then stopped, wondering what in the world he should do.

Until now his only thought had been to come to Pergyth, find Bargah, and somehow . . . somehow Bargah would know what to do. But it was two days' ride to Birn Hall and another three to Welf, with no chance for him to change horses. Then to Pergyth—however far that might be from Welf. Perhaps two days more.

He had thought to find food and shelter in Birn Hall and Welf, but of course he could not stop there. They would recognize the Prince. They would know Kashka. Ande, the young lord of Birn Hall, and his wife Memet had been to Nazor only last year. They had spoken to him often. Before that, they had heard his father, Uncle Camin, Piff, and himself play. Kashka ground his teeth to fight back tears at the memory. What wild tale could he tell them? None wilder than the truth, and who would believe that?

Of his story, they would say . . . that he was seeking revenge upon the Lady Ysene for the beating he had taken. That he was trying to punish the King for having sent him away. The more he thought, the more impossible everything became. He would be caught, hanged, and the Prince, the little Prince, would be returned to Nazor and the terrible power of the Lady Ysene.

He must have time to think!

Kashka nudged the horse to a walk and began looking for some place that he might turn off the road, rest unseen, and try to find some way out of this maze. He soon spied a grassy opening with a trail leading from it into a copse. He turned from the road and in a few moments lifted the still sleeping child to the ground. He laid him in a shady place on the soft grass.

And here was another dilemma.

In all the riding, the galloping of the horse, the dismounting to rest, the lifting of him, moving him this way and that in the effort to find some way of carrying him more easily, the Prince had not wakened.

At first, Kashka was thankful that he did not have to deal with a crying frightened child. Then he began to worry. Now he was thoroughly frightened. By the sun it was close to noon and the Prince had not so much as whimpered.

Who is there to take him? Who is there to wake him?

Kashka had been there to take him. Could he not wake him?

He knelt, bent over the Prince, stroked the hair from his face and forehead.

"Prince Mittai," he said. "Wake up! Wake up!"

But the child did not waken. Kashka sat back on his heels. Something cold on his face—a little water, perhaps.

136

There was a stream nearby. He dipped his hands into the water, sprinkled it on the Prince's face, patted it. Neither did that waken him. He shook him gently. It was no use. He clapped his hands sharply. The child slept.

Perhaps time. . . . Kashka fought the uneasiness that threatened to become panic. Think! he told himself. Make some kind of plan! If they must travel for a week or more—he did not know how long—think, Kashka!

No one had caught them yet. The village of Marle lay between here and Birn Hall. He would stop, buy food. If the Prince was wrapped in his blanket and strapped to his back, it would not appear strange that he slept. Surely they would not send messengers with the news or men to hunt him until they had first searched Nazor. It would take some time. He had best get on as fast as he could. Later . . . later. . . .

He bundled the Prince in his blanket and rigged a kind of sling for him from his own jacket and belt. However, it was impossible to get him to his back by himself. At last he managed with the child before him, partly supported by the sling, partly resting on the saddle in a way that left Kashka his arms free.

He came to the village in the late afternoon, bought cheese and dried apples enough to last several days. While he held out his hand for change from a loaf of bread, the baker said to him, "From Nazor, eh?"

Kashka nodded, hoping the baker would not ask many questions.

"Ay, there's many have left Nazor." He bobbed his head toward the sleeping prince. "Been sick with fever, eh?"

Again Kashka nodded.

"Where are you going, Birn Hall?"

"Yes. How did you know?"

"They say Memet of Birn Hall has healing powers. Good luck to you."

137

"So . . . I've heard." Kashka took the change, shifted the Prince in his arms.

"You'll not reach there tonight, you know. It's a day's ride from here for a well man with a fresh horse."

"I know. I just want to be as far on as I can. The sooner I get there. . . ."

The baker shook his head. "There's another reach of forest between here and Birn Hall. I'd not go through at night. There's robbers preying on the feeble and the sick. Nothing lower among men. They'll cut your throat for the shirt on your back. Ande of Birn has caught two but there are more. We've sent word to the King to ask help in hunting down the rest."

"I'll stay this side of the forest tonight. I thank you for the warning."

With nothing but despair in his heart, Kashka mounted the horse and again set out for the north. Was there no glimmer of hope? Memet of Birn Hall—perhaps she . . . No, he must find Bargah. He would heed the baker's warning and not put the life of the Prince in even greater danger.

"Someone took him! Someone took him! I cannot believe it, but it is so! Impossible, but it is so! He is nowhere to be found in all of Nazor!"

In a rage she would soon in no way be able to control, the Lady Ysene strode around and around through her suite of rooms. As her fury grew, she wanted no more than to destroy everything her eyes fell upon. She had only enough sense left to know that she must let no suspicion fall upon her. As a result, calamity upon calamity fell at random upon folk in the palace and the town.

In the palace kitchen, where the fourth cook was just reaching for a succulent piece of chicken (the third cook's back was turned), a pan of grease on the stove next to him caught fire. The flame rose fierce and hot to the ceiling and scorched the fourth cook's eyebrows. It died down at once, having frightened all in the kitchen and turned the wall blacker.

Lord Benden was indulging in a pre-dinner snack of tiny meat patties, four kinds of cheese, oysters, pickled fish, and bread. He had just filled his wineglass for the third time when such a pain went through his stomach that he threw the glass across the room, pushed everything before him from the table to the floor, and took himself to bed with nothing more to eat until the next morning.

Young Lord Vayn was gazing at himself in the mirror, drawing his comb through his hair for one last touch of perfection, when a thousand snarls entangled themselves in the comb. He could neither pull it through his hair nor free the teeth. At last he had to take scissors and cut away whole chunks of hair, which left him looking anything but neat.

More things happened than can be told. Crocks split, shelves of glassware collapsed, bookcases fell over, pictures tilted on walls, needles pricked fingers, horses kicked, hammers missed nails and struck thumbs, tongues were bitten, cats stepped on, bricks fell on toes, dresses were torn, water spilled, food burned, knees skinned, breeches split—all happening within minutes and continuing on until the lady began to think her strength must be directed elsewhere.

Her fury somewhat lessened, Lady Ysene suddenly knew fear. Not only the child was gone! She turned white and held to the edge of a table to keep herself from falling. *Not only was it gone, but if whoever took the child knew the secret. . . .* No! It must not be! She sat down at once, closed her eyes, drew a deep breath, and held it until she had collected herself.

Then she began seeking, probing, reaching out with her mind, concentrating all her powers upon a thin ring of greenish gold that encircled the arm of a young child. Hour by hour in an arc that spread farther and farther from Nazor, she sought the image. Finally it came to her late in the night. There! There was the ring!

The image grew brighter, stronger. Whoever took the child did not know! Nor in her probing had she sensed another power.

What had it been at Nazor three years ago? Since then there had been no whisper, no shadow of its existence. The country was free of it, as well as the town. She was safe. Her power was safe.

Now she must work! Again she concentrated upon the ring. The shape of the child formed with that of the golden band. He slept. Of course he slept! A shadow lay beside him. Of this she could tell nothing. Whoever it was must be the one who had taken the child from Nazor. She would put a curse upon him! No. The least distraction made the image fade. She drew it to herself once more.

There was no way she could tell from what direction the image came—north, south, east, or west. The distance she had some sense of from how long it had taken her to reach it. The chance that it lay to the west was small. It would be out to sea. But even that possibility she could not deny completely.

How could she find it? How go in all directions at once?

She need not find it! She need only draw it to her. No, not to Nazor. She could not do that. But to Castle Ysene! She could draw it there. Force it! Drive it! Once again her power moved outward, this time not to seek the golden band, but to impose her will upon it.

Kashka woke with a start, sat up, held his head in his hands. What had he been thinking! How could he waste so much time! He must hurry. The one thing he had not thought of— the one person—Lady Ysene! She too would be hunting for the Prince. Forest, robbers—no matter! He could no longer stay here. He must be off!

He bundled the Prince into the sling, mounted his horse, and turned onto the road. In half an hour he had entered the forest. Lady Ysene, he thought. Lady Ysene. . . . I must find her. No! I must find Bargah! Bargah will help. But Lady Ysene knows . . . she knows. . . . I must be careful of her. She will go to Castle Ysene. I must go to Pergyth, to Bargah. Then I'll go to Castle Ysene because . . . because Lady Ysene will know how to wake the Prince! Bargah would not know such a thing. She was no witch. Only Lady Ysene. Why hadn't he thought of her before? He would have gone by way of Nainth. It would have been faster. Now he must go . . .

Some part of his mind cried out against it, but he could not listen. There was no time to waste. He rapped his heels against the horse's ribs. *He would not stop until he had reached Castle Ysene.*

·22·

❧❧❧ "I'm too tired," Kashka whispered. For the third time he had caught himself dozing, almost falling from the horse. He had had no sleep the night before and had ridden that day until he was exhausted. He had perhaps three hours' sleep before he wakened feeling he must go on. Now he had ridden over half the night. The horse too was tired and, when Kashka dozed, it stopped, head down.

"If I fall I'll hurt you," he muttered to the sleeping child. "I have to stop. I have to sleep. Maybe an hour. Then we'll go on."

Kashka dismounted and led the horse from the road. He could hear the babble of water nearby. A drink—he was thirsty. He stumbled, caught himself. Here was a grassy place. He put down the Prince. His arms ached from holding him. Finding the shallow stream almost at his feet, Kashka leaned down to scoop up the cold water.

There was the crack of a dry stick behind him and then a splintering of light exploded in his head.

"Small porridge here. A few coins. Clothes." A heavyset man bent over the boy sprawled on the ground.

"They're better than mine. I'll make the trade." His companion, small, dirty, pulled off his ragged shirt. He untied the bundle. "Here! Here! This is fine stuff! Feel that!"

"A little small for you."

142

"It'll bring a price."

"Ah! Look at this! Gold!"

"No. Brass for sure."

"Gold! I know gold when I see it. I'll have it off his arm!"

"I don't like the look of it—the way it coils around. Like a snake."

"Gold is gold, whatever the shape. How does it open? I'll have to . . ."

"Better to unfasten it, snake or whatever. There's craft in that. I've never seen such. Let me . . . Eh! Eh! It moved. I swear! Like a snake in my hands!"

"You fool! Now you've dropped it. Where—here it is. I'll take it and this stone on the chain too. Eh!"

"What?"

"Strange, that. Some kind of force. I can't . . ."

"The stone? Let me. I . . . oh, that's strange!"

"Don't touch it again! It's . . . it's . . . leave it! Leave them!"

"I'll finish them."

"No! No! Put away the blade! Did you draw blood? You fool! Don't touch them! I'll not have their blood on our hands."

"It is already. I think I've killed that one. This one will die all of himself in these woods."

"No, see? He's not dead. Pull him away from the water. Don't take that either. It makes music. No use to us, and music . . . it's evil . . . calls spirits. We have enough. We have the gold, the horse, the rest. We've done enough. If they die, they die. But I'll not do it and you'll not do it. Come away now. I don't like it."

"What'll we tell the others, that we killed them? Will we share the gold?"

"We'll tell them we left them for dead. And of course we'll share. If they found out, how long do you think we'd have a windpipe to breathe through? There, lead the horse. Hurry! We've a ways to go. Such a ways to go. And all of a hurry. Move there!"

◆ ◆ ◆

Someone was crying, crying so bitterly. Why didn't Cara—
Tettie—Bargah—someone see to it? Why didn't the nurse . . . ?
Kashka groaned. Oh, how his head ached. If only the crying
would stop! He put his hand to his head and winced. What
a lump! How it throbbed! His hair was sticky, crusted. He
tried to sit up.

"Don't cry," he muttered. "Don't cry, Prince. . . ."

Prince! He sat up quickly and opened his eyes.

It was day. The sun came through the trees, the brightness
making worse the pain in his eyes and head. He blinked,
shaded his face.

There sat the little boy. Was he really a prince? He wore
only an undershirt and the amulet around his neck. When he
saw Kashka move he stopped wailing and caught his breath.

"What happened to us?" Kashka groaned again. He could
not believe it! His shirt, his breeches, his shoes—gone! The
horse was gone—everything but his flute! Nearby lay a heap
of rags so filthy Kashka did not want to touch them.

"What will we do? Why did I . . . ?"

The child began to wail and sob once again. Kashka crawled
to him, held him, tried to comfort him, rocking him, patting
his back, murmuring. At last the child grew quiet with only
an occasional long, tremulous sob.

"One thing, you're awake. No doubt of that. Who woke
you? Or was it just time? Are we far enough from that witch?"
He tried to smile. The crying was better than the awful sleep
that had possessed the Prince, but it did little for the pain
behind Kashka's eyes.

"We can't stay here," he went on, glancing at the pile of
rags. "Let's do some washing. We don't have a choice, but
I'll not wear those that way. Come on."

He set the Prince down and the little boy nodded. "Come
on," he repeated.

Kashka smiled at him. "We'll play in the water." He found

144

a stick, picked up the rags with it, and doused them in the stream. He poked them up and down, rinsed and squeezed them out again and again. The Prince played in the water, picked up stones and threw them.

"I make a splash!" he said, laughing.

"You certainly do!" Kashka wiped the water from his eyes. "You make a big splash." He held his cold hands to his aching head. He could sleep for a month!

Kashka wrung out the clothes. There were trousers and a shirt and something else—more holes than cloth—and spread them on the rocks to dry.

Then he looked to see if anything had been left.

"This is luck!" he cried after a few minutes' search. The sack with the bread and cheese and Piff's letter at the bottom of it lay in the grass. They went at it with such enthusiasm that Kashka had to remind himself that there would be nothing for the next day if they didn't stop. He wrapped what was left.

"I think we'd better get on even if our clothes aren't dry. Otherwise we'll spend another night here, and I don't want to."

"We'll go home now," Prince Mittai said.

"I wish we could! Let's find Bargah." Kashka watched the child. Did he know the old woman?

"I'll find Bargah," he said cheerfully. "Bargah's with 'Kama. Bargah has honey cakes."

He knew Bargah! Kashka grinned. "It'll take a while, but we'll find her."

They made a game of trying to find the right holes in the rags they had to wear. Prince Mittai would have spent the rest of the day poking arms or head through first one, then another hole, laughing uproariously when Kashka poked his own face through one, trying to find the Prince inside the tatters. Once the child whimpered and Kashka saw that his arm was bruised, the skin broken. Had it happened when his clothes had been taken? No, they had taken the golden bracelet from his arm.

Why had they been so rough? What kind of brutes were they?

Kashka worried over the Prince having no shoes. He tore strips from the shirt and wrapped them around his feet.

"Raggy-toe shoes," he said. Prince Mittai was delighted. He was a cheerful little fellow! He'd be good company.

When they were dressed Kashka examined the Prince critically.

"We're a pair of vagabonds," he told the child. "Beggars. You're a little beggar and I'm a bigger beggar."

This too delighted Prince Mittai. He trotted along the road holding Kashka's hand and saying the words over and over again, mixing them up, tangling his tongue. Kashka helped with new combinations of leggle biggars and bittle leggars until neither of them was quite sure of the right words.

When the child grew tired Kashka carried him. When he cried the flute soothed him. Now and then he would fall asleep in Kashka's arms. The Prince seemed to grow twice as heavy when he slept.

At evening they came out of the forest.

"We must have ridden a lot farther than I knew," Kashka muttered. He could not understand why he had come into the forest during the night. Something had caused him to feel a terrible urgency. Maybe I had some kind of dream, he thought. It seemed as if I had to go to Castle Ysene. He shuddered. He must have been half asleep. I'll not let that happen again, he told himself.

They stopped to rest at the side of the road. The Prince fell asleep. Kashka gazed across the river. Not far beyond lay Birn Hall. Should they risk stopping there? Even as he wondered, Kashka heard hoofbeats, a rider coming at great speed. As he galloped past, Kashka recognized the livery of the King's messenger. There was no doubt word of the Prince's disappearance was being taken to Birn Hall and everywhere else in the country. He longed to take the child back. If only some disaster would befall the Lady Ysene! That was wishing. He shook his head.

Kashka rose and gathered up the Prince. He would feel safer on the other side of the river, closer to Ande of Birn, even if he dared not go to Birn Hall itself.

He was almost across the bridge when a horse and cart started over behind him. The youth hoped their ragged appearance would put off suspicion.

The cart drew closer. Kashka stepped aside, moving so that the child's face was hidden on his shoulder.

Horse and cart stopped next to him.

"Would you like a ride? You look that tired."

They were an old couple, wrinkled, weathered, sadness in their faces. It took Kashka less than two seconds to decide.

"Yes, thank you." He climbed into the back of the wagon and laid the Prince on the bed of straw. The old man shook the reins.

The old woman turned in her seat. "What a lovely child."

Kashka nodded, held his breath. "He's the son of a friend," he said on seeing no suspicion in the woman's face. "I'm taking him . . . to his grandmother."

"Eh?"

Kashka repeated his answer twice. She was hard of hearing.

"You're from Nazor, then." It was not a question and Kashka did not reply. "We come from there too. We went all the way to bring our daughter and the baby back with us, but we were too late. Both of them. . . . We'd never seen the child." She wiped her eyes. "We'll never go back to Nazor."

She looked again at the Prince. "I envy the grandmother of such a child. He needs a washing."

Kashka agreed.

"You go to Birn Hall, then?" asked the old man.

"No. Farther on. Beyond Welf."

"Welf! And you've already come far from Nazor! Ah, it's no wonder you're ragged as you are." She nudged the old man. "We're going to Welf ourselves."

"So we are. And beyond that."

"They're neither of them fat."

147

"They're not."

"Nor have they great mounds of baggage."

"They haven't that."

"If it were Viny and the baby. . . ."

"They'd weigh the same I'm sure." He seemed to know what she was getting at.

"It's what we'd planned exactly. They'll put no strain on Muffin."

"Will you ride with us? We'll be glad to carry you."

"I . . . I thank you. Yes."

They plodded on. Kashka's head nodded. It still ached from the blow. At last he lay down and slept fitfully, his arm around the Prince.

The old couple went on in silence. They came to a farmer's cottage, stopped, and knocked at the door.

"So, you're on your way back! Did you find them?"

"Yes. They're asleep in the cart. We've covered them with a blanket. It's best to leave them there. We'd not want to bring illness into your house."

The farmer nodded. "You're welcome to sleep in my barn."

The old couple nodded.

"Norry," the old man said turning the cart, "that was no way to talk. You mustn't pretend. You mustn't hope. What is, is. The child has a grandmother."

The next morning the old couple were up before daybreak. Kashka roused as the cart lurched forward.

"We're on our way again," the old man told him. "We'll not be stopping at Birn Hall. We've enough to take us to Welf."

Making certain that the Prince was all right, Kashka lay back in the straw. He wished he might sleep all day, but could sleep no more. He sat up and watched the country pass slowly by.

·23·

Piff stood on the knoll overlooking the meadows and river. The pale green tips of leaves were just beginning to show on the white birches. There was no more to say, no more to do. He had only to bear the numbness of his disbelief, the ache of grief. To accept was more than he could think of as yet.

He looked around once more. This place was peaceful. Kati and Mareth, Camin and Cara. . . . He turned away at last. Halfway down the hill Doro waited for him. They walked together. Piff was just beginning to learn of the number of those in Nazor who bore a like weight.

"Get some rest, lad," Doro said. "And then—"

"I'm going after Kashka," Piff said.

Doro looked surprised. "Have you talked to Sir Andros, then?"

"No."

"I think you should."

Piff nodded and held out his hand. "Thank you, Doro."

The older man took his hand, then embraced the youth. "There's no one in Nazor does not have to build his life again," he said. "You'll find your way."

Again Piff nodded.

As Doro walked away he thought, I didn't have it in my heart to tell him, so I put it off on Sir Andros. It's a coward's

149

way, but after this morning I couldn't. Or has he heard that there's no trace of Kashka beyond Bedlin's Inn? He said he was going after him, as if he knew where he was! Those two . . . Doro rubbed his chin.

Piff did not go to Sir Andros. He must go to Bargah, find out why Kashka had come and gone so secretly in the night. For surely he had taken the letter. Then they must return to Nainth. If there was payment to be made for his coming here against the King's will, he would pay. The look on his mother's face when she had seen him was worth anything they could do to him.

He took his lute from the wall. He had said his good-byes. Those who cared had been with him this morning. Except for . . . That, of course, was impossible. With Prince Mittai missing, who of the royal family would have time to think of Cara and Piff? He was fortunate they hadn't. It left him free to look for Kashka.

He led the horse from the stable. Kashka's horse, his quick eye told him. Why had his cousin been in such a hurry?

Only the smith saw Piff leave. Few knew he had come to Nazor.

The Lady Ysene too was leaving Nazor. She had a letter from her brother, who had left a fortnight earlier, asking her immediate return. Some problems. . . . She explained to the King.

King Darai nodded. "Go, Lady Ysene, where you are needed. We thank you for your help and concern."

The lady settled herself in the coach. The golden band had gone either to the north or the east, for it had grown more distant. It was on its way to Castle Ysene. She herself would go through Nainth, then north toward Gorloth—the shortest way, the roads the best. He—whoever it was—had two days' start, but she could travel through the night, having the horses changed, the drivers taking turns. She would sleep in the coach. Uncomfortable, but necessary. She would be there first, however uncomfortable. *He* must not come to her brother!

It had been odd, last night. How could he have gone on so? She thought he would never stop! But at last he had. She had fallen asleep at once, just as *he* had. And then she had been wakened, jarred, shaken. She called at once to the golden band. All seemed well, though he was moving again, even more rapidly.

In her anger had she given more power to the band than she realized? Or had he become obsessed? If so, she must go with greatest haste. She must also save her strength. She would force the matter only when it was necessary. She did not know what she might have to deal with. Who . . . ? Too much was unknown.

She frowned. There was trouble for her at Nazor as well. The Princess showed no sign of fear, had responded only with a dreadful politeness to her attempts at closeness. Stupid little girl! She wasn't worth bothering with. How could they be so fond of her? Her betrothal to Aciam. . . . It was what she had first planned, but with control of the Princess. Now she would have to go about it somewhat differently. She dared not cast aside her first plan until she had the young prince safely back in Nazor. Then, of course, she would have need for neither Aciam nor Ekama.

Her frown grew deeper. *She must hold the golden band!*

Kashka slept, woke, slept again. The old woman took care of the Prince as if he were her own grandson, holding him, crooning to him, teaching him games.

"You say his mother is dead?" she asked Kashka.

"Yes."

"And his father?"

"He was alone. There was no one else."

151

"How do you know you'll find the grandmother?"

"I was told—"

"It's a long way from Nazor to Welf and beyond. She may no longer be there. What will you do then?"

The old man cleared his throat. "You mustn't talk that way, Norry. Things are hard enough without thinking them worse. Now, lad"—he turned to Kashka—"Pergyth you say? We can't go so far. No, Norry, we can't, but perhaps someone will come to give him a ride. If you need help, we'll be where we're going and you can turn to us. We'd planned on a little one. Norry's already put all the pins out of reach."

He had walked forever and asked where he dared. Kashka's hand trembled as he lifted it to rap. The old woman opened the door. For a few seconds she peered questioningly at the ragged pair. Then astonishment spread across her face.

"Kashka!" she exclaimed. She looked at the child he carried and was speechless. She seized the youth's arm and drew him quickly into the house, closing the door at once behind him.

"Sit down. There," she said, seeing the fatigue in his face. She took the sleeping prince from his arms, laid him on a cot, and covered him with a blanket. Kashka sat down, elbows on the table, and bowed his head into his hands. He had found her! Found her! Found Bargah!

Bargah stirred the embers, added kindling and a log, and hung a kettle over the new blaze. By the time the water had boiled and the tea was steeped, Kashka was able to speak. The old woman listened without interrupting.

". . . and it means that I've stolen him! I think of King Darai and Prince Aciam. I think how they must feel that he's gone. But what could I do, Bargah? What else could I do?" Kashka put his head down on his arms and wept.

She waited until he grew quiet.

"Nothing," she said at last. "There was nothing else for you

152

to do. I would have done exactly the same. And I would weep for the King, just as you do."

"But what can we do now?" he asked. "I've thought and thought and there's nothing I can think of. We can't take Prince Mittai back. We can't tell the King. I don't even know if I can go back. Uncle Camin is dead . . . and Piff. . . . He'll know I was there." Kashka drew the letter from the sack and gave it to Bargah. "I didn't dare leave a note to explain, but he'll understand that I brought the letter to you."

Bargah read the unfinished letter. "Poor Piff. If Cara was that ill. . . ."

After a little more time she said, "I know that you are so tired you can hardly hold up your head. You've walked far tonight. But there is something we must know. We must learn it as quickly as possible. I want you to remember every word the Lady Ysene said that night—everything exactly as you heard her say it."

Kashka sighed. "I don't know if I can."

"I will help you."

Something in her voice made him straighten his back. "How?"

"Sit there. That chair is more comfortable. Fix your mind upon something. The clock ticking, perhaps. I shall talk to you, ask you questions. It is there in your memory, though you may not think so. It will come back to you. Everything just as it was."

"Why must I—?"

"*Because I must know!*" Bargah interrupted, seeing the doubt in his face. "I know it will be painful for you. You have told me of your terror. I understand that. I wonder that you could keep your wits enough to bring the Prince away. What I must know is whether we ourselves can keep the Prince or whether someone who has no knowledge at all of who he is must take him."

"We can't give him to just anyone!" Kashka cried.

"Of course not. But we must protect him in every way. I must know what she said. Her very words! Will you try? We cannot do it if you are not willing."

Kashka still hesitated. We? It sounded as if she would cast a spell upon him. Much as he loved her, trusted her. . . . After Lady Ysene, this was more than she should ask!

"There are times when you must choose," the old woman said. "It is what you do when you are a man. You make choices, always trying to choose the best, but often not knowing, not absolutely sure that you are right. Sometimes you are wrong. You learn from that. You learn what reasons are important for your choices.

"You have started on that path. You chose to bring the Prince away, not to run and hide yourself and be safe. For you would have been safe—for a time. Now we don't know who is safe, but for the moment she does not have the young prince. We have him."

Kashka rubbed his hands together. They were cold and wet. "I shall try."

Bargah nodded. Kashka made himself comfortable in the chair and began listening to the ticking of the clock.

"Fix your eyes on the candle there," Bargah told him, and then she began talking to him. She said nothing strange, muttered no words that were foreign to him. His fear grew less. After a time she asked him to think back to the moment he came to the top of the hill and looked upon Nazor and the palace.

He was able to do that, to tell her of how the darkness reached out to him and of his feelings. He told her everything until the moment the Lady Ysene cried, *"He is mine!"* Then, as if he had been plunged into cold water, he cried, "I can't! I can't anymore! I know she said that he must be taken from Nazor before the cock crowed, that if anyone in the royal family knew where he was, she would find out. But I can't remember her words. The exact way. I only remember 'Who

is there to take him? Who is there to wake him?' Then—
something about her power. I don't know!"

"Let us try again," Bargah said quietly.

Twice more he tried.

"Something stops me. Something won't let me. I know there
was more after she touched me. I don't know what. It was so
cold!" He shuddered.

Bargah said nothing. She sat quietly, looking at him, nodding her head.

"I want to!" Kashka insisted. "I don't know what stops
me!" When she still said nothing he asked, "Is there any other
way?"

"Yes," she said at last. "There is. I had hoped we could do
it this way. This way you knew what you were saying, you
would remember what you said. You would not say anything
you did not wish to say. But I see you cannot do that. That
does not mean that you do not want to do it. It means that
you cannot. Don't look that way! I'm not displeased."

"And the other way?"

"The other way you give yourself to me. You give me your
mind. I learn what I must know from it."

"Give you my mind? Everything? All of it?"

"Yes. Though I don't want all of it. Only that which has
to do with Lady Ysene."

"But if I can't remember, how can I give it?"

"I shall take it. You will know nothing of my taking it."

"I'll know nothing of it? Once it's started, I . . . I can't stop
you?" If there was anything that was truly his own it was his
mind, his thoughts, how he felt.

"You cannot stop me."

Kashka's heart beat so painfully in his throat he could not
swallow.

"Do you want to give it? Give me your mind? Your thoughts?
Your memory? Surrender it all?"

Bargah truly was a witch! She had just told him as much.

How could he give himself up to her? He clasped his hands
tightly, trying to keep them from trembling. At the same
time. . . . Bargah—was—Bargah. And the Prince. . . . Better not to think about it.

"Yes," he whispered. "What must I do?"

"Nothing, just yet. Let me fix another cup of tea for us.
That will calm you. I'm not going to hurt you."

Still Kashka's fear grew. "Will you . . . will you give it
back?" he asked finally, his teeth almost chattering.

"Give what back?"

"My . . . my mind."

Bargah smiled. "Of course! I'm not taking it to keep. It will
always be yours. I am only borrowing it. Just for the time that
you lay there in the passageway. Those few minutes that Lady
Ysene spoke."

Bargah brewed the tea, talking a little of this and that, as if
what she were doing was something one did every day . . . like
washing her hands. Her calmness terrified him all the more.

"There, now," she said, setting the cups on the table and
filling them from the pot. "I'm having honey in mine. Would
you like some in yours?" She stirred a spoonful into one steaming cup.

Kashka nodded.

She pushed the honey pot toward him and he helped himself, his hand shaking. He stirred the tea. She asked him about
Piff, what they had done in Nainth. How they liked the Duke
and Duchess. His mouth was so dry he could scarcely answer.
He clenched his teeth to keep them from chattering. She sipped
at her tea and he took a sip of his. He was glad for the honey.
She had brewed it strong. He began to feel a little better. The
hot drink warmed him. It went through him as if . . . as if . . .
How heavy his arms were! How heavy all of his body felt! He
could not move. He was warm and . . . and . . . She had
tricked him! He looked at her across the table. She was watching him. What had she done?

"You could have said no, Kashka," the old woman said softly.

He tried to shake his head. He tried to say that he couldn't have said no because he knew of no other way to save the Prince.

He was unable to form the words.

·24·

The candle had burned down, died. Only a few embers remained in the white ash of the fireplace. The pale light of early morning crept into the room. Bargah sat quietly, her elbows on the table, her head in her hands. She was tired. Across from her Kashka slept. He had not moved since he had put his head down on his arms, since that look he had given her.

He had expected something different. There were, of course, other ways. However, Bargah was in a hurry and words, with Kashka, would take much time, be difficult. He would have fought her, however hard he tried not to.

"Just as well," the old woman murmured.

She had held his wrists, bowed her head, and closed her eyes. Then she questioned him. It took time. Bargah knew it would. But Kashka had already taken her to the very moment she sought, so that once again there it was not too long before she thought she had learned exactly what she wanted to know. His whispered words repeated all that Lady Ysene had cried out.

Bargah was about to draw away her hands when something stopped her. She would probe a little deeper, follow the thread of Lady Ysene back yet farther. Then she moved forward in time, again to the Prince, to the flight from Nazor and all that had happened until this moment. Again there was little Kashka had not told her, but that little made her lift her head and murmur, "A golden band upon his arm—stolen!"

A golden band? The Prince wore no such ornament.

She held Kashka's face in her hands and once more began to question him.

"This golden band, what did it look like? Was it jeweled?"

"No. Yes. Two small stones—like eyes."

"Was it a single band?"

"Yes. No." He had paid little attention to it, yet he had seen it.

"It is there before you on his arm. Will you look at it? Will you describe it to me?"

"A single golden band. Plain. No. . . . Double, like snakes twined together. Snakes— No, different. A . . . a pair of lizards . . . strange red-eyed fish with teeth . . . like birds of prey . . . talons . . . boars . . . with tusks, long, vicious . . . It's always different. But—I don't remember it changing. It seems the same. Plain. Gold . . . with eyes. Green stones . . . I don't remember. I didn't see . . ."

Bargah raised her head, pressed her lips together, drew a deep breath, counted, fought to keep her hands quiet at the sides of his face. The golden band of Eddris! She knew of it, though she had never seen it. Who had—in her lifetime? Who had seen it in five hundred years! The power of the Lady Ysene is greater than I dreamed! *The circle of my power!* That was what she meant! Its time had once again come around. Somewhere she had found it!

That was what had driven Kashka in the night. Though he did not wear it, he had held the child close, slept with him in his arms to keep him warm. And the child was possessed by the band.

Why had the lady risked it out of her hands? But how else could she overcome the power of the royal family, the amulet, the stone of Megrath? Doubtless she believed she must surrender the band to the Prince. She thought it worth the risk,

159

for she believed that there was no risk. The child would be there—asleep. Would she waken him, take it before anyone saw it? Or did its power let her keep it from all other eyes there in Nazor? Yes! *"Let it blind those who sleep. . . ."* She was so sure of herself, so certain! Why not, with such power?

Such a fear ran through Bargah at the thought of that power that for a moment she was almost unable to breathe. She closed her eyes. It was all she could do to keep her hands at the sides of Kashka's face.

Yet there is much the Lady Ysene does not know about the band of gold or she would never have let it out of her hands, Bargah told herself when she once again had hold of her thoughts. She would have kept her hand upon it, even on the Prince's arm, until dawn. Two hours more!

"I am spent. . . ." Had the use of its power drained her that much? Or had the stone protected the Prince by just that much, made it just that much more difficult for her? Perhaps. The Prince still lived, though it had been taken from his arm by another. "How can that be . . . ?" Bargah shook her head. There was much *she* did not know about the power of the band. Ancient books had been lost. Scrolls that must have told much more of its immense power destroyed—or stolen?

And yet—though touched by that power, the Prince was here, safe.

And Kashka? He too had seen the golden band, been driven by the power of it. If he should come again under its power. . . .

She bent over the boy. "Hear me, Kashka! Listen to me! If ever the golden band comes to you, cast it away! Be rid of it!"

Now she had given a command. She could question no more. No matter. She had finished. But suddenly she was filled with a sense of foreboding. She put her hand upon the boy's forehead. "Sleep now," she murmured. "Rest. You will need every ounce of strength, of will. . . ."

Bargah withdrew her hands. The past, the present—these came to her. The future, the spinning out beyond now, was not open to her. Doubtless the lady had planned to control every thought of the child prince. What she had not reckoned with was a boy. Two boys, one who had fallen asleep in Nainth, and one who hadn't. For if Piff had waited to go to Nazor. . . . But I cannot start that, for that goes back to the beginning of time, Bargah thought wearily. And what will be goes on to the end of time. How do we untangle it, this knot in our own time?

The first rays of the sun came through the window to shine on the copper pots hanging on the wall.

"We must start with the little Prince Mittai," Bargah murmured. "How . . . ?"

There was a tap at the door. Bargah glanced quickly at Kashka. She could open the door and no one would see him.

She rose, unbarred it, but left the chain in place. She had taken more than one precaution. She opened the door just a little.

"Piff!" She could not believe her eyes.

"Well, yes. But aren't you going to let me in? I've come a long way!"

"No. No, I'm not going to let you in. Wait!" She peered through the crack. "You have a horse? Take him around to the back. There's a shed. I'll come out to you, but you must keep a distance. Neither a hug nor a kiss nor even a hand-shake!"

Piff was mystified.

"Close your mouth," Bargah told him, "and hurry."

Piff came from the shed to see Bargah cross the garden with a child in her arms. She set him on his feet and, with a little push, sent him across the way where a neighbor child played in a puddle left by the night's rain.

Piff stared at the little boy. It was . . . It was . . . He went numb from head to toe.

"Sit there, Piff. We can see him from here Now, listen to me!"

161

All the while she spoke Piff tried to make sense of her words. Kashka—Lady Ysene—the little prince. . . . He shook his head.

Now she was saying, ". . . and until you have done this, I dare not let you come into the house. Do you hear me? You must—"

"Look, Bargah!" he interrupted. "That woman—she's taking him. . . ."

For a woman had come from the house next door, crying, "Rob, Rob, are you in it again? And who is this with you?" and snatched up both mud-spattered children.

"It's all right, Piff. That's Mistress Potry. She'll bathe him. It's the best thing in the world she could do for us! And now, did you hear what I said? You must take him to the old couple that brought them through Welf. They know nothing of who the child is. You say that the grandmother is dead and you cannot care for him yourself. You must also explain the stone—the amulet. Piff! Are you listening to me?"

Piff nodded. His mouth had gone dry. The sound of his heart beating in his ears almost drowned out Bargah's words.

"Now, go and get the child from Mistress Potry. Quickly. I'll come behind you. I knew she would dress him. She'll burn the rags too. Bless her! Piff! Get hold of yourself!"

He took a deep breath. Two. It would help his legs to hold him up. This was far worse than the first time he had played his lute by himself before the King. No wrong notes, he told himself, or if you play one, pretend you didn't and hope no one notices. No, it's a play with Gamel. It's my time. Kashka's carried his part off. What are the lines? *I've come to take a maker of royal mudpies, Mistress Potry.* Royal mudpies! He didn't dare say even that much!

"So he's yours, is he? Here he is all clean! I've put some of my Rob's old clothes on him. I couldn't make top nor toe of what he had."

Piff took the child and held him close. He still could not believe any of what was happening.

"It was terrible," he heard himself say. "We were robbed on the road and left with rags. They took everything. Who can think—a child's clothes? He was asleep when we came and we didn't want to wake him. Then he got out to play without our knowing it. He's a scamp."

"I didn't know who it was there with my Rob in that mud puddle. When Bargah called over to ask if I'd seen . . . Well, I already had them both in the tub."

"I thank you."

"Oh, it's nothing. I have my Rob in the tub three times a day sometimes. Especially after a rain shower."

"I'll return the clothes as soon as—"

"No, no. They're too small for my Rob. I was going to give them to my sister, but she likes new things. I'm glad if you can make use of them. I've more. Here, let me give you a few more. It's hard needing everything at once."

She tucked another little shirt and jacket into Piff's arms.

"Will you be staying with Bargah, then?"

"No, we've still a ways to go. I'm taking him to his grandmother. She's an old friend of Bargah's. Then I'll be back. How far a walk is it to Glidden?"

"Why, you can't walk all that way with such a little one! You'd not get there for the harvest! You say you're coming back? It's only three hours with a pony cart. If I were sure you'd return it. . . . If you can be back before sundown, so my man didn't know I'd lent it. . . ."

"I'll be back before that if I leave at once. Three hours, you say? I'll be back well before supper and with a kiss for you, good mother! Oh, thank you!"

In no time the pony was harnessed and Piff was down the road with the little prince beside him.

The woman watched them on their way. "What a charming boy! What a charming boy! If my Rob grows up to half of that he might marry a princess!" She turned to Bargah, who stood beside her. "I hope what you've said is true—that I can trust him. If I lose the cart and pony. . . ."

"I would trust him with the King's gold," Bargah told her. I'm trusting him with metal more precious than that, she added to herself. "You're kindness itself, Mistress Potry. They've had such bad luck."

"I've heard it's better to stay home these days. That's what I'm doing. What a sweet child! What a charming boy!"

"Yes, they are what you say. Now I'd better see to things in the house," Bargah said. "I've this and that yet to do, what with having to take care of those two."

"Do you need help? I've quick hands for setting things right."

"I can see that! No, thank you. I've just to take a few things from my cart. He could have used mine rather than borrow yours, Mistress Potry, if I'd been quicker yesterday. I'll finish before he returns this afternoon. And I've honey cakes started. I'll bring some to you for your Rob."

"Well, if you need . . . Ah! Oh! Do you see what I see? There's my Rob in the mud again! It's another tubbing for him! Rob! Rob!" And off she hurried.

Bargah returned to her house, closed the door, and leaned against it for a moment. "I need a good cup of tea," she said aloud. "It's been a night and day to age me ten years. I've never seen anyone go so white as Piff when he saw the Prince! But he carried it off with Mistress Potry."

They've had training, Piff and Kashka, and it's serving them now, she went on to herself. It's serving them and me and the King and all the country!

If only I could have gone with him! But some power of hers will stay with the Prince for seven years. That golden band— if she can trace back through whoever took it. . . . She will search for him. We must break every connection we can, leave no trail from Nazor through Kashka to me to the child. . . . Mistress Potry and Piff. . . . The old couple. . . . Will it be enough? I wish I knew!

The pony trotted along at a good pace. Piff did not continue on to the village of Glidden, however. A little distance beyond a curve in the road he turned onto a less used road that wound upward. He walked beside the pony where it grew steeper until at last they came out into a broad high valley. Here the river that tumbled beside the road started in the high marshes. In another hour they should come to the village.

Now he could see the curve in the road that came up from Welf. The one the old couple had told Kashka about. And here was a lane that cut through the fields to that road. It would be wiser for him to come into the village from that side. Wiser? Was anything wise? Again he went over all that had happened to turn his world upside down in an instant.

Prince Mittai! The whole country was looking for him! And Lady Ysene . . . she was looking for him too. That's why she had come on the morning his mother had died and he had wanted to . . . to kill her! If Doro hadn't held him. . . .

He chewed his lip. This thing he must do. Would he be able to do it? Give the Prince to someone he had never seen? Say to them, but not say to them, "Here. Here is the King's young son. Take him. He's yours. For seven years, he's yours. We must never see him in Nazor or let the King know where he is because . . . because . . ."

Just as Kashka had to take him, you have to give him away. You have no choice! Bargah's last words to him.

There was the cottage ahead of him. How quickly they had come to it! The second on the right. It was a neat cottage. Clean. There was a garden. It reminded him of Bargah's little house in Nazor.

He stopped at the gate, made himself get down from the cart. Made himself tie the pony to the post. Made himself lift down the child.

He opened the gate, and the door to the house flew open. The two old people came running down the path.

"Look who's here! Look who's here!" cried the old woman. She scooped up the Prince. "Ohhh! He's all clean and washed! Did you come all this way for a visit or . . . ?"

Piff shook his head. He could not speak.

165

"You've brought him to us, then?"

He nodded.

"There, lad," said the old man, putting his arm around the boy, "you mustn't feel so badly. You're not a man yet that can rear a son. We'll love him and care for him—we already do—as if he were our own. And you can come and visit him whenever you want. Why, if you'd stayed in Nazor or gone back with him, he might have died of that fever. Now come in, lad, and rest. Stay the night if you will. We've room, though it's small."

Piff shook his head. "I can't. I borrowed the pony and the cart. I . . . have to . . . to take them back."

"Come in and rest a minute all the same."

Still Piff shook his head. "I just . . . want to say, his father is . . . was . . . a scholar. If there's a master in the village, let him learn to read and write."

"Now! You didn't tell us that before! But I'm glad to know. We'll do our best."

"And . . . the stone he wears around his neck. It's very old. There's a charm. You must never take it off."

"I knew there was something strange with it," said the old woman.

"It's . . . it's for the good it does for him. It keeps away what's evil." Piff found it more and more difficult to keep his words straight. "He . . . he's a prince . . . to me. . . ."

"We'll take care of him. You don't know how Norry cried when we let you off on the road. We didn't think we'd see you again as long as we lived."

"Come back and visit us. Come and live with us, if you will."

Piff turned away. He could not bear to stay another minute. They watched him turn the pony, start down the road.

"Poor lad! It near broke his heart to leave the little one."

"He couldn't bear even to touch him, to kiss him goodbye!"

166

"I know how the lad felt. He would have taken the child with him if he'd picked him up."

"Did you notice?" asked the old woman. "I can't say for sure, for he had tears in his eyes. But before, his eyes were so blue. I'm sure they were blue. And today they looked brown."

"It must have been the tears, Norry, or your own eyes that are growing old. But it's no matter the color of his eyes. It's the inside of him that counts. There was no change in how much he cared for the little one."

·25·

ꙮ Bargah put a penny on the table. "Toss the coin, or you'll be here trying to decide where to go until the sun grows cold."

"Two out of three," Piff said. "Bargah tosses the third time."

The coin twisted in the air.

"So it will be Nainth, not Nazor. I think that's best myself," Bargah said. "You will return to the Duke and wait until the King sends for you. He *will* send for you, I am certain. He has missed you. Tell the Duke of Cara's death. He'll know of the Prince's disappearance. Tell him you did not see the King— everything as it was except for what brought you here. I doubt he will question you closely. Too much has happened to take his attention.

"Kashka, you were robbed of your horse. Piff met you on the road. You returned to Nainth together. It is the truth as far as it goes.

"But it is not the story you tell so much as the one you do not tell that matters. Three things!

"First, not only must you never whisper a word of this to anyone, but even between you, *never a look, never a word that you have any knowledge of the Prince!*" She looked from one to the other.

"Next, *never a word of where I am.* Who can say what has happened to an old woman on the road from here to Nazor?

168

Again, silence! Keeping silent may be the most difficult trial of your lives. It will also be the greatest service you can do for your king for the next seven years. I cannot be too insistent."

They nodded.

"And the third thing?" Kashka asked.

"Stay away from the Lady Ysene! Her powers are formidable! Kashka, you know. Piff, you must take my word for it.

"Avoid her in every way. If by some chance you find yourselves near her, let your minds turn to the most trivial things in the world. The lint on your sleeve, a hole in your stocking! Anything that has nothing to do with the Prince. Learn to do this now. Practice it. For the lady can put herself into the thoughts of another. If she is the least suspicious, she will pick the knowledge from your minds as easily as you take the meat from a walnut. *She must never have reason to question you.* I cannot be there to help you. Stay together. Help each other."

Again they nodded. Piff looked at his cousin. Kashka had gone white.

"Now then, pack these last few boxes into the cart for me. There's Nanalia crying again! She'll miss you. You've spoiled her already."

"You've not told us who she is, Bargah. Where did she come from?" Kashka and Piff bent over the infant, feeling the grasp of the tiny fingers over one of their own, making faces at her to see her laugh.

"She is my reason for coming here," Bargah said. "She is the great-granddaughter of—never mind. It's too long a story. But, as many children now are, she is an orphan. I shall look after her and you will take those boxes out!"

"You first," Kashka said, lifting the chortling baby.

"No, you." Piff took the baby from him. "You'll make her spit milk, bouncing her that way."

"I'll take her," said Bargah. "She needs changing. Get at those boxes. I want to be off before sundown!"

◆ ◆ ◆

They watched Piff's horse draw the cart up the road into the mountains.

"Even if my horse will make it easier for her than that old mule she had, Bargah will have her hands full," Piff remarked.

"It doesn't seem to worry her."

"You never know what worries Bargah. She's not like anyone else."

When Kashka did not reply, Piff looked at him. "Did you just find out? Didn't you know before?"

Kashka shook his head.

"My father told me. I always thought Uncle Mareth had told you."

Again Kashka shook his head.

"It's something you don't talk about," Piff went on thoughtfully. "Bargah never uses it for herself. Only to help others. She's not like Lady Ysene."

Their eyes met. Piff had never seen such fear in his cousin's look. It frightened him even more than Bargah's warning. He brought his lute around from his back and struck a chord. "We're out of practice. If we're going to play for the Duke and Duchess. . . ."

"Especially the Duchess," Kashka said, wetting his lips. "She has an ear like my father's." He pulled his flute from its case and they began playing.

The Lady Ysene was forgotten—for the moment.

But Lady Ysene was much in Bargah's thoughts. What will her next step be? The old woman absentmindedly patted the baby in the basket. She will search for the Prince, of course. And then? Will she turn again to Ekama? I cannot be in two places at once. I would not have come away when I did except that she was to leave that very afternoon. Did she suspect what it was that kept her from the Princess? I don't think so. But she changed her mind and stayed. Why? I don't know, unless, with me gone, she sensed a freedom she had not known before.

170

If she thought the time was right, she would change her plans. Yes. She would act. She is not one to hesitate when an opportunity is at her fingertips.

Ekama and Aciam . . . without little Mittai, the lady dares not touch them.

Ekama and Aciam, yes. It's good Piff was gone for the winter. Ekama needed the time to grow. But she is still such a child! She does not see what is in Aciam's face when he looks at her. One day she will wake to it.

The old woman sighed. At least Darai is aware of Lady Ysene. He will watch.

Bargah had learned much of the Lady Ysene through the winter. She is like a dark whirlpool, the old woman now thought, trying to fill her emptiness with those things she lacks. The joy of being alive, beauty, love. . . . Cold and grasping, she does not understand that these are not things to be taken. These are things one gives one's self to. She can leave nothing alone to be cherished for what it is, but must force it to submit to her—like grinding a flower beneath her heel because she would have it a different color—to do her will.

While Kashka . . . all the warm and happy things. . . . I cannot believe that each time it just happened to be Kashka. But what draws them together? I fear for him. He has no power from that world she draws from—or I. Indeed, he fears it, and who can blame him after what has happened? Now that he knows more of me—that look he gave me before he fell asleep— betrayed! It will take time to heal.

She rubbed her eyes with her fingertips. I have kept the knowledge of my powers from others. Agrom knew, of course. But he is dead and so is Tarmedo. Mareth knew and Camin— yes, I am sure—perhaps Cara. And they are all dead. King Darai knows. Kashka knows, and I think Piff too, from his look. Let it go no farther! The Lady Ysene must not know of me or— She glanced at the baby, then turned the basket to shade the infant from the sun.

The golden band. . . . Even now the lady is driving it,

willing it back to herself. Bargah frowned. "Once she has it, she will never let it out of her hand again," she murmured aloud. "Seven years! What can I do?" Seven years to wait, to wonder—to watch over the little prince, for if I cannot have him myself, still I can never be far from him. I too must choose. Piff and Kashka must find their own way. Mittai *must* be kept from her power.

Will I be able to do it? The band of Eddris . . . its power. The lady herself is powerful. This golden band will magnify that power a thousand times! I am old. She shook her head. Those spinners and weavers and snippers—what have they in mind? "I don't know," she whispered. "I can only do what I can."

"I have done all that I can. It is on its way and so am I," Lady Ysene murmured to the cushions of her coach. She leaned forward and tapped loudly on the window.

"Faster!" she commanded.

"The horses are tiring, my Lady."

"Bah! They were fresh from Bedlin's."

"It's been all day, my Lady. Where will you stop for the night?"

"We will go on to Wellwood. I'll not stop."

"But it's Sansnom Wood, my Lady. There's a place not far ahead—"

"We'll not stop!"

"Yes, my Lady."

Sansnom Wood! Cowards! What power was there left in Sansnom Wood? Superstitious fools! What did they know of it? Ah! They were going faster. Good!

Foam from the horses' mouths spotted their sides.

There was a sudden crack, a creaking and splintering. The coach tilted, the lady was thrown forward and back in the shaking coach. The coachmen shouted.

At last the grinding and shuddering stopped.

"You're not hurt? It's an axle, my Lady. Broken." The driver helped Lady Ysene from the sagging coach.

The second coachman turned his face away as if to protect himself from the lady's tongue.

"It was sound when we left Nazor, my Lady," the first protested.

"One of you will take a horse and ride to Wellwood for help."

She looked from one to the other. The answer was clear. Not through Sansnom Wood alone. Not at night. Not even for her. Lady Ysene struggled to keep her temper. This was no place to lose it. She would deal with them later.

They waited. Someone came riding through the night so furiously that if the horse had not sensed the blocked road and swerved in time, the rider would have been killed. The lady called to him to stop. But the rider scarcely paused. He shouted over his shoulder, "I'll tell them at Bedlin's!" The cry faded.

She waited. The next day brought a sad little man with a patched wagon and a horse that longed only to be left quietly in the nearest pasture.

"Oh no, my Lady. A faster horse would only shake my wagon to pieces. We're still in Sansnom Wood. To spend another night here would be too much. Last night the trees whispered so I could not sleep. But I'll take you to Wellwood."

She ground her teeth. Another fool! It was a day to Wellwood and another before anyone would venture into Sansnom Wood, and yet another before the repair brought the coach to her. The lady would have ridden a horse to Nainth. But horses were no friends of hers, for she was no friend of theirs. They were deaf to whatever oaths she might shout into their ears.

When she came to Nainth at last, more unpleasantness awaited her.

"Mogrud and his brother are gathering their forces to the north, east of the river. Hundreds and hundreds of men, my

Lady. More, surely, than there are in Byrrhad. There is no doubt they plan to attack. Word has been sent to Nazor. Stay here—better, return to Nazor. I can spare you no men to give you protection." The Duke of Nainth was surprised to see Lady Ysene grow pale. Surely she knew that her brother added his forces to those of Byrrhad?

"I will go to Castle Ysene. At once!" Her wrath was such that the Duke put his hand to his forehead. "Go, Lady Ysene. The risk is your own."

Her contempt that she might need his protection was clear. The Duke's polite wish that she have a safe journey in no way expressed his true thoughts. Your deceit is convincing, Lady, he told himself. Yet to feel so safe you must know those extra hundreds under Mogrud are men of Xon. If they aren't, I'll eat raw oats with my horse.

The Duke was only half right. The lady had no sense of safety from the forces across the river. Hers was an even greater fury toward them. She braced herself in the swaying coach. "The kingdom of Darai is mine to take as I wish. That my brother should plot with Mogrud . . . ! Unspeakable!" Her fingers plucked at the wool of the blanket that lay across her knees. As for her sense of safety, it lay in her own powers. By those powers she had sent for an escort from Castle Ysene.

·26·

⬊⬊⬊ Princess Ekama stood alone in the center of the empty courtyard at the palace of Nazor. They were gone. All of the young lords and the older ones too. All of the young men of Nazor, lords or not. Leading them were Prince Aciam, the Margrave of Tat, and Sir Andros. Through the east gate on the road to Nainth.

There had been such a stir and bustle, the finding of armor and arms and horses and fittings of every kind. Loaded carts and wagons had been sent off as quickly as possible, one after the other. And now the men too were gone. Emptiness, like a clear night sky with no stars, stretched around her.

She had not known how empty that would be, or how terrible emptiness was until now.

In those last three days Prince Aciam had had only a minute for her. "Look after the King," he had said. She nodded. He took both her hands in his. "Someday we are to marry."

Again she nodded. This marriage—Tettie could do nothing but talk of gowns and celebrations, but Ekama did not want to think about that. She preferred to play with the young prince in the garden. But Prince Mittai had vanished. The sick feeling again came over her.

Perhaps it was all right to think of a beautiful wedding, but *afterward* . . . besides, Prince Aciam was going away.

Going away!

In all the busyness she had not thought of how it would be with him gone. Before, when he had been away, Piff and Kashka had been here. Now . . . she looked up at him and then felt even more shy. She looked at her shoes. They were scuffed.

Prince Aciam put his hand under her chin and lifted her face. His look was sober. There was a question in his eyes.

"You know I want to marry you," he said.

She had not thought about that either. Surprised, she looked into his face and a thousand things suddenly went through her head. The next to the last was that she wanted to be with him always. The last turned into words.

"Why can't I go with you to Nainth?"

"Because the King needs you here," he told her. But her asking seemed to have answered the question in his look, for he smiled. It was the smile then that made the emptiness now so terrible.

She went to the King. She read to him. At least he was a little better, his speech a little clearer than it had been at first. If he were better yet tomorrow and the next day, perhaps she could find a way to go, to be with Prince Aciam.

After she had read for a few minutes, she saw that the King was not listening. "Would you rather I didn't. . . ." she began.

"All the warm things," he said suddenly and turned his head slightly toward her. "The warm, the bright, the happy things."

She leaned forward to understand better.

"My queen . . . my princes . . . even my scape . . . graces. All . . . gone. All but you."

"Prince Aciam will come back. We'll find Prince Mittai. Piff and Kashka will come whenever you send for them."

But the King just looked at her.

When he had fallen asleep, the Princess went out into the garden. Only the oldest gardener had remained behind.

176

"I'll do what I can, Princess Ekama." He carried a spade and a rake. In his wheelbarrow were new young plants.

"Show me how," Ekama said suddenly. "I'll help you plant them."

"It's not just the planting, Princess. It's the tending, the weeding, the watering and the feeding and the pruning. It takes care to raise a fine flower."

While Princess Ekama knelt on the ground and turned over the soil with a trowel in the palace garden at Nazor, she thought now of Prince Aciam and the danger he must face, now of the flowers that would bloom.

While Prince Aciam rode toward Nainth with the men of Nazor, he thought now of the Princess Ekama, now of the battle to come and the men who would die.

And while the men of Nazor moved toward Nainth on the road through Sansnom Wood, two youths traveled toward Nainth on the road from Pergyth. Sometimes they walked. Sometimes they rode in a cart with a traveler. They always made the journey cheerful with their music.

This day they came upon a pair of wagons stopped by the side of the road. In the hope they might be offered something to eat in exchange—they were always hungry—they began to play at once.

There was a sudden roar, a sound like that of the mountain falling upon them. One of the wagons shook from side to side. The flap at the end was thrown into the air and a huge bearded man leaped to the ground.

"Aha!" he shouted on seeing them. "Didn't I tell you so! Didn't I wager a thousand gold pieces that it was Piff and Kashka? But who believed me, eh? The whole lot of you has nothing but tin pot lids for ears!" He pounced upon the two boys, an arm around each with such a hug that both were certain their necks were broken, their ribs splintered.

"Suvio!" Kashka gasped.

"You remember me, eh?"

177

"The great Suvio! How could we forget! But how is it you remember us?" Piff tried without luck to dodge the great thump on the back that Suvio delivered.

"Remember you! Ha!" He ran his hand over his thick black beard. "How could anyone forget such a quartet as I heard two years ago in Nazor? Eh? And how does the world treat your fathers? Both well?"

He looked from one to the other. "No," he said then and shook his head. "I'll not believe that. Both? No, no. Oh, what a loss to the world! But what are you doing here? Was there no place for you with King Darai? Has he lost his wits?"

"Not at all," Piff assured him. "We're on our way to Nazor now."

"Only by way of Nainth," Kashka put in.

"Then you're in luck! Then we're in luck!" roared Suvio. "You'll join us! We'll go together. Oh, what a show we'll give them on the road from Gorloth to Nainth! You're hungry. What boy is never anything but hungry! That's what makes a man of a boy—eating!" He thumped his wide paunch, then delivered another of his blows, which Kashka was no luckier to avoid than Piff had been.

Suvio seized them both by the collar and half lifted them into his wagon. "Silvi! Is there any stew left? No? Bread? A few raw carrots? Parsley? What a pair of young sparrows you are! Meat on your bones is what you need. We'll put it there, won't we?" He turned to the group that had gathered around them. "We'll have a time of it with Piff and Kashka! Hitch the horses to the wagons!"

Kashka rubbed the back of his neck. Piff gingerly ran his hand down his ribs. No, they weren't broken. In half an hour they were on the road once more, traveling slowly to the east.

The next day they stopped in Carth. On the second day they arrived in the village of Merne where the road they traveled met that running between Nainth and Gorloth.

The troupe lost no time. The horses were unhitched. Boxes

were trundled out and carried swiftly to the grass in the center of the village square. In no time two booths were set up. From one Suvio would sell that which cured everyone of everything, all from a single bottle. From the other, Silvi would sell a sweet that made it necessary to buy Suvio's cure.

Barden lit the torches that he would put out in his mouth. Cazza set up the rope he would walk on. Cazza's wife and child danced on their toes and led the little dog that danced on its hind legs. Cazza's brother played a raucous but rollicking horn. The pony pranced in a circle, Kila standing on his back.

"See, ladies and gentlemen!" Suvio shouted when the sales of his miraculous elixir slowed. He drank a full bottle of the cure and tossed the empty container into the air with a snort and a roar. The muscles of his arms swelled, those on his back rippled. He leaped from the booth, lifted Kila from the pony, then lifted the pony to his shoulders.

"See what it does for a man who is a man! But there are few who can drink so much without exploding with the strength of it!"

Quento, the deaf mime, began his wildly exaggerated imitation of all the others, even to a sorry attempt at lifting the pony. When he found he could not, he picked up the discarded bottle, shook a drop into his mouth, and, with a flourish and great show of strength, pulled a straw-stuffed toy pony from beneath his shirt and perched it on his shoulders. He strutted proudly before the laughing crowd. Those who didn't buy from belief bought for the fun of it.

Piff and Kashka played the music of the dancing at Gandy's. Kashka tumbled, Piff juggled. It was far different here from performing in the palaces of Nazor and Nainth. The restless audience must be caught, wooed, beguiled, held with a promise of yet better to come or it would turn away. Folk were more excited by a high leap or impossible catch of the balls than by a polished turn on lute or flute. Something not well done was hooted. Something done well drew cheers and clapping and stamping that knew no limits of politeness.

The cousins found it exciting in a way Nazor had never been.

There were interruptions, distractions. Folk from the country came and went, for it was market day. Some pressed through in a hurry to be about their business. Others jostled to the front where they might see better. Some came on foot, some on horseback. The crowd moved forward, drew back, grew, diminished. Young boys turned somersaults on the edge of the green, jumped, clicked their heels, threw balls into the air, vied with one another if not with the performers.

The two youths were near the end of their act. Piff and Kashka took turns, watching each other with exaggerated interest, tried to copy, then outdo the other with their different skills. The high toss of a ball, a high leap. A toss, turn, and catch—a leap, turn, and handspring. Two balls in the air— a double somersault. On it went, each time more elaborate. At last they worked together, whirling around each other in as carefully timed a pattern as any dance set to music. Yet to those who watched all seemed by chance.

There was yet a minute to go when a coach followed by six horsemen rattled through the street, scattering the crowd. There was no stopping for Piff and Kashka. They were working too closely. A misstep, a bad fall, and a sprain or broken bone would be the end of it for weeks.

The coach drew suddenly to a stop. An order was given and the horsemen turned.

Now they were finished, just in time to see the riders coming at a gallop toward the green. Breathless, they turned, racing for safety out of the way of the galloping hooves. Piff threw himself on the ground, rolled beneath a wagon. Kashka leaped for the doorway of a shop. But in that instant he felt hands seize his arms. He was drawn up, thrown roughly over the rump of a horse with a blow that knocked the remaining breath from his lungs.

180

In half a minute the riders wheeled, galloped away behind the already disappearing coach.

Piff rolled from beneath the wagon and looked across the square.

"Kashka!" he called. "Kashka!" He ran to the center of the green while Suvio and the others gaped at the splintered booths.

"Where's Kashka?" Piff cried, looking frantically in all directions.

There was no sign of him.

Several of the villagers gathered to sympathize over the broken booths, the scattered candies and bottles.

One man put his hands on Piff's shoulders.

"They took your brother," he said.

·27·

➷➷➷ "Who? Who took him?" Piff cried. "Why?"

The villagers looked at one another.

"There's always been talk of the like happening," said one.

"I've never heard of it done in the white light of day," said another.

"Who took him?" Piff pleaded, now almost beside himself with fear.

"The horsemen of the Lady Ysene."

Faces, village square, sky—all tilted then darkened around Piff. Voices grew distant, then came back as the world turned flat again.

"I'll go after them!" he cried, and would at once have run out of the village, but Suvio caught and held him. Struggle as he would, he could not escape.

"Be quiet, Piff! Be still! Give us a minute to ask a question. To think."

More villagers gathered around. A small girl began to cry.

"Now, we'd like to know what it is we're up against," Suvio said, still not letting go of Piff though the boy had stopped fighting.

One man cleared his throat. "There've always been tales about Lady Ysene. When someone disappears in the night, there's always the story comes back. She takes folk. She sees one she fancies. She takes him—or her."

182

"What for?" Suvio asked.

"Who knows what for?" said another. "Who goes to Castle Ysene to find out?"

"Nor does anyone come back from there to say. Four vanished from hereabouts just last year, all at the same time."

"And three from near Carth we've learned since," said still another. "There's been never a word of any of them. Seven of them."

"She has a way of keeping folk."

"She may need servants," a fourth joined in. "They don't live long at Castle Ysene."

Piff's despair grew with every word. "Suvio, help me find him!" he begged.

"The place is a fortress," said the man who had first spoken. "A slime-green moat, thick walls, guards. They say . . ." His voice trailed off.

"What do they say?" Suvio asked.

"They say there are other . . . beings at Castle Ysene. It's better not knowing."

Piff looked at the faces around him. He needn't ask them about her. He knew more of the Lady Ysene than they did. I'll find him, he thought. We will come back from there. There has to be a way. I've only to think of it.

Suvio let go his hold on Piff and muttered, "I don't know. We can't . . ."

Then, as they stood there, a horseman came riding even faster than those of the Lady Ysene had come. He pulled up before the knot of people.

"Mogrud's brother has attacked Nainth!" he cried. "Prince Aciam asks the help of every man and boy in the country!"

"Mogrud's brother! Prince Aciam! What of Mogrud? What of the King?"

"The King lies in Nazor, struck down by an illness. He cannot move from his bed. Prince Aciam leads our men along with Mittai of Nainth, the Margrave of Tat, and Sir Andros. Mogrud is camped where the rivers join between Byrrhad and Xon. His forces there grow larger each day."

"There is fighting at Nainth?"

"They were battling at the bridge over the east branch of the river. When I left, the men of Nainth held them back. But it's a day and a half since. Mogrud and his brother have more men in arms than we have people in the country. The Prince needs you, every one. And I need a fresh horse. I must go on to Gorloth."

In three minutes the rider was off.

The villagers argued among themselves.

"We should go!"

"What of the bridge here? Suppose Mogrud comes north to Merne?"

"The bridge here would not bear an army."

"Mogrud would have to cross Xon. The lady would never permit it."

"Her brother might."

"She'd not let him. If there is aught we know it's that she hates Mogrud."

"The Duke fears his sister. He'd not dare cross her."

"I'm going to Nainth," Suvio said, "and all my troupe with me. I'll not hang back and be called a coward."

Piff listened in an agony of indecision. What was he to do? Suvio left the splinters of wood on the green and led the way to the wagons. Men turned away to seek weapons, saddle horses, say their good-byes.

Piff stood alone. He had disobeyed the orders of King Darai when he had left Nainth for Nazor. Now, and this was far more serious, he must decide between trying to help Kashka and obeying the call from Prince Aciam.

Then another thought came to him. What of Prince Mittai? If the Lady Ysene should learn from Kashka where he was! Bargah's words washed over him. *Avoid her. Help each other.*

Keeping this secret will be the greatest service you can do for your king for the next seven years.

Suddenly he ran after Suvio. "Suvio! Suvio!" he called. "Wait! I must have a few days. I *must* go after him. If there is nothing I can do, I shall come back and go with the men of Gorloth to Nainth. *I must go after Kashka!*"

"I can't give you leave," Suvio said, looking Piff up and down. "That's for you to decide. By your size, you're only half a man as it is. I don't know that the Prince will miss a string plucker."

Stung speechless, Piff watched Suvio's retreating back. In that instant he understood what it was that drove Kashka to leap from a roof or explode in a fit of rage.

His own rage at the moment gave him time to ask only one question. Where was Castle Ysene? Then it drove him to run north from Merne to the bridge, across the bridge, and into the country of the Duke of Xon. Not until then did he remember that he had left everything he owned—his lute and along with it, Kashka's flute and what few clothes they had between them—in Suvio's wagon.

The horsemen rode fiercely for a short time, then stopped. Kashka had scarcely regained his breath when he was hauled from the horse, bound tightly, and thrown again over the back of the animal. Off they went across a long wooden bridge and then onto a road. The boy was choked with dust. He closed his eyes against the grit flying up from the horses' hooves.

Only one thing he knew. He had glimpsed the coach and recognized it. He was a captive of the Lady Ysene.

He thought they would ride forever. His only efforts were to get a breath of air when possible and to try to keep his neck from being broken. Later he wondered why he had struggled so to keep alive.

Forever came to an end at last. The light was growing dim. It was evening. He was aware only faintly of the hollow sound of another bridge beneath the horses' hooves, of the smell of stagnant water. There was a clanking of chains and rusted winches. The air turned cold and damp. At last the horses stopped. He was pulled down, dropped on the ground.

"Leave him there for her."

Only half conscious of what was happening, he was at least able to pretend he was not at all conscious. No more words were spoken. The sounds of footsteps, of horses being led away, were all that came to him. Beneath him was stone. Cold settled around him, through him to the marrow of his bones. More horses came and the sound of wheels with them. These also came to a stop. There were other sounds and finally a voice.

"Bring him to my rooms in ten minutes."

There was no mistaking the voice. She knows! Kashka thought. She knows that I . . . Desperately he turned his mind to the feel of his flute against his lip. A scale. A simple scale. The first he had ever learned from Master Wondry.

Her footsteps faded.

Kashka had no need of trying to lie still. All of his joints turned to water at the thought of what was to come.

It seemed only ten seconds before he heard the boots, felt the hands upon his arms. They dragged him he did not know where. Up stairways, through corridors. At last they stopped before a door. Again they let him fall. Kashka lay still. Angry voices came to his ears. He recognized those of the Lady Ysene and her brother the Duke of Xon.

"I don't understand why you permitted it! You were not to invade!"

"I did not invade! Nor did I permit it! Mogrud is strong. Much stronger than either of us knew. These are his doings— his and his brother's. How was I to stop his brother? Did you expect me to invade Byrrhad? Let them fight. Let them weaken themselves against Darai. If matters go poorly for them at Nainth we will cut them down in Xon. If the battle goes their way, we will help them—"

"Never! In no way will we support Mogrud! I shall hope to

186

hear of his death at Nainth. And what do you mean? Cut them down in Xon? Does he plan to invade Xon?"

"Mogrud is not at Nainth. It is his brother who is there. Mogrud is camped where the rivers join between Byrrhad and Xon."

"*What is he doing there?*"

"Waiting."

"What for?"

"To see which way to go."

"What do you mean? He would be a fool to battle in two places at once."

"He wishes to cross the bridge at Merne. Come down on the other side of the river to attack Nainth from that side." The Duke's voice was sulky, angry.

"He would not dare come through Xon without our agreeing! He will set no foot in Xon! If he does I will have him in chains. My way! All of his doings are casting doubt upon us!"

"Why should they?"

"They believe Mogrud is strengthened by forces of yours. Is that true?"

"Why should I give him help? I gave my promise to you—"

"Your promises!"

"Calm yourself. Your anger is no pretty thing to look on. And here—see here what I've done for you. This is yours, is it not?"

There was silence. It grew longer until it seemed to Kashka it said more than any words. What was it he had of hers?

Then her voice came. A whisper, it seemed, but a sound to it that penetrated the walls, echoed through the roof to the sky, sent chill after chill down Kashka's spine.

"*Where did you find this?*"

"Where did you lose it, sister?"

"I did not lose it! Where did you find it?" Her voice rose in a sudden shriek.

He did not answer.

"Where?"

"When you can speak to me as a sister, not as a witch, I shall tell you."

"Tell me." Her voice dropped.

"A band of men—a pack of thieves—came to the castle gate. Called to enter. The leader wore it around his neck on this same chain. I recognized it. I saw it once when you—"

"Where are they—these men? These thieves?"

"Where do you think?"

"Take me to them at once!"

"You have mistaken my meaning. They are dead and buried."

"Dead!" Again a shriek.

"There was no doubt in my mind they had stolen it. Why should they live? However they stumbled upon it, they were ignorant of its worth to you, had no sense of its meaning. I could see that myself."

"What do *you* know of its meaning?"

"What do I know of any of your baubles? I only know that you valued it. They stole it. Why should they live?" he repeated.

"And suppose I valued them? What did you know of *their* worth? You must kill everything that crosses before your eyes! Why do you think I—?" She stopped suddenly. "Never mind. We have talked enough. Leave me!" The darkness of her rage was closing in upon her. She might kill him. Yes, she would. . . .

The Duke of Xon stepped back quickly and opened the door. He found himself face-to-face with two of the lady's men, an unconscious boy, head drooping, between them.

"What is this?" he asked, reaching to lift the face.

"My lady's," said one of the men.

"Bah!" growled the Duke, dropped his hand, and strode away.

Lady Ysene saw them. "Chain him below." Her voice trembled.

"A band, my Lady?" asked one.

"A band?" Her voice rose for a third time to a shriek. "Yes! A band! Here, this will do!"

Kashka felt the cold touch of metal across the back of his neck. A chain with some kind of pendant had been dropped over his head. With it came a feeling as if he had been struck. It drove the air from his lungs.

The weight of the pendant bled him, suffocated him, pulled him into darkness.

A gray consciousness crept through him. He tried to think where he might be. Who he might be. There was only confusion, despair, fear. *Where was he? Who was he?* His mind groped, questioned.

There was nothing. Only coldness. Darkness.

He had known coldness and darkness. He was drawn away from now, from here. Back . . . back . . . a long time back. It was there, the coldness. The darkness too. But the silence was not there. There had been sound, noise, a terrible confusion of it that destroyed his senses. He had pressed his hands to his ears, trying to shut it out. He could not do it. It grew worse and worse. Soon it would possess him, fill him with it alone. All else would be shut out to the end of time.

Then a voice came through it to him. At first there was only the sound of it, a single tone like a straight line through a mass of tangles or the clear tone of a flute through a deafening cacophony. Words took shape like separate notes of a melody. What were they? If he could remember, then he might learn who he was.

Listen to me! Hear me!

He was listening! How could he not hear in the deathliness of this silence?

Open your eyes! Look at me! Look at me!

There had been a lamp to light the room, a fire to warm him. Here it was darkness. Did he not have his eyes open? What brought such blackness? There were eyes in the dark.

189

Whose? Did he see them or did he imagine them? Either way, he must hold them before him. They were all that he had in this blind night.

Look at me! The eyes looked deeply into his own.

But it was only a dream. A dream of eyes and a voice. The voice. . . . Now it said, *Cast it away. Be rid of it!*

Be rid of what? What did he have?

A weight lay across his neck and shoulders, a heaviness that kept him from moving. A chain that bound him to the cold stone on which he lay. It was drawing all of his strength from him, all of his thoughts, his memory, all of himself. He must be free of it!

He tried to move his hands, to touch the chain, but something held them. Something hard and cold around his wrists. He pulled, heard a clanking.

You can! You must!

Again! He pulled himself forward on his elbows. There, he could just touch the side of his throat. His fingers felt along his collar, under the edge of it. He had hold of it. The chain . . . it was so heavy. A terrible weight as if he were trying to lift the whole world with the fingers of one hand.

You must!

"I . . . I'm trying."

He fought with it. Pull it now, lift it. He turned his head sideways, drew back the chain. Slide it over, then . . . push it away. Push it away across the floor as far as you can. Push it away from whoever you are.

That was good, Kashka!

Kashka! He was Kashka!

The stone beneath his face tipped and turned. Far away he heard a creaking, a heavy door slam—far away, as if from distant thunder in the sky.

·28·

Kashka woke, cold to numbness, aching in every muscle, his bones painful against the stone floor. There was no way he could turn that would give him comfort.

Was it still night, or was he blind? The darkness was as great as it had been when he groped so desperately for some knowledge of himself. This time he knew who he was, where he was. He strained to see his hands, some glimmer, some sliver of light. There was nothing. The silence weighed upon him as heavily as the darkness. There was only despair.

One faint speck of hope came to him. That was that the lady had not come to question him about . . . He fixed his mind upon the image of his father's harp. Of his father's hands moving across the strings. Why hadn't she come? Or had she come while he slept. Taken his mind as another witch had? He shuddered, his hope dissolving. He had no recollection of that first questioning. Might not Lady Ysene have been here and gone? Taken his mind while the chain hung around his neck, while he was powerless to think, to know who he was?

His despair suddenly turned to anger. What right had she? What right had any of them—anyone at all—to bind another person, to probe, to pry, to steal him from himself? He was filled with such rage that tears came to his eyes. He pulled and twisted the chains, but there was only pain for trying.

191

After a time he grew quiet. If she had come and gone, if she had taken all he knew from him, he had only to lie here in the dark until the end of time.

Strange thoughts began going through his mind. He imagined someone opening the door and bringing light into the room. He was surprised he could invent an image with such detail. He had never seen the person before. He did not know if it was a boy or a girl. It was thin, small, dark-eyed. Dressed in a ragged tunic, hair cropped short, barefoot, it brought soup and bread.

Kashka turned his face aside.

"You eat it," he said and was stunned by the sound of his own voice. Then he watched, marveled as bite by bite the bread was eaten, the soup drunk as if what he saw was real. Recalling the taste of bitter tea with honey, he felt he would be sick. He would eat nothing in this place, even that of his own imagining.

The person vanished with the light.

Kashka imagined he heard the sound of his flute. He filled his mind with music for hours. When he had exhausted everything he knew, he invented music of his own. He talked with Piff about how it should be played. He questioned his father, but his father did not answer. He only looked at Kashka. At last he said, "She has the eyes of a snake," and Kashka found he had been turned into a mouse. A snake with the eyes of Lady Ysene came toward him. If only he could run! But he was paralyzed, his wrists and ankles held by burning circles of fire.

The dark-eyed person came again with the bowl and the bread. Again Kashka turned away.

The third time the person appeared, Kashka knew that of all his dreams and nightmare fantasies, this was not one of them. This was someone who set a candle on the floor, brought food, and offered it to him.

"I'll never eat it," he said. "You eat it. You're alive. You're free." Once more he did not recognize the sound of his voice, an unfamiliar hoarse whisper. What had happened to it?

The person raised the bowl to its lips, drank, and set it down.

Kashka twisted, propped himself on his elbows, and stared.

"Do you know what it is to be free?" he asked, wondering himself what it was, if he had ever known it.

There was no answer. He . . . she . . . was so small, so thin.

"It's running in a field with no one to chain you," he said. "It's thinking what you will with no one to tell you. It's everything of your own running through your head and no one to take it from you. It's your fingers on the flute and not even notes to worry you. Only music. Music for you to have and to give away. Free. Free for whoever will take it for their own. Giving it because you want to. Because you're free to give it!"

He wasn't sure what he was saying, but he could not stop talking.

"I want to be free!" he cried. "That's why I won't eat your bread. I would rather die than eat bread and be in chains!"

By the light of the candle he saw the stones of the cell that surrounded him, saw the chains that held him, the manacles on his wrists and ankles. He pulled at them, but the fire of his dreams was as painful when he was awake.

The person wiped a hand across a mouth. Bread and soup were gone.

"Why don't you go away from here? You're free," he went on. "There are no chains on your arms or legs. Run away! Anyplace in the world is better. Go to the Princess Ekama. Did you know her? She was here once. How . . . ?" He stopped speaking. His head was spinning. How had the Princess been able to live in such a place? Even the best room in the castle must be a horror of cold stone and chains.

He closed his eyes, put his head down on his arm. What

was the use? This person was deaf. Why should it know what he was talking about when he didn't know himself? There was no such thing as being free. There was only stone and iron. Iron and stone. The only way out of here was to die. How long did it take?

The door closed. The light was gone.

There were dreams again, more confused than before. In this one something soft, cold, stroked his face. A snake. . . . He woke suddenly, pulled away.

But there was no creature. There was light. He could see. It was the small person touching his face. The candle was there, but no bread, no bowl.

Kashka shook his head to clear it. Again the person reached out and touched his face, looked into his eyes. Kashka stared back and then became aware that the person held up something before him.

It was a key.

Unbelieving, Kashka watched as the key was turned, the manacles opened one after the other. He could sit up! He could stretch, rub the numbness from his arms and legs. Oh, how he ached! He got to his hands and knees, then crept to the wall. He stood, hands against the wall until the dizziness was gone.

"Who are you?" he asked.

There was no answer, only the shake of the head.

Kashka looked more closely at the face. The features were fine, delicate. Scarcely more than skin covered the bones.

"You're a girl?"

A nod.

"Can't you speak?"

She shook her head no.

Had she been born mute? He wondered. Or had the Lady Ysene . . . Kashka shuddered.

While he rubbed his legs and arms the girl had locked the empty manacles. She picked up the candle from the floor, picked up a parcel Kashka had not noticed, and then bent to scoop up something else. Kashka saw the glint of gold.

"No!" he cried. "Leave it!"

She shook her head and, looping the chain over her arm, backed away from him through the door. Kashka stumbled after her. She locked the door, hung the keys beside it, and turned down the dark passageway. Slight as she was, he did not have the strength to try to take the chain from her or make her throw it down. It was all he could do to keep on his feet. Limping, he followed her.

The light from the candle was enough only to keep them from walking into the walls of a narrow passage. They turned and Kashka's footsteps echoed. Was it a room? A cavern? The girl held the candle high, looking, searching along the wall. There were tools. Peculiar instruments of—what? Cold went down Kashka's spine. There—against the wall! Chains and a mound of bones. The girl took something from among the tools and walked on.

The youth felt the passage slope downward. His heart fell with each step. He had hoped they would come to a stair leading up. It was so dark they must be underground. Where was she taking him—perhaps to Lady Ysene? But he would be lost for eternity if he did not stay with her!

On they went, feeling their way, a turn, another, a spiraling stair. The walls were damp, the air foul. Now the passage ran straight, now it sloped upward. The candle flickered. If it should go out!

Then Kashka caught a breath of air with a taste of freshness in it. Again the flame bent low. The girl stood still and sheltered it with her hand. They climbed a steep stairway, so narrow they could not walk side by side. At the top of the stair was a door, the wood rotted and broken, the iron rusty. The girl pushed against it. It did not open. Kashka put his shoulder to it. Together they pushed. It gave way, creaking and groaning.

Damp night air rushed over them. They stepped out of the castle and under the night sky.

Kashka drew breath after breath of fetid air, sweet to him after that of the dungeon. If he could have held it in his hands, caressed it, he would have done so.

A touch on his arm brought him to look around. They stood on the edge of a pool of water, the stone wall of the castle rising from it. There was no path leading away.

The girl gave Kashka the candle, then knelt down. After feeling about she began drawing on a rope, pulling it carefully. In a minute a small boat half full of water appeared. Kashka shook his head. It would sink with their weight. But the girl leaned over and groped in it until she brought up a small bucket. Silently she began to dip out the water. Kashka bent to help her.

At last the shell rode high, and though it leaked, the water came in slowly. The girl disappeared down the stair and returned with a long pole. Kashka nodded and motioned for her to get into the boat. She shook her head, pointed at him and then pointed across the water. She placed the pole and the parcel she had brought into the boat, pointed once more to him and to the direction he must go.

Kashka could not believe that she did not want to go with him. She stooped to pick up something from the ground, then put the tool she had taken from the wall into his hand. If he had been in Nazor, Kashka would have taken it for some kind of shears the gardeners might use to prune rosebushes. What use had it here? His stomach turned.

The girl touched his face. He watched the movement of her hand as she pushed back the sleeve of her tunic. He could just see it against the white of her upper arm. A dark band. She took his hand, pressed his fingers against it. It was of metal, cold and hard. Then she motioned toward his other hand.

Suddenly he understood. She wanted him to cut the band

196

upon her arm. He nodded quickly, raised the tool. He felt her tremble. She was afraid! What did she fear? He paused and put his hand against her cheek. "Don't be afraid," he whispered close to her ear. "I won't hurt you."

She held his hand for a second. He drew it away and felt carefully of the ring and of how he could slip the blade beneath it. The next moment he pressed with both hands. The metal was hard. He pressed harder. Suddenly there was a crack as if lightning had struck at his feet. The metal split. The tool was jarred from his hand and, with the broken ring from her arm, fell into the pool and sank.

The girl gasped and fell against him. Stunned by the sound, Kashka held her. Then he lifted her quickly and put her into the boat. He stepped in carefully, took up the pole, and pushed away from the castle wall.

The boat rocked, turned, bobbed a little, and then slowly began drifting. A slight current carried them farther from the wall. Kashka lowered the pole into the water, feeling for something to push against. The pool was too deep.

Lady Ysene woke suddenly. She knew the sound of it—the sharp crack of metal sundered. Someone had died. She glared at the canopy. It annoyed her when they died in the night and woke her. It annoyed her especially now after three nights of sleeplessness and anger. She would lie awake once again, fuming, infuriated with her brother.

Tomorrow the last of the remains of those who had brought the golden band should be found. She would go over them, see if those of a small child were among them. They must sift the soil carefully for any trace. By the end of the day she would know. By the end of the day her brother would be here again. Her brother! That she must call him kin!

Not only had he killed them, but had buried them here, there, everywhere! Why not a common grave? Because it was his whim! What a waste of time! And if they did not find the child, she still would not know!

Oh, she would question him tomorrow! Had there been any women or children among the robbers? The idea of a woman would throw him off. He would answer. If he had not killed the child, what had he done with it?

Her anger doubled. Where had he gone? Was he playing games with her? A double game—one with her, one with Mogrud? So far the news had been . . . what should she call it? Good or bad? Mogrud's brother had crossed the river but Nainth still held out. There were losses on both sides that might affect her plans. Had Aciam been killed? That must not happen until she found the young prince! Aciam *must* marry Ekama! It was the wedge she sought. She would have Nazor! She would have Nainth!

Nainth! Why was Mogrud sitting halfway between Nainth and Castle Ysene? Why did he not put all his strength against Nainth? Had he really ideas of coming this way? He would regret that! Once she had spoken with her brother, she would make her own plans for Nainth.

Now she must sleep. Who was it had died? She ground her teeth. There was no way to punish such a one. Someday she would learn all the secret powers of the golden band. Then she would be able to reach beyond the grave, punish those who were foolish enough to die in the night! The incompetent half-wits and imbeciles who cluttered the human race—she would see them all to their graves and beyond!

The girl remained huddled, unmoving in the bow of the boat. They had drifted from the pool through a narrow channel and into a river. Kashka was too busy keeping them afloat in the swift current to go to her. Now and then he scraped half a bucket of water from the bottom of the boat.

He worried at her stillness. When they were caught under a bank in an eddying pool, he crept to her on hands and knees.

He whispered to her, shook her slightly. She did not respond.

"She's fainted," he muttered and rubbed her wrists. He trailed his hand in the river to scoop up water and splash it on her face.

At last she sighed and opened her eyes. Kashka leaned back relieved.

She sat up.

"Don't move so fast!" the boy warned her. "You'll tip us over."

She turned her face toward him. He could see the gleam of her eyes.

"You fainted. We're on a river. I don't know where we're going."

She reached out to touch him.

He took her hand. It was colder than his own. "You'll be all right. I couldn't leave you there. I couldn't believe you didn't want to come away."

She held his hand, pressed it against her face. She was crying. He put his arm around her.

"It's all right," he said. "We'll find our way. We'll go to Nainth, to Nazor. You'll have friends. All of my friends will be your friends." He looked up into the night sky. Stars shone through a break in the clouds. It was forever since he had seen them. "The stars, the moon, the sun!" The sense of his freedom grew. "The King himself!"

He pushed the boat back into the current. He would find his way to Merne. How long would it take? Two days? Three? A week? It didn't matter. Piff would wait for him there.

·29·

"Do you know enough to unload fish?" The driver looked at the besmirched dull-eyed youth who stood gaping in the road. A half-wit, he thought.

The boy nodded.

"Then climb up here. And watch you don't fall under the wheels the way the last one did." The boy clambered awkwardly to the seat. The driver swore. He could never find a boy with any wits about him, for who with any wits would ride a wagon to Castle Ysene, even if it was only to unload fish or cabbages?

"Where are you from? I've never seen you before."

"Omwheray." The boy turned, pointed behind him to the sky more than to the river valley.

What was wrong with him? Cleft palate? There was no harelip.

"Just stupid!" the driver muttered, and shook the reins.

There was no use trying to make conversation. The boy could not be understood. He was also slightly cross-eyed and tended to drool from a mouth that hung slack most of the time. He couldn't seem to breathe through his nose.

They crossed the moat and waited for the iron gate to be raised, then drove into the yard and around to the kitchen entrance.

"Here it is," the driver said.

The boy looked around.

"You get down here!" The driver was losing his patience. Castle Ysene always put him in a foul mood. "You take the fish. Carry them through the door there. They'll show you where to put them."

The boy got down, limped to the side of the wagon, and waited.

"The sack there!" shouted the driver. "Put them in the sack, carry them through the door." He drew back his foot, but did not aim well. He missed as the boy moved suddenly to fill the sack with fish.

"Slow until they see a kick coming," muttered the driver.

The boy carried the filled sack through the door and stood waiting until someone might speak to him. It was several minutes, for there were whispered words going through the kitchen, furtive looks, fear on faces. Word had filtered down from the rooms above. Something was amiss with the Lady Ysene.

"Fish, eh?" Someone finally noticed. "There. Over there. In that tub."

The boy carried them to the corner of the kitchen, dumped them in the tub. He stood waiting.

Suddenly the door flew open. Lady Ysene herself strode into the kitchen. She looked from face to face. Her eyes came to rest on the boy beside the tub.

"Who is that?" She pointed to the cross-eyed, drooling youth with the turned-in foot and crooked back.

"Driver's boy. He brought the fish."

"Imbecile!" she snorted in disgust. "Who took food to the boy in the dungeon? The one I brought with me four days ago?"

The cook cleared his throat. "The mute."

"Where is she?"

Heads turned. "She's not here."

"When did you last see her?"

"Night before last."

"Who took food to him last night?"

"No one. She didn't come to the kitchen last night."

There was no mistaking the lady's anger. She picked up a crock, threw it, smashed it on the floor.

"I want her found!" She turned and vanished.

Looks were exchanged. A mop and broom were brought.

"She's not the only one missing," muttered the cook.

"Who else?" asked the woman with the mop.

"The boy."

"What boy?" The woman looked around the kitchen.

"The one she brought. The one in the dungeon."

"How can anyone be missing from the dungeon?"

"Who can say?" the cook muttered. "But he's not in the dungeon. The door was locked, the chains locked. The keys outside. But the boy was gone."

"*He* took him?"

The cook shook his head. "The Duke just returned. The boy was already gone."

"There'll be a bad time for that!"

"He'll not get far. Nor can the mute hide for long. She'll find them both."

"You think it was the mute?"

"Who else? She was never like the rest of us. Always off by herself. No one knew where. The lady'll call her now."

"She must be up there calling both of them." The woman shuddered.

The driver's boy passed through the kitchen, reloaded the sack, and brought more fish to dump into the tub. The driver waited impatiently. When all the fish were gone, he touched the horse with his whip. The sooner he came away from Castle Ysene, the happier he was. But his happiness must wait this day, for as the horse lurched forward, a wheel fell off the wagon.

"Get some help!" the driver shouted at the boy who sat

202

clinging to the tilted seat. The boy started to climb down, fell, picked himself up, dusted his breeches in a halfway manner, and limped toward the kitchen. He stood for some time waiting for help. While he waited a pair of guards entered and asked for something strong to drink.

"Did you find him?" the cook asked in a low voice as he filled mugs for them.

One guard shook his head. "No, but we found the way he went out."

"How? Where?"

"All we know is that he's gone. Devil knows how or where," said the other, wiping his hand across his mouth. "She'll have to use her own way of finding him.".

"What of the mute?"

"No sign of her down there."

"What will you tell the lady?"

"We'll tell her that there's no sign of him or her. If they went out that way, they must have drowned. Otherwise, who can say? There may be others who will know for certain." He swallowed his drink quickly.

No one in the kitchen offered to help the driver's boy. He limped away to find that the driver had taken care of the wheel himself.

"I'd leave you here for all the good you are," he grumbled. However, he was a man of mercy. When the boy was again beside him on the seat, he drove through the gate and across the moat. When they were well down the road, he drew a handkerchief from his pocket and mopped his forehead. It was a cool evening but he was sweating like a freeholder hoeing a field under a July sun. He would not spend a night at Castle Ysene for all the fish and cabbage in the world.

Lady Ysene sat with her hands clasped. No. There was no need for her to call them. They could not have left the castle. There was no way out. They were hiding somewhere, or, more probably, lost in the maze beneath the castle. The guards were still searching through the tunnels—four of them at a time. Cowards! Lamps and torches! She would send her own down to look, but these men would die of fright if she did. If the mute and the boy were not found soon, she *would* send her sisters down. What did it matter what men died of? What a relief it would be to be free of them at last. They could not even see in the dark!

A knock came at the door. A word was spoken, an object given to her. The bearer was dismissed.

Lady Ysene stared at the small piece of clothing. It erased all other matters from her thoughts. In spite of the dirt she could see the fine cloth, the elegant embroidery. She held it in her hand, her fingers twitching.

This was all. It was enough!

She ground her teeth. First the golden band, now this. The band had been taken from the child while he lived, of course. Whoever had taken it might have lost it to others—to those who came here, or who knew how many between? This she had gone over a thousand times. But the shirt! Why would they have the shirt unless they had taken it themselves? Oh, how she would have questioned them! Now there was no tracing where they had come from.

She thought back to the night in Nazor, the night of her searching. When *he* had slept at last, she too had slept. Then she had awakened suddenly. Yes! That was when they took it, for they could take it only while she slept. Had it been on the road to Nainth or the road to Birn Hall? Or some path into the mountains?

The child? Doubtless they killed it, buried it in some ditch.

Yet. . . . She could not bring herself to believe it. She could not *risk* believing it. She must comb the country.

Lady Ysene chewed her underlip. Agh, here was the Duke of Xon. How would he explain himself today? Hunting? Fishing? Perhaps a journey to talk with Mogrud in his camp where the rivers joined? She snorted. He wouldn't dare do that! But whatever the truth, it would be the one thing he would not tell her.

The driver wiped the back of his hand across his nose. "They say the Duke has agreed. Mogrud will come to the bridge at Merne in spite of her. She won't like that!"

"Aaow!" Piff turned as much of an interested look as he dared upon the man to keep him talking.

"It'll be a surprise for Nainth when Mogrud comes down through their own country. He'll be sitting on the throne at Nazor before you can snap your finger against your thumb. I don't say I like it. More power for Mogrud, less for Xon. Too bad for King Darai. I've been across the river. It's a pretty country there. But who's to stop Mogrud? I'd say the Duke's letting him through to keep him from burning and slaughtering here. Hummp! Who's to say that he won't turn on Xon a week from now? My road turns off here. Do you go this way?"

"Hownway." Piff waved vaguely toward the road ahead and climbed awkwardly from the seat.

"Watch out for the men of Mogrud. They say there're thousands camped where the waters meet." The driver looked at him curiously, then shrugged and turned his horse down the other road.

·30·

↘↘↘ There were fires. Hundreds of them covered the land in the triangle between the two rivers. Kashka stood up carefully and stared across the reeds into the low country. At first he could not imagine why there were fires. Then he remembered the words of the Duke of Xon to Lady Ysene. The meeting of the two rivers—Mogrud's forces! Hundreds and hundreds of men!

The attack upon Nainth! His stomach turned. He loved the Duke of Nainth, his quick-tongued duchess, and their three young daughters. If Mogrud should win, he would kill them, destroy Nainth with its beautiful spires and gardens.

But Mogrud was here. Here was Byrrhad. Across the river where they had come from was Xon. And *there*, ahead of them, was the yet wider river. The dark strip beyond the silver of the water was his own country.

The fires—he sniffed the air. They were cooking! He was hungry almost to faintness. The loaf Trista had brought and two fish eaten raw were all they had had in the three nights and two days they had been upon the river. What he wouldn't give for a bowl of stew!

The sky was growing light behind the dark mountains of Xon, the folded shapes of the lower slopes emerging from the mist. Trista stirred and opened her eyes. Kashka had given her the name, for she could give him no name for herself. He pointed to the forests far across the river.

"When we come there, we'll be safe," he told her. "We've only to—"

Trista put a hand on his arm, finger to her lips. Though she was mute, her hearing was keen. They lay flat in the boat, hidden by the tall reeds. Kashka strained his ears. There were voices. Men were bringing horses to the river to drink. How many? Five? Six?

". . . glad we're going to Nainth at last. I'm tired of this waiting."

"There were still more coming. Mogrud knows what he's doing."

"Held back by the men of Xon! How do we know they'll fight?"

"Are you calling us cowards?" A fourth voice.

"Why don't you wear your own colors, then? You hide in Byrrhad's. Are you ashamed of being from Xon?"

"I'm ashamed to be taken for a man of Mogrud! It's not for soldiers of Xon he's waited. He's afraid! Of what? Nainth is soft. The Duke there with his music, his flowers, his statues, his pictures on the walls! Smears of paint—I would slash them to bits! Break the noisemakers' hands! What good are they in battle? Soft as new cheese, all of them. Yet Mogrud's brother can't take the city! What kind of soldiers does he lead?"

"The word that Nainth was soft came from Xon." The voices were angry. "There was a message last night. The walls of Nainth are stronger than we were told. The men of Nainth fight like demons. And with them the men of Nazor. Your duke lied. Xon wants us killed. Mogrud's brother is sore weakened."

"Men of Xon die at Nainth too."

"Do they!"

There was a scuffling.

"Stop them! Hold them! Can't you remember orders? What do either of you know?" A new voice spoke harshly. "Mogrud has plans. Half of us will go south to his brother at Nainth on this side of the river. Half will march north to the bridge at

Merne, cross there, and come down upon Nainth on their side of the river. His brother will hold off further attack until then. Mogrud himself will lead those crossing at Merne. Nainth will fall in a week."

"How do you know so much?"

"I listen."

"To what men? Idle talk! Mogrud won't do that!"

"Why not?"

"For one thing, the bridge at Merne won't bear an army. For another, there's Castle Ysene. *She'll* not let him pass through Xon."

"Hmmp! He'll cross the bridge one man at a time if he must. What's a woman and her castle? Her brother need only give his word."

"Why hasn't he?"

"Because he fears his sister."

"Why? What can she do? What kind of army does she command?"

"That's food for thought."

"You talk riddles—like the lies of Xon! Everyone knows the Duke can't be trusted. Everyone knows Mogrud and that sister of his hate one another."

"What do any of you know of Xon? Hear this! There was a messenger yesterday. The Duke promises to persuade his sister. Mogrud has answered. If the lady agrees to a meeting of the three of them, he will go to her. He waits now for a reply."

"He is a fool to trust her."

"He will go whatever her word. He. . . ."

They left, the bitter argument continuing.

Kashka sat up. If only Mogrud might be delayed! If only they could be warned at Merne! If only . . . His eyes fell to Trista's feet.

There lay the dreaded chain, fallen from Trista's arm when he had lifted her into the boat. He had not dared touch it—

had even avoided looking at it. Nothing would have pleased him more than to pick it up with the pole and drop it into the river. But though she would not touch it either, Trista had insisted it stay in the boat. What did she know of it?

Now, for the first time, he dared look closely at it. A shock of recognition went through him. *The golden band that hung like a pendant from the chain was the same that had been stolen from the Prince!*

In that second of recognition a confusion of memories, of words, of meanings flooded through him. Trista had explained with many gestures how the band he had cut from her arm was a way of the Lady Ysene to control those she brought to the castle.

A band, my Lady?

A band? Yes! A band! Here, this will do!

Then had come the touch of the chain and the wave of darkness that engulfed him. The frightening sleep of little Prince Mittai—he had not wakened until the golden band had been stolen!

Cast it away! Be rid of it! Try, Kashka. You must!

The eyes, the voice in the darkness—they were Bargah's! Somehow she was helping him, being with him, giving him strength. How did she know? What did it matter how? A mixture of love and gratitude toward her washed over him. What she had done, in taking his mind, she had to do for the Prince just as what he had done in taking the Prince from Nazor, he had to do for him.

"Trista," he whispered, "you must wait for me here. I'm going . . ." He pointed. "If I'm not back in an hour you must take the boat, cross the river, and somehow find someone to help you. No! You can't come with me. Lie flat so they won't see you. Stay here. Wait for me. Be ready when you hear me coming to push the boat into the current. We may need to be quick. I need you here. Do you understand? Wait for me, but no longer than an hour!"

As she nodded, he leaned forward, snatched the golden chain from where it lay at her feet, and slipped from the boat into the shallow water. Trista, her eyes dark with terror, watched as Kashka pushed through the reeds to the bank. She had felt the sleeping strength of the band when she had picked it up. It was a hundred times that of her own. If it had wakened, it would enslave him.

When he had run from sight, she crouched in the bottom of the boat. She would wait for him for more than an hour. She would wait forever.

"Leave me!" was all the Lady Ysene said.

She did not rage as everyone had expected when the word was brought early in the morning that neither the mute nor the boy could be found. But her calm was more chilling than her rage.

She locked and barred her door. There was little need for her to do so. Today no one in Castle Ysene would venture even to the same floor as her chambers.

First she would find the mute.

She needed only a moment for that one. She was dead. The band lay at the bottom of the pool that skirted the south tower. Where the band was, she was. Had she led him out that way? How could she have learned the way? The lady frowned. The girl's thoughts had always been a haze because she was mute and did not think clearly. There had been no depth to probe. What a disappointment she had been, her work as a mime fading almost at once.

Her death was no loss.

The other—he did not lie in the pool. Doubtless he could swim. He must have enticed the mute, promised her—and then let her drown. So much the better. There was less to fear. For Lady Ysene had known fear when she heard of the locked door, saw the empty manacles.

"Is he a spirit? A wraith? How is it he appears and disappears?

How is it I have never seen his face? How is it he can vanish wearing a band?

"What did I do to hold him?" she continued to mutter. "I was so angry with Xon!" She had done *something*. She could hear her own words in her ears. *Yes! A band! Here, this will do!* But what was it? How had she done it? That terrible fury Xon had brought upon her! She could not remember. Think. Close your eyes. Think back to the day, the hour, the moment. Xon had given her the golden band. She had put it away . . . after he left . . . Where had she hidden it in her anger? Had she dropped it in the stone vase? She started up. How could she bring it up from there? A lodestone would not attract gold! No. She was certain she had not done that. She had such a strong sense of it being in a safe place. She knew in her blood that it was safe. She had not even thought to hold it since she had locked it away. Locked it away, yes. In her cabinet where . . . No!

She had . . . She had . . . *She had dropped the chain with the coiled band over the boy's head!*

"No! No! I could not have done that!" She went quickly to the cabinet, took out a casket covered with writhing figures, and opened it.

Empty!

How could she have done that!

Her anger—now she remembered thinking *where will it be safer than in the dungeon of my own castle, chained to the wall? Locked . . . !*

"Yet I put no hold, set no limit! If he is the tool of some greater power?" She paled. *"If he knows its use!*

"No! I will not permit it! The band of Eddris is mine! I will bring it back to me!"

In the dreadful calm between fear and rage, carefully, slowly, so that nothing might go amiss, disturb her way, she set her thoughts, her mind, her will.

The image came to her.

He does not know its power! *It is still mine!*"

She must have it in her hand as quickly as possible. She would give him no rest. She would drive him with all the furies of her power.

"I will bring him to me. You will come to me!"

Kashka ran as if he were pursued by fiends. The thought of such a pursuit did not occur to him. What he feared was the fiend he held in his hand. It ran with him.

Straight into the camp he ran. There were shouts and in less than a moment he was seized.

"Take me to L-L . . . Mogrud," he gasped. "As fast as . . . I come with word from the D-Duke of Xon!" He was so breathless, so frantic, there seemed no reason to hold him or question him. He was not armed.

He was hurried to Mogrud's tent.

"He says he comes from the Duke of Xon." Two soldiers pushed the boy forward.

A dark bearded man sat behind a table of boards covered with a wide map. Three others bent over it with him.

The soldiers pushed the boy to his knees.

A wave of darkness went through the youth. Get up. Bend low. Run between them. Out. Up the river. Go back. Take it to Castle Ysene. Quickly!

"Stand up!" Someone was speaking to him.

He was on his feet. Now! Run!

But there were hands on his arms, pulling at him, forcing his hand to the table. He fought them, but a twist of the wrist made him cry out, open his fingers. The chain fell to the table.

The darkness grayed, faded, left him trembling and covered with sweat.

"It is . . . for Mogrud," he gasped. "Only Mogrud."

"I am Mogrud." He was heavy-browed, his black beard streaked with gray. He looked at the curiously entwined double band with the shining chain running through it. All gold! It gleamed as if it were molten! He raised his eyes to the boy. "What is this?"

"It is from my lord, the Duke of Xon." *Be rid of it!* The youth stretched out his hand, touched the chain, pushed it across the map, drew back his hand quickly. "A . . . a sign. He sends it, having . . . having received your word." The youth's gasping for breath sounded more like a deep sigh.

Mogrud leaned back in his chair, his look cunning.

"Give me your message," he said. "And all of the circumstances of it. I'll decide then if I believe you." His eyes pierced the boy, then slid to the coiled gold upon the table. It glowed as if possessed of some kind of life.

"My Lord, all I know of the circumstances is this." The boy's head tilted slightly to one side. Mogrud had never seen so open and innocent a face upon a messenger of the Duke of Xon. It was almost enough to erase suspicion.

"The messenger he sent to you returned bringing my lord, the Duke of Xon, your word that you would be willing to enter Xon and meet with him and his sister if she were so willing." He stopped for a breath. "She has been reluctant, it is said. But he found—my lord, the Duke—found a means of gaining her confidence, of assuring her that it would be for the best. Now she agrees to a meeting with you. My message—my exact message—" He closed his eyes and recited carefully. "Come as quickly as you will. Bring as many with you as you feel the need for your own protection. We will discuss terms. I can promise you passage through Xon."

Mogrud's eyes gleamed. Still he was cautious.

"What made her change her mind? Only three days ago . . . Eh?" He leaned forward. Stretched a hand toward the chain, drew it back again.

The boy shook his head, looked aside.

"What does he hold over her?" Mogrud's voice was compelling.

213

The boy glanced up and flushed. Again he looked away.

"I . . . I don't know, my Lord. He . . . he . . . perhaps he has something she wants. And she . . . she has what he wants—her word. They have . . . have come to an agreement." He looked up, his eyes troubled, and met Mogrud's gaze.

Mogrud nodded his head slowly. "That is how agreements come about." He held the boy's eyes with his own. "And what of you?" he asked suddenly. "You are not the usual messenger I have from the Duke of Xon."

"I am fast," the boy said simply. "I go where no horse can come through."

"You are fast," Mogrud agreed thoughtfully. "And you will return to the Duke of Xon?"

"I will bring him your answer. I leave the chain or—or return it to him."

"Ah!" Mogrud's hand reached out, covered the golden chain. "And if you do not return?"

Fear showed in the boy's eyes. "I *must* return!"

"Why?"

"He . . . he is my master."

Mogrud was watching him. Kashka looked down. He must be careful.

"You are free of him now. Or have *you* reached an agreement?"

"My Lord?"

"Perhaps he has something *you* want. You will return to him for it?"

"My Lord!"

Mogrud leaned forward, watching him even more closely. "A brother? A sister? A sweetheart?"

"My Lord . . . I . . . ."

Mogrud leaned back again, drawing the chain toward him. He had touched the sensitive spot. A face like that—so easy to read! Still. . . . How could he be certain? Had *she* sent the boy to trap him? Which did he serve? He fingered the golden

214

links. A quick march to Castle Ysene. Yes! He dropped the chain. Wait! The slaves of the lady wore a metal band. He had seen one once.

"Take off his shirt!" he ordered.

Kashka fought, twisted, turned, but he was held and the shirt torn from his back. There was no need for him to pretend fear. However, Mogrud merely glanced at the pale youth. There was no band, no sign of one. Recent chafing on his wrists not yet healed—he had been in chains. The scars on his back were the mark of the Duke. It was no trick of Lady Ysene.

"Give the shirt back to him," he said. A waste that Xon should have him! Or would his sister have him? Might that be part of the agreement? What did it matter? Whichever had him would destroy him. It wasn't Mogrud's affair.

Mogrud waved his hand as if to brush away messenger and thought alike. Then he spoke to one of the soldiers.

"Give him bread to carry." He looked again at the boy. "Don't be surprised if the Duke of Xon breaks his promise to you."

"But . . . but he is a lord . . . a duke! His word . . ."

Mogrud waved his hand once again to dismiss him.

Kashka slipped from the tent and started toward the river. The soldier called to him and handed him a loaf. Kashka nodded his thanks, began walking swiftly, then trotting. If his luck would hold only a few minutes more! The last of the tents were just ahead of him. A hundred paces to the river and . . .

A loud whistle sounded behind him.

Kashka broke into a run. Three men rose to their feet. He dashed between them, straight ahead.

Another whistle!

Faster he ran, leaped into the water. How it pulled at him, the reeds tangling in his feet. There was a splashing behind him. The boat. . . . Trista sitting straight, the pole in her hands. . . . He floundered, threw himself forward, caught the side of the boat, pushed it, leaped into it. A sharp jolt threw him down. The boat rocked. Kashka twisted to his knees, trying to steady the shell. He looked up to see Trista clutching the pole. Behind him a soldier bent double. She had stopped him and given them a good push as well! Kashka took the pole, dug it into the riverbed. The boat slipped forward.

Now only a swimmer might follow. Trista pulled at Kashka and bent down. An arrow flew over their heads. He lay down quickly and pulled her flat beside him. The current caught the shell and carried them into the wide river.

Mogrud fingered the golden chain and examined the band that hung from it. The boy had gotten away. He was fast, but that fast? How had Xon had time to return and send him back so quickly? He would have questioned him further. The scars were old. No, one that young could not be so deceptive. If *she* had sent him. . . . What an actor he would be! He was too young. Still, the lady was known to have a taste for fine things. Her collecting. . . . He pulled at his beard. An intense desire to go to Castle Ysene filled him. He pushed the chain aside to study the map.

He would trust the strength of a silk thread to hold a wild horse sooner than trust either the lady or her brother. His hand closed over the chain.

Even for that, he would go to Castle Ysene with half of his troops—his horsemen. No trick they held could stand against his mounted forces. The rest he would send to the bridge at Merne to wait for him. His brother must be patient. A messenger must leave at once for Nainth.

How heavy this gold was!

Yes, he would go. He must go! At once! Yes, to the Lady Ysene. Let them see who is faster, who will get there first, he or that hapless boy!

He gave orders.

216

·31·

⟍⟍⟍ Lady Ysene ground her teeth.

How he resisted! No one had ever opposed her with such strength!

I will have him! I will have him!

Mogrud woke in the night. He knew well enough the men and horses were tired. He had pushed them hard. He fought his desire, his need to move. He sat up. His world would come down if they did not move more quickly! This matter with Xon must be agreed upon, settled!

The soldier in him fought the unexplained fear. The battle left him exhausted. He rose finally, his eyes dark with fatigue, to waken his troops before dawn. They would finish the journey to Castle Ysene today. Then to the river—the bridge at Merne.

To Merne, Piff thought. Again he was off at the steady jogging trot he had set for himself the day before.

He-got-away-he-got-away-she-does-not-know-she-does-not-know. Jog-trot-jog-trot. The words kept pace with his feet, around and around in his head. They alternated with to-Merne-to-Merne. And then he would add, I-hope-he-did-I-hope-he-did-I-hope-he-got-to-Merne. For the bridge at Merne was the quickest way for Kashka to return to the realm of King Darai.

The hypnotic words and the exhilaration of knowing that his cousin had somehow escaped Castle Ysene kept him running on and on. He wished he might go faster but knew he could not.

He paused at the top of a hill to rest when the sun glinted on something near the river far to his left. There! There it was again! He watched. Again! It was a line moving—armed men. Coming down the road beside the river.

With a cry he leaped forward. To-Merne-first-to-Merne-first. He dared not think of Kashka. Only of Merne.

Kashka stood up in the boat and looked across the swiftly flowing current. The white foam curled around the rocks jutting from the water.

"We can't risk crossing, Trista. We found out fast enough you can't swim the first time we tipped over. Even if you could, the boat would never come through *that!*"

Tired, wet, hungry, he again pushed the frail shell away from the bank. "We'll have to try to come to the bridge at Merne and cross it ahead of Mogrud. We have to warn them at Merne." With the pole and a paddle improvised from a flat piece of wood he had found, they set out again down the river.

Stop them at Merne! Stop them from coming to Nainth!

The Margrave of Tat hurried to the Duke of Nainth where he stood watching the gathering of forces on the plain beyond the wall.

"They're preparing for another attack," the Duke said wearily. "I think of my duchess, my daughters. . . ."

"Add to that another," said the grim margrave.

"What? Who?"

"The Princess Ekama."

"The Princess Ekama! What about her?"

"She is here."

"What are you saying!"

"I scarcely know myself. But she is here. In Nainth. With the Duchess and your daughters. Don't ask me how she came.

I only guess that she hid herself in the last wagon of supplies that came from Nazor. Rags! Covered with dust and dirt! Hungry as a wolf pup!

"I never would have known her myself, but Aciam knew her at once. I have never seen such a look . . . of . . . The best I can say is . . . mixed. I'm not a man of words. Ah, the young! Delight and agony! Delight to see her, agony because he fears for her—what might come if we cannot hold them off." The Margrave strode away . He would find another place to view more of the enemy camp.

The Princess too! No delight, only agony for the old, thought the Duke of Nainth in despair. Agony for knowing surely what will come because we cannot hold them off. One more attack. . . .

If only we might divide them, split them in half! But their numbers will be doubled instead when the rest of Mogrud's men come. More than doubled—by four if the reports we hear are true.

The Margrave returned. "No matter how they form, I have the same answer for them. We can stop half of them. I don't know why they're waiting. They keep forming again and again, as if they would rehearse every possible way. This last—but we cannot meet them hand to hand. There are not enough of us. The trenches, the stakes, all of our traps will only slow them down. Our gates cannot take another battering, yet they hold off an attack."

"They don't know we are weakened by Sir Andros' leaving for Merne."

"Merne!" The Margrave exploded. "Who would have thought the whole town would come and leave the bridge there open?"

"They are farmers, shopkeepers—not planners of battles. You heard their reasons. They did what they were asked to do. They're here and they will fight. They did not believe Mogrud might come that way."

"That's the whole answer to Mogrud! You must believe he

219

will do anything you can think of, for the chances are not that he won't but that he will! I need the trained men of Sir Andros here, not on the way to Merne. If Mogrud has already crossed, Andros and all of them are lost.

"Are you listening to me? No? Thinking of your wife and daughters? They should have been sent from Nainth at once. If we knew that Mogrud would not be at our backs within hours they might still be sent, the Princess with them. If I had my way, Prince Aciam would go too."

"The Prince?"

"Yes. There is no doubt Darai will not live long. Young Mittai has vanished. There is only Aciam. He is too young for heavy battle—only sixteen. Though the young fight fiercely, we should not risk him."

"He has proven himself these last few days."

"Of course he has proven himself! I trained him! He is skilled, but he is little more than a boy. Would you set him against Mogrud's brother? He does not yet have a man's wrist or arm."

"He will never agree to leave Nainth. But I should have risked Sansnom Wood or the mountains. . . ." The Duke spoke half to himself, half to the Margrave. "Yet, is even Sansnom Wood safe? When Nainth falls, Nazor is doomed."

The Margrave listened with only half an ear. He stared over the plain. If he could lure part of them to the south where the marshes were. To send men . . . to weaken Nainth even more. . . . He frowned. He should give all of his mind to strategy. So should the Duke. This man was too concerned with the tender things of life.

"Women and children," he grumbled to himself.

·32·

↘↘↘ "Women and childen—that's all there are. A few old men too feeble to walk and Quento here. He didn't understand Suvio. He wouldn't go with him."

Piff listened to the innkeeper's wife. She had brought the women of Merne to the inn. They sat around tables, stood against the walls.

"There was no holding any of them back. Who would be called a coward?" A young woman carrying an infant in her arms spoke sadly.

"Did no one think Mogrud might use the bridge?" Piff asked.

"They talked of it. But the Lady Ysene has never been a friend of Mogrud that she would let him cross Xon."

"Unless she thought it to her advantage."

"If we could stop them at the bridge. . . . I've been wondering but I can't think of a way." A stout middle-aged woman with a quick eye folded her arms. "We can't tear down the bridge or build a barricade in a day. Nor have we any weapons but pitchforks—those of us who've turned the hay. What's a pitchfork against an army?"

"There's a great deal of brush and wood along the riverbank. I saw it when I crossed," Piff said thoughtfully. "We might pile it on the bridge."

"They'd clear it away soon enough."

221

"The piers beneath are of stone," he went on, "but it's all wood above, and the very center span has no stone even beneath it."

"That's true. After the great flood of the time of Damien the center piers were never rebuilt. It's weakened the bridge, that."

"The brush is dry. There's been no rain. It would burn if we . . ."

"Why are we sitting here like gossiping old men?" asked the innkeeper's wife, rising abruptly to her feet. In five minutes the room was empty.

Piff went with them, tired though he was. Someone pulled at his arm. It was Quento. The mime drew him aside, a question in his eyes. Did he wonder what they were about? Quento moved his hands.

Piff watched. He had worked enough with Gamel to understand quickly. Quento was asking him about—a woman? A girl! Quento, watching Piff's lips, nodded eagerly. At Castle Ysene? She did not speak? She *cannot* speak. A mute! Again Quento nodded. Who was she? His—daughter!

I did not see her. Piff touched his eyes, shook his head. I heard of a girl who was mute. He touched his ears, made a sign of talking, and nodded. Quento seized his shoulders, a look of both anguish and hope on his face.

At last Piff was able to make him understand that the girl and Kashka had both vanished. No one knew where or how, even Lady Ysene. But they must hope that somehow the two had escaped together. That somehow they would come to Merne, or somewhere in the country. Somehow he and Quento would find them.

Quento's eyes filled with tears. He embraced Piff.

A strong bond between them, they worked side by side dragging brush and logs to the bridge with the women of Merne.

The innkeeper's wife paused a moment to look at the grow-

222

ing mound. "Here's something we all know how to do," she said. "Gather wood to build a fire against a cold night."

It would freeze the fires of hell! What a cold tomb this castle was! Mogrud curled his hand around the hot cup.

"Your request was that I come. That is why I am here."

"I sent no message."

Xon! Lying as usual! He's covering himself before his sister. "You sent two. The second was especially convincing."

Lady Ysene pushed aside her plate. So my brother *is* tickling toes with Mogrud! She put her hand on the Duke's arm. "This is very curious as neither of us sent a messenger. Yet I think we must consider it carefully."

The Duke of Xon would meet neither his sister's nor Mogrud's look. Had *she* sent a messenger?

"The messenger said you were in agreement, my Lady." Mogrud spoke politely. Which of them was lying? The Duke, of course. The boy had come from him. As for the lady. . . . He gritted his teeth. It made his stomach ache to dine with this woman. Had she poisoned him? He had eaten almost nothing. How he hated her! One never knew what she was thinking.

He knew what it was to lie, to cheat, to deceive. Xon he could trust to think in ways he himself would. But she—her deviousness was beyond comprehension. It was impossible to consider anything connected with her word! He dreaded a pact with her. What treacherous ends it might lead to were completely unknown. Yet . . . yet he could not help himself! This agreement *must* take place. If he were strong enough what could she do? He *was* strong enough! He had brought the better part of his men with him. She could see his strength. He had told her that the rest of his men were already in Xon on their way to the bridge at Merne. What could she do? She spoke of agreement. She must be afraid!

"There would be advantages." Mogrud glanced toward the Duke.

The Duke of Xon could not keep his eyes from the circle of gold lying against Mogrud's chest. It gleamed now a red-gold, now green.

How had it come to Mogrud?

His sister had not left the castle in the past week. She would never trust that bangle to the hand of a servant, even to one of her own kind. It had to do with her power, he did not know what. But he feared it. Should he have returned it? She would have found out. All of his life, she had found out. This band of gold—it made him ill. Better for him he had given it back to her.

But her power! That it and Mogrud's should be joined! The thought made him flush hot and shiver in turn. It was *he* who had planned to use Mogrud's strength. *He* who would play those two against each other to his own advantage. How that scheming, conniving sister of his . . . Never had he been so shaken. He turned his face away. He must gain control of his feelings!

Lady Ysene twisted the dark jeweled ring upon her finger. She had overcome her first shock at seeing the golden band. How in Hecate's name had it come to Mogrud? She had fought all night to bring it to her! And the day as well!

What had happened to her sprite? Her wraith? Her—whatever he was! Had Mogrud killed him—if it was possible to kill him—for the gold? She would have known. What a fool Mogrud was to think there was value in a chunk of metal! If he knew what he wore around his neck. . . . But he did not know. It was hers as much there as if she held it in her hand. And Mogrud was hers as well. She would stay close to him.

Mogrud's forces and her brother's—how tempting it was to show them. But it was better that neither knew. She would not push them. Let them believe they were masters of their own thoughts. Resist as he might, the gold around Mogrud's neck enchained him more than the fetters of a dungeon, more than his lust for any treasure dug from the earth.

"Tell us if you will, Mogrud, what is your mind where the realm of Darai is concerned? Is it the gold in the mountains you seek? The jewels of his crown? Such gold does not interest us. Perhaps we are already in agreement."

The Lady Ysene smiled.

Both men shuddered.

"What is this?" the Duchess of Nainth asked her husband. She eyed the box Derenth had set upon the table.

"Every woman and child in Nainth is being armed." Mittai's face was gray, his lips tight.

The Duchess put her hand into the box and drew out a blade. She looked at it thoughtfully, then laid it on the table.

"Oh, Mittai, can you really see that in the hand of Licia? She is only seven! Try to imagine it!"

"Imagine! What I see haunts me! I curse my imagination! If I were like Tat, with none, I would sleep peacefully. I cannot die knowing I have left you with nothing to defend yourselves."

"Your imagination is one of your virtues. But you're so tired that now you're losing your good sense. We are not condemned to death. You've held them off so far, why not another day? And another?" She put her arms around him.

"Why not?" He sighed. "How are the children? I've not seen them for three days."

"They're well. They adore the Princess. Today Arianne was fretting for fear Mogrud would take her gold locket from her. 'Give it to him,' Ekama told her. 'Who cares for gold? Give it to his brother and let Mogrud fight him for it. Let them all sink in the marshes for it weighing them down! Do you know what I would do then? I'd dance on the wall with Prince Aciam. I'd rather dance with him than have all the gold in the world.' Do you know what they did then? See here."

She took a small box from her writing desk. "They've put

all their rings and chains and lockets and bracelets in here. Look what they've written on the box. 'For Mogrud who is so stupid he thinks gold is worth more than dancing.' "

The Duke laughed and held the Duchess close. "I wonder," he murmured, "What if . . . ?" Suddenly he kissed her.

"What if what?" she asked.

"Something the Princess said. What if . . . ? Yes! I'll talk to the Margrave! See what he thinks!" He was already at the door and opening it.

"What are you going to do?" the Duchess asked.

"Make plans for a dance for the Princess!" he cried over his shoulder.

"What did you say?" The Margrave of Tat looked at the Duke of Nainth.

"I said we shall celebrate."

"Celebrate? What?"

"The news we've just had that Mogrud has gone to Castle Ysene."

"You would celebrate our funerals ahead of time?"

"No, no! The victory! Flags! Banners! Music! We shall dance on top of the walls. Everyone will dress in bright clothes— men, women, children. . . ."

"And what will we gain by this?"

"Time."

"For what?"

"For seeds to grow that I shall plant, my dear Margrave. It's spring!"

"I think you've gone mad."

"Ah, I am disappointed. I thought you would ask what kind of seeds."

"I'm not a man for word games," the Margrave growled.

"Seeds of doubt, my friend! The kind that take less than a day to root, sprout, blossom, set, ripen, and be reaped." The Duke waved his hand toward the distant camp.

"We know that Mogrud's forces are strengthened by those of Xon. But the men of Xon wear the colors of Byrrhad. Why? Because as usual, Xon is playing a double game. Mogrud knows that. So must his brother. So must every man of Byrrhad in that camp. How can they trust each other? It's not a happy family over there. Suppose—just suppose—that they saw us celebrating the death of Mogrud at the treacherous hand of Xon!"

"But that isn't the case! They would find out soon enough!"

"But that *is* just the case, my dear Margrave. They will have just heard."

The Margrave shook his head. "If we might lure them to the marshes. . . ."

"The marshes! My idea exactly! I shall take half a dozen youths through the marshes. We shall creep into their camp, then shout the word among them. 'Mogrud is dead! Xon has killed him!' They will see the celebration here upon the walls of Nainth. Think of it!"

The Margrave chewed the end of his mustache. Finally he nodded slowly. "Mogrud's brother is as hot-headed and quick to act as Mogrud is cool and sly. He's had the news of Mogrud's going to Castle Ysene."

The Duke of Nainth and the Margrave of Tat looked at each other.

"He will smell treachery."

"We shall add to its aroma!" The Duke saluted the Margrave and turned away.

The Margrave stared after him. "Half a dozen men with words! He is mad. Who ever won a battle with words but a sharp-tongued wife? Still . . . if they turn on one another, the men of Byrrhad and those of Xon. . . ."

The Duke of Nainth walked quickly toward the suite of rooms where he knew he would find his lady.

"Only for a moment now," he murmured. "And then, if we're lucky, I may yet have another dance with my duchess."

227

·33·

↘↘↘ Piff, Quento, and the women of Merne worked the rest of the day. The sun set and they worked into the night. The bridge was heaped with brush and wood as far as the center span. Mounds were made on the bank on either side of the bridge and around the end of it, ready to be added to the blaze. The small fishing boats of the village were loaded with brush and kindling, floated under the sloping end of the bridge, and chained there. Behind a clump of trees a fire was tended. Brands were set to burning. They would be kept burning throughout the time of waiting.

The hours slipped by.

Piff could not sleep. He ached in every bone and muscle. One thought weighed upon him. Kashka had not come to Merne. If the bridge was burned, he would be trapped in Xon. Where might he cross the river? Each time he dozed a nightmare stole his sleep from him. He was running and running, Lady Ysene and the Duke of Xon just behind him. The slime of the stagnant moat rose around him. Kashka's face in the water, the look of fear. . . . At last he rose.

"There's fog on the river," he said in a low voice to the three women keeping watch by the fire. "I'm going across to see if there's anything doing."

"How can you get through all of that?" The innkeeper's wife waved a hand toward the bridge.

228

"The rail is clear. I can walk on that to the center. It's clear beyond."

"Do you have to go?"

"If they send a scout to find out if it's guarded—I don't want them to have any advantage. We may have to burn it sooner than we think. If I don't come back, at any sign of them, set it afire! I can swim." He forced a smile. There was still the smallest hope that Kashka might . . .

"Don't fall!" But he was gone.

The cobbler's daughter fed ends of wood into the fire. "I wonder if he slept at all tonight?" she murmured. "He was restless."

"I wonder if he learned anything of his brother? He said nothing of that." The stout woman warmed her hands over the blaze.

"He's such a gentle-spoken boy." The cobbler's daughter sighed. "I should like to see Suvio walking on that rail between a tinderbox and the river to find out if the men of Mogrud were waiting for him."

The innkeeper's wife snorted.

The tip of the boat rested in the mud near the bridge. Kashka pulled it higher so that the shell would not float away. Then he untied it. There might not be time to meddle with knots. He stared at the dark murmuring water.

"Trista!" He shook her gently, whispered in her ear. There was no fear that she would make a sound on wakening.

"I'm going onto the bridge. I don't see a guard there. There is one a little way up the road, and Mogrud's men are gathered farther up behind the trees. I couldn't tell how many—on and on up the road.

"Wait here. Be very quiet. I'll have to swim and then climb . . ." He gestured toward the bridge. "They'd see me if I went up the bank to it. I have to warn them on the other side, to wake the people of Merne. I'll be back for you. We'll cross the bridge if we can. Otherwise we'll have to chance the river."

She sat up and nodded.

Trista watched as Kashka slipped into the water and vanished in the thin fog that drifted on the surface. Now it broke and she could see the bridge almost above her. Now the fog closed in and it disappeared. Silently she lifted the pole in both hands, listened to the rush of the river, waited.

While he waited for word from Xon that his men were in place, Mogrud went through his plan once again. First scouts to cross silently, discover what defenses there were, take care of any guards on the other side. They must leave within ten minutes. If all was clear, men on foot, rags tied around their boots to muffle the sound, would follow. Why rouse a sleeping village, perhaps armed men? Until enough had crossed, they must be careful. Then burn the village quickly. Finally the horsemen, a few at a time. Silence would no longer matter—only that too many did not cross together.

He stared at the mist drifting over the river. Was he being overcautious? No. Why should he lose men the way his brother did? He would need them all—at Nazor!

Mogrud struggled to possess himself. Sometimes he felt that he had won. Won what? he asked himself. Must I fight myself? My own knowledge? My own experience? Am I not known for the brilliance of my tactics? When have I lost a battle? *But what was he doing here at the bridge to Merne with all of his forces? He should have sent half of them to his brother at Nainth where they were needed!* Instead he had ordered them all to come here. It was madness! He should have . . . Still, the march on the other side of the river would be easier, quicker. There would be little resistance. They would move swiftly upon Nainth. His brother need only wait where he was until Mogrud arrived to attack from the other side.

He was right to have done it this way. If only it were possible to move more of them at a time across the river. But the bridge would not bear a great weight of armed men and horses.

Mogrud rubbed his hands across his face and eyes. They must move within half an hour. He raised his head. Where were the scouts? Men were waiting. His own strongest mounted here with him near the bridge, then the men on foot. Then his horsemen. The Duke of Xon's men behind all. Why behind him? Why at his back? He shook his head as if to clear it. It did not make sense.

Where was Ysene? Once they were across the river he would be free of that accursed woman. Why had she insisted upon coming with them? This was no place for a woman! She had no reason to be here that he could fathom except that she did not trust her brother. Who did? What other reason she might have he was too tired to want to know.

The Lady Ysene dismounted and walked silently past the guard and on toward the bridge. If all went her way. . . . If? Of course it would go her way! So far it had gone exactly her way. Who was there to oppose her? Mogrud was exhausted, though he was strong. Oh, he was strong! Never had she fought so! But she had worn him down. He would do every bidding of hers now. When he had gained what she needed there would be an end of him! Her brother? He had come around. He would hold back the men of Xon. They would not be tied to Mogrud, but would save Nainth from him. Let Mogrud clear the way, then—but neither must her brother come to Nainth! She would have it for herself! The beauty of Nainth, the power of Nazor!

What was that? A deer come down to the river? A fish jumping? She must stay calm. She too was tired, her temper thin.

A tatter of mist rose and drifted across the bridge.

Then she saw him.

The boy. The wraith. The spirit. Coming from the river, swinging himself easily up over the side of the bridge, rising

231

to his feet and vanishing into the fog with never a sound. She recognized the ease, the grace of how he moved.

Lady Ysene had known fear, never terror. Now she felt the hair rise on her arms, her scalp prickle, a feeling of lead stopping the flow of blood through her veins.

Who was he?

The answer to her dread came in one word.

"Mogrud!"

It was the sepulchral voice of her kind. The call filled the air, penetrating the forest behind her, sweeping across the river before her, rising to the sky above her.

"Mogrud!" Her will was in his mind. The image of the sword. The image of the boy beneath the blade.

"Mogrud!"

He could not resist the third call.

With a harsh cry, Mogrud spurred his horse and it leaped forward. To the bridge! Across the bridge to find him and strike him down! The silence was shattered. There was thunder in his mind, thunder beneath his horse's hooves, and thunder behind him.

For the men surrounding Mogrud, waiting, spurred, armed, tense, the cry was a signal. They followed him at full gallop. Those on foot pressed after their leaders.

Piff had dropped from the rail and started across the center span of the bridge when he heard the cry. He paused. Was he so tired that he imagined a voice? Then the boards beneath his feet trembled. Horses! The men of Mogrud! Behind him was certain holocaust. Beneath him, the river—dark, swift. . . . Which way should he choose? The end would be the same. Which way? Numb with fatigue, he stood irresolute.

Kashka heard the cry. He heard the horses on the road. They were coming! The bridge shook. He bounded forward. Out of the drifting fog he ran, behind him a huge horse, a rider dark in the night, arm high, the glint of metal above it. Before him—a figure, immobile, as if frozen.

There was no instant for a word—even a name. Only an instant to seize a hand, give a great pull to the side of the bridge. The sword of Mogrud whined as it split the air. At the same moment fire roared to the sky from the bridge, from the riverbank, from the river itself.

·34·

↘↘↘ Piff! Kashka seized his hand, pulled him to the side of the bridge, pushed him even as the sword hissed over their heads. He heard the thwack of the blade splitting the rail as he leaped beside Piff into the swiftly flowing river.

They came up side by side, gasping and blowing, to a world turned red by high leaping flames. The image of fire flickered around them in the water as they were carried down the river and away from the bridge. They fought to keep their heads up in a current that tumbled them, drew them down.

"There!" Kashka gasped. Something dark bobbed and turned just ahead of them. A log, perhaps. If they could gain it! He kicked, reached out. His hand touched the smooth end of a stick. He clung to it, grasped wildly at the disappearing head of his cousin, and drew him back to the surface.

"Hold to me!"

"Too tired. . . ." Piff could say no more. The water again washed over his head.

Kashka locked his legs around his cousin, turned on his back, and held up Piff's head with one hand while he clung to the stick with the other.

A hand grasped his wrist.

"Trista!"

At Lady Ysene's call for Mogrud, Trista had leaped from the boat, freed it from the mud, and pushed her way out into

234

the river. There was not only her terrible fear of the lady but also the knowledge of what Mogrud must wear that she called him that way. In her bones she knew that Kashka could not return. In the instant of the rising flames she saw Kashka—two of him! Was the flickering light the cause of it? Saw him leap from the bridge. Frantically she poled and paddled. When the two heads appeared in the water, she was just in front of them, carried in the same swift current.

She held out the pole.

Trista drew them slowly to the back of the boat where it would tip less easily.

"Piff. . . . I can't lift him. Pull him, Trista!"

Together they tumbled him headfirst into the boat. Kashka scrambled after him. Trista bailed water. Kashka looked back. He had a glimpse of the bridge, an arc of fire low on the water that stopped in abrupt darkness midriver. Then the boat was swept around a point of land and, where the river widened, turned into calmer water.

Lady Ysene stood on the riverbank, unbelieving of what her eyes saw. The bridge exploded in flame. The mass of men on foot and on horseback, pressing forward, trapped those on the bridge. The terrified neighing and rearing of the horses to the front, and then—then a creaking, groaning, splintering of timbers as the weight of armed men and horses was too great for the span. The center of the bridge collapsed into the river, carrying all there with it. Others too fell and fell from the press of those behind who could not stop.

She sucked in her breath, holding to the power of the golden band. Holding, holding—until it began to fade and fade and then was gone. She knew that Mogrud was dead. That the golden ring of power lay somewhere in the mud and slime at the bottom of the river. That it too was dead.

She had lost it forever.

◆　◆　◆

The Duchess of Nainth walked the length of the wall. It was still an hour before dawn, but she preferred walking in the cool darkness to lying on her back and staring at nothing. She climbed the stairs to the point of the high watch. Perhaps Mittai was here. Instead she found the Margrave of Tat.

He looked at her, grunted, and turned his face again to the east. They had different views of the world, he and the Duchess, but they were much alike in the *way* they looked at it. They stood side by side. The Margrave spoke first.

"We should have a sign any minute."

The Duchess did not reply. She too looked to the east.

"It's a wild scheme, but it might work," he went on. "It's worth trying. He said he knew the marshes, the Duke."

"He knows them." The marshes?

"They should be there by now." He turned and scowled at the Duchess as if it were her fault if they weren't. He could not see how tightly she clasped her hands beneath her cloak. "It was no pleasant task, stripping dead men of their clothes," he went on, "nor putting them on either. I would have thought him too squeamish. Nor is it a boy's game where he's gone. There's more courage in the Duke than I guessed."

"When you look at a man you guess at the size of his muscle, Margrave. You only know courage when it shows itself. Then there is no need to guess."

"He's not been overeager for battle, Madame!" The Margrave flared, feeling the sting of her words. "Though he's a better swordsman than I knew."

"He is a superb swordsman. As for battle, do you fight to win or fight for show? If you expected to put on a glorious battle with every man of Nainth throwing himself upon ten spears of the enemy, you will find a poor audience here to play to."

"Madame," the Margrave began angrily, "I have never risked—Wait! Look! Did you see that? A light! A torch! And there's another! And another! The bells! The trumpets! Why aren't they sounding? Ho! There . . . !"

236

Even as he shouted, the bells in the town of Nainth and in the towers of the palace began to ring. Trumpets sounded and torches were rushed to light the tops of the walls around city and palace. Men gathered to shout and cheer.

The Duchess stared across the darkness of the plain to where a small tongue of fire suddenly rose. Then another and another.

"He's done it!" cried the Margrave of Tat. "At least he's there! Now all we need do is hope."

"What . . . who . . . ? What has who done?"

"Why, the Duke, of course. He didn't tell you? He's there!" The Margrave pointed as another column of flame rose into the air. "And none too soon! It's almost dawn. But he should be coming away now. Get out! Get out!" The Margrave began muttering. "Morning is coming! I can smell it. You've done enough. You've roused them. You've brought the news. You *must* have done enough by now."

He fell silent and watched with the Duchess.

The noise coming from the towers and walls on Nainth beat against their ears. More fires rose, their color paling against the growing light of the sky behind them. Smoke thickened, drifted over the camp.

"Devil knows what's happening there now," grumbled the Margrave. "The orders for here are that we are to dance! Where are those musicians?" he shouted, then turned away muttering, "What a wretched time for music! Who wants to dance at five in the morning? He's mad!"

More people gathered on the walls. Flags and banners appeared.

The Duchess remained by herself on the wall. The shouts behind her finally sifted themselves into a chant. "Mogrud is dead! Mogrud is dead!"

Then Prince Aciam's voice was in her ear, his arm around her. "Here you are, Auntie Duchess!" He kissed her cheek. "I've been hunting for you. There was a messenger in the night. Mogrud is dead! They say Xon turned against him!

Murdered him! What a welcome piece of treachery!" He kissed her again.

She drew back to look at his glowing face. The Princess was at his side, dressed, but her hair still rumpled from sleep, her feet in slippers.

"They're playing music!" cried Ekama. "We're going to dance!"

"Come and join us," Aciam said. "Where is my uncle? Where is the Duke?"

"Go on! Go on! Do your dancing!" She pushed them off with a laugh and watched as Aciam swung the Princess away in such a dance as they had never done within the palaces of Nainth or Nazor! After a moment the smile left the Duchess's mouth and she turned again to watch the growing mantle of smoke.

"Madame?" It was the Margrave of Tat. "You understand now?"

"Yes."

"I thought him overconcerned with women and children."

"What do *you* fight for, Margrave, a pile of stones?"

"I want him back, Lady."

"So do I."

"I don't dance, Madame."

"I should turn you down if you did. I shall wait to dance with my husband."

"By the King's crown, Madame, if ever *I* have a wife I hope she will be like the Duke of Nainth's! I know what I like in a woman."

"By the Queen's crown, Margrave, if ever *I* have a war, I shall put you in charge of it. You also recognize a good man when you see one."

Silent now, they stood side by side. The sun, pale through the haze of smoke, rose higher.

·35·

↘↘↘ The Duchess of Nainth stood alone upon the wall, her back straight, her hands clasped. She looked upon the smoke that hung like a pall over plain and river, tinged red now by the setting sun. She did not hear the occasional clash of arms or cries of men that came from the distant camp. She did not hear the music and laughter that echoed now and again in the palace or town. There was a silence within her that would be filled by the sound of one voice only. She had waited for it since the dawn.

"Why aren't you dancing?"

The Duchess whirled around. "Mittai!"

He put his arms around her. "I promised myself a dance."

"I promised a thousand."

"Selfish. And now I shall have to make another promise."

"What is that?"

"A new dress for you."

The Duchess looked down. "Mud! And . . . blood? Are you hurt?"

"No."

"The Margrave said you were only to slip into the camp, start the rumor. Then you were to leave, there was to be no fighting."

"I was so close to him. He came out with his sword in his hand. . . ."

239

"Who?"

"Mogrud's brother."

"And?"

"He is dead. But it . . . delayed me."

"And those who went with you?"

"They waited for me. I know the marsh better than they. Come, I don't want to dance in these clothes. I don't really want to dance. Not now. I want to bathe, to sleep, to forget what I've seen. I'm not fond of slaughter. Tomorrow. . . ."

"Look then at some of those you've kept from it for at least one night more. Here are Prince Aciam and Princess Ekama. Why aren't you dancing?" the Duchess asked the Princess.

Ekama wrinkled her nose. "I'm so tired! I've been dancing all day. I think I shall hold a funeral for my feet! I'm just going to listen to the music."

"It was better earlier. They're out of tune now. Where have you been, Uncle? You've missed the best of the music. It sounds as tired as we are."

"We've never had the *best* music," said the Princess. "We would have that only if Piff and Kashka were here. I wish they were. It's been such a long winter since I heard them play! They could play and dance three days and three nights without being tired."

"Didn't they play for you when they returned to Nazor?" asked the Duke.

"To Nazor? I thought they were here. But they weren't. I've been afraid to ask where they might be."

"I see you knew them well."

"When did they go to Nazor?" Prince Aciam asked.

"When we had the unhappy news of the Queen, your mother, Piff left that night. Kashka followed the next day. They never arrived?"

The Princess shook her head.

"Perhaps they were afraid to tell you. The King had not sent for them."

Again Ekama shook her head. "He asked for them—his scapegraces. If they were in Nazor they would have come—at least to me. I know they would! It's so long ago now. . . ." There were tears in her eyes. "Where are they? Piff . . . Kashka . . . If they weren't together?"

"It's not so long ago. A month? Six weeks? No more than that! I know them. Surely if they found each other . . ." Aciam put his arm around her.

"Leave me alone, Trista," he begged. But she continued to shake him.

Kashka sat up at last, trying to drive the sleep from his mind, his body. He opened his eyes and blinked at the men standing around them. The agony for sleep twisted to fear. But no, they were neither men of Mogrud nor men of Xon.

"Here are two not dead," said one. "What about him?"

Kashka leaned over and shook Piff. Piff groaned and turned over.

"He's alive! All three! The first we've found! What are you doing here?"

Kashka sat on the ground, elbows on his knees, head in his hands, his eyes closed. "We're on our way to Nainth to fight for Prince Aciam," he mumbled.

"You're what?" There was a burst of laughter.

"Let's take them along," said another voice. "It's true there's not much flesh, and scarcely any life, but I call that spirit!"

Kashka was dragged to his feet. "Come on, boy! If you're going to fight, you have to be able to walk in your sleep. The men of Gorloth can fight in their sleep!"

Someone picked up Piff and hoisted him over his shoulder. "And this one? This one will fight too?"

Kashka took Trista's hand. "This one brings all the luck."

"We can use that!"

They scrambled up the riverbank to the road.

"Put them in the wagon there. Let them sleep until we need

241

them at Merne. An hour's sleep does wonders for a soldier."

The wagon jerked and jolted. I'll never be able to sleep, Kashka thought as he fell asleep.

The men of Gorloth arrived at Merne. With Sir Andros, the Baron of Gorloth watched the steady licking of flames, paled by the morning sun. "We saw the glow in the sky last night. I thought to find Merne itself in flames. Who . . . ?"

"The women of Merne," Sir Andros told him.

"How is it at Nainth?"

Sir Andros shook his head. "There was little hope when I left. Who knows how it is now? At least Mogrud won't come down this side of the river." He turned his horse. "There's no need to stand and stare."

But the Baron continued to gaze at the bridge. "It wasn't fire alone did that."

"Too many came. The fire stopped them. It collapsed from the weight."

"Would Mogrud have such poor judgment?"

"It must have been another's judgment. As for Mogrud, he may be in Nainth by now." Sir Andros touched his heel to his horse. "I've sent a messenger. We'll rest a while in Merne and then go back. We may yet be of use."

The messenger came to Nainth with news of the bridge at Merne.

"It's rumored that Mogrud is dead, that the forces of Xon fell upon those of Mogrud, that the strength of each has been cut in half and halved again. But there's no proof of that. We know only that a goodly number were lost when the bridge fell."

"Mmmm." The Duke of Nainth looked sideways at the Margrave of Tat.

"Your own invention brings an echo faster then the sound travels out," said the Margrave. "What of Sir Andros and the Baron of Gorloth?"

"They are on their way to Nainth. They have left a small garrison at Merne, though there is little to fear from there. There is no other place to cross. The Baron destroyed both bridges farther down the river and left a force of men in Gorloth as well."

"So we've only to wait for Mogrud."

The messenger nodded. "Yes, my Lord."

"Mmmm."

·36·

↘↘↘ Piff and Kashka were awakened by the sound of
laughter. They had slept through Merne and halfway to Nainth.
It was evening. There were fires and men gathered around
them, the smell of meat cooking. Again there was laughter.
The cousins slipped from the wagon to push their way through
the good-natured crowd.

It was Quento and—Trista! Kashka stared, his mouth open.
"Her father!" Piff told him. "Only her name is Nanya."

Quento saw them and drew them into the center of the
circle. Soon the laughter was doubled.

After a few moments Kashka found his flute in his hands
and Piff his lute. "He kept them for us when Suvio left," Piff
explained. "They kept them at the inn."

But Kashka could not play a note, for the smell of the
cooking food made his mouth water so that he could not blow
into the flute. Piff doubled over with laughter at the sight.
Nanya and Quento imitated both so that the crowd soon understood. Such a roar of laughter went up that the Baron and Sir
Andros came to see what it was about.

Sir Andros's jaw dropped. "By the stone of Megrath! Where
did *they* come from? From the women of Merne I thought
Piff . . . As for Kashka. . . ."

No one could tell him.

And so they came to Nainth.

244

But Mogrud did not come.

Still, they kept watch in Nainth, waiting for Mogrud. They strengthened the gates and walls, fortified the bridges even more. Another day went by. Two. Three. . . .

Rumors came, tales, gossip, stories, until on the fifth day the Duke of Nainth sent again for Sir Andros. Then, after questioning this one and that one, Suvio was sent for and several others of Merne. Quento and Nanya were called before him with Kila, who was able to talk to them with her hands. At last he spoke with Piff. After he had left, the Duke sat thoughtful.

"Your Highness!" It was Derenth. "A soldier of Byrrhad has been found wandering in the deserted camp. He says he is looking for Mogrud. He is not quite clear in his mind and has a strange story to tell—it may be a wild fancy—of the death of Mogrud. Do you want to question him?"

The Duke looked up. "Yes. Let us have Prince Aciam, the Margrave, and Sir Andros here as well. Then I want you to bring Kashka. . . ."

"I give you good day, my Lords," the soldier said and bowed. "I am told you have taken pity on my king and put him to bed with a dose of salts for his fever and a hot brick at his feet. I am his aide and have come to tell him how matters go."

The Margrave pursed his lips. Sir Andros and Prince Aciam exchanged looks.

"I have been searching for him ever since we were separated at the bridge at Merne," the soldier went on. "For it was there I lost him. Tra-la, they say that Nainth will fall, the Duke and Prince, Nazor and all!

"No, my Lords." He leaned forward. "You are mistaken. It was before that that I lost him, though I did not truly lose *him*. He lost *himself*. You ask how? When?

"He lost himself, I tell you truly, on the day that boy brought the message from the Duke of Xon. Yes, from that day my

245

king was lost. I know, because I stood beside him on that day and heard that boy's words and took that boy's shirt from his back because my king ordered it for whatever his reason. Everyone there will swear I tell the truth!

"That boy gave my king gold for trust with his words. A golden toy to bring him joy! Then he ran away—that boy—and took my king with him. For though he left behind a shell, the King was gone from it. Only his beard remained to prove he was our king.

"We were deceived, my Lords, and thought he still was there behind his beard."

"The man is mad!" exclaimed the Margrave.

"Mad? *Perhaps* that was it, my Lords. I would not argue with you. But I myself think in my mind that he was divided. Yes, he was parted from his senses. Certainly parted from his good sense, for instead of doing what he would have done, should have done, could have done, tra-la tra-la tra-la, he went to the east instead of the south and talked with the beast and burned his mouth. . . . My Lords, forgive me, for I have discovered rhyme but still have found no reason."

"What *is* this?" The Margrave scowled and turned to the Duke of Nainth, but the Duke only motioned for one of the guards.

"Bring Kashka," he said.

Kashka was brought in, and, on looking around, his expression was one of even greater bewilderment than that of the Margrave of Tat.

When the soldier saw him he cried out, "There he is! The very same who brought the message from Xon! Who brought the gold! Beware he does not steal you from yourselves, my Lords! I know him!" He turned suddenly from Kashka to look at the men seated before him. A sly look came over his face.

"They *told* me you were men of Nainth, men of Nazor. Duke! Prince! I did not believe, for Nainth will fall, Duke and all! But *now* I understand!" He nodded his head up and down, up and down, and then pointed to Kashka.

246

"He said he brought the message from the Duke of Xon. He said he was the Duke's messenger and we all believed him. Except we *feared* he was from that Lady Ysene. You know her, my Lords?" He paused, shuddered. "But he ran away and we could not catch him. Now I know. *He was from Nainth! From Nazor!* That is why she said, 'Kill him! Kill him!' "

Tears began to run down the soldier's face. "For you see, my king was not lost from all of his senses. 'Watch her,' he told me. 'Watch her every minute.' And that is why I did not follow my king onto the bridge, though all the rest did. I stood behind her at the river and saw him"—again he pointed to Kashka—"come out of the water like a river spirit to climb on the bridge. I heard her call Mogrud, my king, then. Three times she called him, and he came and they all followed him because he was our king. But I watched her and I heard her say, 'Kill him, kill him, Mogrud!' They all rode after my king onto the bridge and then the men of Xon fell upon us. But we fought them. We fought—except I watched her. I watched until she went away. Now . . . here he is and . . ." The soldier stopped speaking, stared at Kashka, his face suddenly blank, his eyes fixed.

"Take him out." The Duke's quiet voice broke into the silence that followed. He turned to Kashka. "I have heard many pieces of this story. From Piff, from Suvio, from the mute girl, from Sir Andros—now from this soldier. Though he is deranged, there is meaning in his meanderings. We want the rest of the story from you. *The truth!*" he added firmly on seeing Kashka tilt his head slightly, the look of innocence appear. "Did you—?"

"Did you carry a message from the Duke of Xon to Mogrud?" the Margrave of Tat broke in. "What kind of treason—"

The Duke stopped him. "Let us hear what he says before judging."

"My Lord, I carried a message to Mogrud and *said* it was from the Duke of Xon."

"You . . . you walked into Mogrud's camp, told a lie, and stand here before us? Alive? What did you say to him?"

"My Lord, I . . . I told him Lady Ysene was willing to make an agreement with him. I had heard her say she would have him in chains if he entered Xon. I . . ." He paused. When no one spoke, Kashka swallowed. "I . . . But I didn't walk, my Lord. I ran."

All eyes were fixed upon him. Still no one spoke. Kashka rubbed the back of his hand across his lips.

"We heard the soldiers talking beside the river, Trista—Nanya, that is—and I. They were to leave that day, half for Nainth, half for the bridge at Merne. If . . . if they might be delayed. . . . If the people at Merne might be warned. . . . But we were too late at Merne. The soldiers were already there. The river winds. We tipped over twice—three times." He looked from one face to another.

"You gave him gold, the soldier said. And Mogrud went to her? Where did you get gold?" The Margrave's look was fierce.

"It was a chain, my Lord. The Lady Ysene . . . let it fall. Nanya brought it. I knew it was gold. It was heavy. At first I didn't want her to bring it. I would have dropped it in the river. But she . . . And it was useful, my Lord. If I hadn't had it . . . I *hoped* it would convince him. I *hoped* he would go to her. It would give us time."

"Yes. Mogrud's love for gold!" The Margrave continued to stare at Kashka. "But I don't understand. He could have kept it and not gone. How did you come there in the first place? When did you—?"

"I know much of the story, Margrave," the Duke interrupted. "I shall tell it to you. It was only this I wondered about, what he said to Mogrud. I think we have heard enough. Prince Aciam?"

"I should like to hear what you have to tell us, Uncle," replied the Prince, who had also been staring at Kashka. "Why don't you go and practice your flute?" he said to him suddenly. "I thought I heard a mistake last night!"

"Oh, Your Highness, only my own variation!" Kashka protested. "But I'll practice!" he added quickly, more than pleased to be free of the questioning.

"I would like to know," the Margrave said when he had left, "how a man of Mogrud's experience could show such poor judgment. He sent none of his army to his brother, took the word of a boy he had never seen to go and make an agreement with a woman he hated and mistrusted, tried to cross a bridge that he knew would not hold him—all as mindless as that soldier of his. It makes no sense. There is no reason. I knew him! He was a man of cunning, of infinite care with his plans!"

"There is something missing," said Sir Andros. "Something we don't know of. Perhaps in time we shall learn it. Now all we can say is that Mogrud lost his reason."

"And Kashka had something to do with it," Prince Aciam murmured.

"We should question him further. I should like to know the reason—"

"We will question him. But not now. I would return to Nazor as quickly as possible," Prince Aciam interrupted the Margrave. "The king is ill and we are a drain on the stores of Nainth."

"Come, Margrave." The Duke of Nainth put his arm over the shoulder of the Margrave of Tat. "You have not seen the gardens. There are some fine pieces of sculpture in my favorite rose garden. There are other reasons in this world that you should know of. Of course there are still many questions to ask Kashka. But he won't vanish." The Duke paused, then frowned. "I don't *think* he will vanish!"

·37·

⬎⬎⬎ They had helped him into the chair and now he sat looking through the window into the garden. The bells were ringing again.

"Prince Aciam is returning," they had told him. "The battle is won!"

Aciam! He will be wise, just. But what will he do without Ekama? She is ill, they told him. Every day—she is ill. He began to fear. Yes, it was so long, and Bargah was not there to cure her. Aciam is young, strong, capable—better that he wear the crown. It has grown so heavy. It was not so heavy when I had my queen. Ekama—she had grown so sad. Gone now, with the others, with little Mittai, with . . .

All gone, gone, gone.

What was that?

Music came up to him, up from the garden. Fluting and the sound of the lute. He lifted his head, unable to believe.

"I am dreaming!"

But the music continued. His pleasure grew, his wonder with it. Shades of Mareth and Camin! He leaned forward to look down.

There they were, in the garden! Heads tilted back, eyes on his window.

"Sire!'"

Oh, those voices! It had been so long! Why had they left him?

"Sire! May we come up?"

Yes, yes! They would turn to the doors, come up the stair, the corridors. Could he wait five minutes?

Instead, heads on one side, that look between them—he had forgotten that! He watched as one, lute on his back, and the other, flute tucked in the leather case and slung from his shoulder, ran to the wall. Together they leaped up and, hand over hand in a mad scramble through the ivy, head first, heels following over the balcony rail, laughing, panting, they stood before him.

"Sire!"

So there was still joy! There was still laughter! A king could weep for joy! They were his own!

The next minute they turned his chair around. They pushed tables and chairs against the walls, flung open the wide double doors to the room adjoining, and in a trice had cleared that too. Then Kashka laid aside his flute and Piff swung his lute around under his hands, struck a chord.

"For King Darai!" they cried in one voice, and then the music started.

There was the old delight returned to him. His joy, his pleasure in the skill of others! If only his queen were here. . . . But who . . . ? There beside him was Aciam, on the other side, Ekama. He must have dreamed . . . ! For she was not sad, but laughing. And her nose was sunburned!

There was the harvest dance at Gandy's, the biggest of the year, with all of the town of Nazor there. All would wear masks. All had spent hours making dresses and shaping false faces to hide behind, to tease, to tantalize.

Darcie too planned and cut and sewed and smiled and teased. For she had a young man to dance with. Never would she tell him the color of her dress or the shape of her mask.

Who was to say she did not go as a princess?

Who was to say there was not a princess there who went as something other?

251

Who was to say who anyone was who hid behind flour-paste and paper masks all shaped and painted with the fantasy of dreams? One was a lamb, another a bear, another a wolf. There was a dragon, fearsome enough to call for a shriek when someone found *that* head resting unexpectedly on her shoulder!

When the dancing started the secret was often lost, for who could not help but recognize Master Pindy's jogging step, or the peculiar uneven hop of Roby Mardle, or Dame Fogg's waddle?

There was one couple—who were they, the milkmaid and the shepherd—who danced only with each other? who had masks turned only toward one another? who danced with such lightness and grace as had never been seen at Gandy's? No one knew.

And who was the harlequin who seemed always to be in two places at once? Darcie wondered when he asked her to dance. She was whirled away so quickly from her young man, whom she had known at once, that she hardly touched a foot to the floor.

At the end of the dance, a voice she did not quite know murmured in her ear, "That was one, Darcie!" And he disappeared.

She had scarcely turned around when there he was before her, leading her off in another dance, this time with a gentleness and lightness that made her feel as if she were a true princess. At the end of that dance he said, though in a somewhat different voice, "That was two, Darcie!"

She had just found her young man to tease him again, for he had not yet found her and was growing a bit sulky, when an arm went around Darcie's waist and a hand took hers and off she skipped, to turn and whirl. At the end of it the harlequin said, "That was three, Darcie."

"How do you know . . . ?" she cried, but he slipped away. Though there he was in front of her in an instant to dance

252

with her—quickly, lightly, until, "That was four, Darcie."
Somehow he knew who she was, but who was he?

Breathless, she found her young man, who stood talking
with—the harlequin! But . . . Darcie looked at the crowd. He
had gone toward the other side of the room. How had he . . . ?
Then off he took her again in such a dance that at the end of
it her head was turning so much she did not hear the
whispered, "That was five, Darcie," before he was off.

She was not surprised to find him at her elbow half a second
later. She was surprised when suddenly, in the middle of the
dance, her own young man came between her and the harlequin.

"I'll teach you to dance all night with my girl!" he cried
and swung a fist fast and hard. But Harlequin was quick as
light and ducked the blow. It was Nowl Gronder that caught
it on the side of the head.

Nowl Gronder was not a tall man, but he was as wide as
he was tall and as strong as the pair of oxen that pulled his
plow. Besides, no luck for Darcie's young man, Nowl had a
temper as short as himself. So he asked no explanation for the
blow, but picked up Darcie's young man and tossed him broad-
side into the line of dancers behind him. That brought at least
fifteen dancers down on Nowl, which was the limit that he
could handle. So more joined in, to help and for the fun of
it, and for the warmth of the aged cider that had gone to their
heads.

Darcie felt herself hurried through the crowd. She had scarcely
time to think before she found herself in a back room with
not one, but two harlequins, the shepherd, and his milkmaid.
A window was opened. One of the harlequins was through it
in an instant. The shepherd lifted the milkmaid through and
the harlequin caught her on the other side.

Behind them the room was in a roar and there were cries
that Gandy had sent for the palace guard to come and stop
the fight. At that moment Darcie felt herself lifted through

the window and caught on the other side. Then came the shepherd and finally the second harlequin.

There was a quick whisper, and she would have sworn it was, "Are you all right, Your Highness?" But she might have imagined that. The harlequins seized her hands and, with the shepherd and the milkmaid, they ran as fast as they could up the hill, dodging into a doorway when the palace guard went marching by.

When they came to the bakery, one of the harlequins said, "I still owe you half a one, Darcie. I'll pay it when you want, for you're rare on your feet. But if you'd rather, I'll settle with a kiss."

She was so out of breath she could not say no or even protest when her mask was lifted. The kiss was something more than she was used to, for her young man was well behaved and hadn't much practice. So she was even more out of breath at the end of it when the second harlequin said, "I've paid my three, Darcie, so I don't owe you any but I'll add a kiss, for it was a great favor you did us."

When Darcie went up the stair to the rooms above the bakery, her father called out, "Why are you home so early?"

"There was a row," she answered.

"Did Jory see you home?"

"No."

"Who did?"

Darcie only sighed and thought of the smiles that were a little higher on one side than the other.

There was a day in the late fall when Kashka sat with his back against the far wall of the garden. Piff sat beside him, fumbling for the right notes to the words he had in his head. He stopped playing suddenly and said, "You've never told me what it was about the chain you gave Mogrud."

Kashka glanced around the deserted garden.

"I gave him . . . nothing."

254

Piff was still for a moment and then he said, "The horseman who came across the bridge behind you wore a golden chain with a pendant—a circle of gold—hanging from it that glowed in the dark like fire. I saw it."

"I didn't see him. He was behind me."

There was silence between them again until Kashka whispered. "Then he *did* wear it! *He took it and he wore it!* That means . . . *that means she's lost it!* I gave him—*nothing*, and for that she's lost. . . . I don't know!"

" 'Nothing?' 'I don't know'? Is it a riddle?" Piff asked, watching his cousin's face.

"Yes. Because to wear it is to be—nothing. But to lose it—*I think she's lost—not everything, I'm sure—but oh it must be a great deal. I don't know how much!—I don't know!*" Kashka murmured and then he began to laugh. "It *is* a riddle! I'll tell you more of it and see if you can guess the answer. Not now, though. It's too much to tell you, for there's Ekama. But it's good news! Oh, it's good news for the King and Prince Aciam and the Princess and for—"

"And for the lint on your sleeve, Cousin Kashka?"

"Yes! And for the hole in *your* stocking, Cousin Piff!"

They talked with the Princess for a moment, then left her there. When they were out of sight, Prince Aciam swung down from the wall.

"What's the matter?" she asked. "You look . . . odd. Is something wrong?"

"They've been talking in riddles. I've been trying to guess the answers."

"Why don't you ask them?"

"And let them know I was eavesdropping? Would you like to know that someone was eavesdropping on *us?*" He kissed her.

"What was the riddle?" she asked after a moment.

"What is good news for the lint on your sleeve and the hole in your stocking?"

"What a queer riddle!"

255

◆ ◆ ◆

It was spring. There was the night of the death of King Darai. Those he loved were near him. Two he hated were in the palace. The Duke of Xon came to pay his respects to the dying king. The Lady Ysene talked of the coming wedding with her stepsister.

In the middle of a sentence the Lady Ysene suddenly paused. "He knows!" she exclaimed. "The King knows!"

Startled, the Princess looked at her. "Knows what, my Lady?"

"You must excuse me, Ekama. I must go to my room at once. I am not well." She hastened away.

But by the time she came to her room, the King was dead.

"I must find out who it was," she said to herself. "I must find out at once!"

Swiftly she went through the corridors to the King's suite. There were guards at the door. Sir Andros was standing near.

"I am sorry, my Lady. No one is to enter just now. The King is dead."

"I know. I mean, how tragic! Was he alone?"

"No. The Prince was with him. Indeed, my Lady, your brother left only two minutes before he died."

"My brother? *My brother!*"

In the King's chamber Prince Aciam lifted his head and looked through his tears at the two he had grown up with.

"What did you tell him?" he asked. "I knew you would say something to take away the bitterness of the Duke of Xon's visit—something to make him want to laugh. But that is not laughter on his face. That is joy! Happiness! As if you told him the best news of his life!"

"Just a word, Your Majesty. A bit of—fluff, lint, no more."

Aciam closed his eyes against his tears. "You must leave, of course. Both of you. At once. For Nainth. I don't know why he was so insistent, but the King—my father—said you must never be here when the Duke of Xon and the Lady Ysene were here. I promised him. I didn't know they were coming or you would have left yesterday. I . . . I . . . ."

256

"We shall leave, Your Majesty. We shall be gone from Nazor in ten minutes. We shall return the minute you send for us."

The sky was blue and the sun warm. The air was sweet from the meadows of clover blooming beside the road to Nainth. The two young riders did not push their horses.

"What's six and sixteen, Cousin Piff?" Kashka asked.

"Twenty-two."

"Twenty-two! I'll be an old man by then!"

"So will I!"

Then Piff began to hum. In a few minutes he started singing.

O I lost my love to a prince's brother,
So I took to the road to find me another.
I came to Nainth—down the palace stairs she ran!
Who did I find but the fair Arianne!

O the weavers weave and the spinners spin
I've lint on my sleeve and no beard on my chin.
But what my sweetheart found most shocking
Was my toe coming through the hole in my stocking!

Kashka leaned over, took the lute from his cousin and struck a chord.

O I met a witch in her castle gray.
She asked me to dinner, invited me to stay.
But she'd a wen on her ear and seventeen toes
And the chains were so cold I almost froze!

O the spinners spin and the cutters cut,
And my sweetheart stitched my lips tight shut.
But stop pointing fingers, and stop your mocking
Just because she wouldn't mend the hole in my stocking!

Piff took back his lute, sang another verse, and then they sang it together.

O my stockings are gone and my heels worn down,
So I walked barefoot through the town.
I laughed with my sweetheart, we laughed at your mocking.
You can't have a hole if you don't have a stocking!

O the cutters cut and the players play,
And that's all the tale we'll tell today. . . .